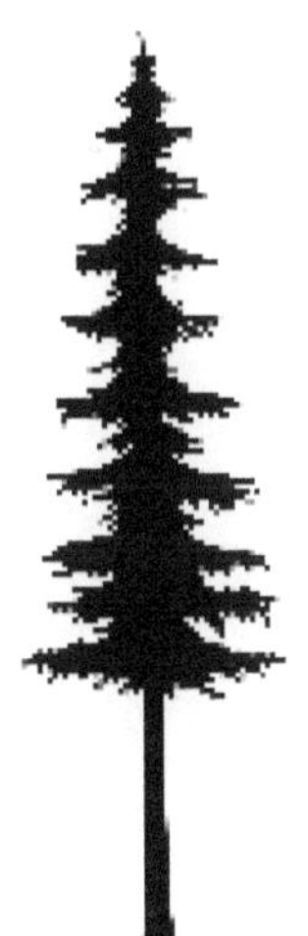

Lone Pine

Sarah Lengler

Book II in the Pine duology

Dedication

For the ones still **searching** through the fog.

May the light lead you through the **trees**.

Acknowledgement

Special thanks to my alpha readers, especially Paula van Kerken for all her detailed and constructive feedback. Thanks to my family for their support. Thank you to my nephew for contributing his handwriting to the Christian chapter headers. Thank you to all Veterans for all that you have done. Most of all, I'd like to thank God for the inspiration and visions for my writing… and everything else He does for me on a daily basis.

Contents:

Prologue

Todd sits behind his desk. Tina perched on his lap. They await the news—where did Shea go? She had only been gone from the property for ten minutes, but the Donoghue's grow impatient.

A knock on the door startles them both. Tina stands and moves to the right of Todd's chair.

"Enter," Todd calls.

A man in a black suit walks through the door followed by three more men wearing tactical gear.

"Report," Todd barks—fingers fiddling with his ring.

Tina places a hand on his shoulder in an attempt to calm him, but he immediately slaps it away.

"Sir. She ran, as you predicted. Team Alpha followed her to a busy intersection and unfortunately lost visual. When they zeroed in on her location, she was gone. A puddle of blood and this was all that remained."

He holds up a shard of glass and her neural implant for Todd to see.

Tina takes an instinctive step away from the desk.

Todd's eyes darken and his face reddens.

"FUCK!" he screams.

1 | Shea

Four months after

Shea reclines in a lounge chair on the porch of the cabin, watching Diesel and Christian hop over downed trees and chase bees below her. Though Diesel is still young, he is a born guard dog and sees Christian as his main charge. *Lose Control* by Teddy Swims plays through a solar powered speaker.

"Boys, be careful with the bees. We need them to pollinate our garden and all the berries you two love to eat all the time. If you drive them away, what will you snack on?" she asks from her lounged position.

She watches Christian's face lift toward her, then he slowly says, "Wal-Mart?"

Shea laughs. They've been working on his speech since she arrived at the cabin all those months ago. But this was not a word she remembers teaching him.

"Who taught you that?"

He looks away, the perfect example of bashful, then points to his head, saying, "Memories."

"Ah, I see. Well, you better manage your beast over there. His mouth will swell up if he messes with the wrong bee and it stings him."

Christian turns to Diesel, who sits and calms at the boy's attention. Christian points out his index finger and taps the dog's nose three times, saying, "No," with each tap.

Shea chuckles to herself and continues lounging. These times are few and far between, so when she gets the opportunity, she enjoys it.

Earlier this afternoon she walked two of their many acres in search of berries, dandelions, chaga, wild herbs and plants for herbal remedies. She got several loads and sweet talked her adoring husband Gregg and loving friend John into carrying the loads to the cabin and returning to the forest for the next batch. Now, they are fishing, and she can dry herbs, flowers and berries only so fast. So, relaxy time it is!

This is one of the last days this will be possible. Winter will be here soon and bring with it hunting

There is already a chill in the air, and as it passes over her, she shivers. Groaning, she gets up and approaches the railing that surrounds the porch.

"Hey, you two, could you bring up some of the firewood Gregg and John cut yesterday? We need to restock the supply up here, and I'm going to build a fire in the woodstove."

"Yes, mam-am," he smiles up at her.

"Good try. You're getting there, bud," she says with a single wave over the railing, before turning and walking into the cabin.

Crouched in front of the stove, she prepares a fire, just like Gregg taught her. She places small kindling in the shape of a log cabin, leaving plenty of gaps for air to circulate, so the flame isn't suffocated when it ignites. Once her masterpiece is finished, she uses a long match, about six inches in length, to place the flame into the stove. When she sees the fire begin to spread, she drops the match and closes the thick ash-stained glass door. She remains there, to make sure the flame fully catches.

Hearing quiet footsteps behind her, she closes her eyes and takes a deep breath. She immediately gags—sure, she's smelled better—but Gregg stands behind her soaked in river water and fish guts. His odor is on another level.

"Hey, beautiful. Can I get a kiss?" He puckers his lips and makes kissy noises in her direction, slowly making his way toward her.

Shea's trapped. Behind her is the wood stove, which butts up against the living room's far wall. The only way out is through.

Standing, she gives her wonderful husband a huge smile, and says, "You know, if John's available to babysit, the two of us could go down to the river, just the two of us, and wash away all that stench."

The closer she gets to him, the worse it is. She holds her breath and puts her arms out, as if to hug him. But when she reaches him, she places her hands on his hips and gently pushes him out of the way.

She walks out of the cabin quickly. Back on the porch, she giggles and watches John leading Christian up the stairs with more firewood.

"Well, don't you guys just exceed expectations, every day?"

"Yup," Christian says, passing her.

John laughs through his nose, and says, "Yup."

"Hey, John, how come you're all clean? Didn't catch any today?" Shea taunts.

"Psh, please. I caught 'em all. Your man just wanted to prove he did some physical labor today," he answers.

"Come on, John. What he's doing here with the little tech we have is amazing. The auto-waterers from the river, the plants love that fish water. Plus, he always takes the risk of going into town. Don't be a hater!"

Gregg grabs her from behind, and says, "Yeah, man, what's with the roast?"

I wonder how long I can hold my breath

"Man, I'd love to apologize, but my lunch is about to make a comeback. Get out of the cabin. We're gonna have to smell you all night long!"

"It's not that bad!"

"Um, your wife is turning blue, and I know I don't stink."

Shea releases her breath. Apparently, she needs to practice her neutral face.

She walks forward and turns toward Gregg, holding her hand out to her stinky husband.

"C'mon Greggy-poo, you need a bath."

He smiles and takes her hand. "I already have our toiletries and towels on the four-wheeler."

"Of course you do." Shea feels her face and body relax as they descend the stairs and board the four-wheeler. Just before Gregg mounts, he pulls off his hip waders and hangs them from a hook in the wood of the cabin's exterior next to John's. Underneath, his basketball shorts cling to his legs and bunch in his crotch.

He plants a kiss on Shea, who immediately wipes her mouth with the back of her hand.

Salty fish, blegh!

A five-minute ride later, Gregg parks the four-wheeler on the large rocks of the riverbed. They unpack what they need, undress, and tiptoe into the ankle-deep, frigid water. Gregg scoops up a handful of water and flings it at Shea. Her whole body locks up as she squeals.

"Gregg! What have I told you?"

Gregg pouts. "Naughty boys don't get river-booty."

Shea chuckles. "Get over here. Hurry up, it's cold and I need you to wash my back."

After her hair and body are clean and Gregg smells like desert cedar—apparently naughty boys do get river-booty—they make their way back to the cabin to prepare for dinner.

2 | JOHN

Setting up the fish-fry station outside, several feet away from the cabin, John fillets the fish alone. He tried to teach Christian when they first came out here, but it's difficult for the kid not to get attached to the fish, when he's seen its whole life. Instead, Christian peels potatoes and preps other veggies for dinner. Diesel sits below Christian, eating peels and cuttings.

"You gonna eat some fish tonight, little man?" John asks him.

"Ummmm…." he says, his index finger pointed to his chin.

"You don't have to, bud. Just asking."

"No. This," Christian says, holding a potato in the air.

"Okay, that's cool. Miss Shea might have used the last of the sour cream for her cake. Gregg doesn't go into town for a couple of days." John batters the fillets and carefully drops them into the oil. He keeps one raw and plain for Diesel.

"Nah-uh," Christian sing-songs, stacking his veggies in a bucket and heading up the stairs to rinse them off.

"Well, you can look, but either way you're eating your veggies!"

Christian sticks his tongue out at John and walks up the steps, Diesel following diligently behind.

John hears the four-wheeler approaching behind him as he pulls the first batch of fish from the fryer and batters the next. Once the four-wheeler goes quiet, he calls over his shoulder, "Took you long enough. The kid's upstairs with the veg. Fish is almost done."

"Took a while to get that smell out of him," Shea says, heading up the stairs.

"I bet. His waders have a hole, letting that water soak in, marinating his ass. I'm surprised he didn't get hypothermia."

He hears Shea's laughter as she walks into the cabin.

"Served its purpose though, didn't it?" Gregg says, clapping John on the back and chuckling to himself.

"Whatever works. You should add new waders to your order this month though. That water is only gonna get colder."

"Good idea."

3 | GREGG

After everyone is full and Diesel is licking the last of the fish from his bowl, Gregg organizes everyone in front of their 'go' bags.

"As you guys know, I'll be going to pick up our monthly order in a couple of days, so it's time to cycle out the goods," Gregg instructs.

"And Christian, I'm putting you in charge of Diesel's bag this time. You got it?"

"Yup."

"Take out all the dried goods this time too. I have plenty to put all new ones in," Shea says.

"Did you add some 'go' phones to the list? I have six left in my bag, but you know how fast we can tear through those," John says.

"Got it," Gregg replies, jotting it down on a list.

The group empties their bags onto the floor and repacks them. They carefully remove old food items—to be replaced with new.

"This?" Christian asks, holding up a vacuum-sealed bag of moose jerky.

"That can stay, bud. The seal is still good, and I'm sure even if it wasn't Diesel wouldn't care anyway," John says.

Shea organizes the dried fruit pouches into piles and hands new ones to each of them for their packs.

"Getting up at three a.m. is bad enough, man. But now you're giving me work to do?" John asks, rubbing his eyes. He stands next to Gregg, who is hitching the meat wagon to the four-wheeler.

"We need to be prepared for the winter. We got lucky we got here right at the start of spring, but winter is gonna be rough and we aren't prepared yet." Gregg loads a bag of cash into the trailer and secures it with a carabiner.

"Dude, we'll be fine. We got this. I just need a few more hours."

"John, I don't want Shea involved in the stuff we were talking about, or Christian. That kid picks everything up. Plus, now that he's talking, there are no secrets. It's important, John. Please, just get it done!" Gregg says, placing a hat with a sasquatch in front of a mountain range onto his head. His hair has grown enough that it flips up at the ends.

"Why can't we just fill her in? She was in the dark for so long. We don't have to do that anymore."

"John, she's been through enough," Gregg says, starting the four-wheeler. "This is a burden we can carry for her. Just do this, please."

"Alright, alright, man. She's your wife, I'll follow your lead. No problem."

"Thank you. I'll be back before dark." Gregg mounts the four-wheeler, puts his sunglasses on the brim of his hat, for later, and pulls away from the cabin.

Hours later, he pulls into a secluded alleyway in town. He revs his engine twice, then turns it off. A tall man enters the alley and approaches Gregg.

"Hey, Matt! What's the news?" Gregg asks.

"Nothing here. All good," Matt replies.

"Good. Where's my order?"

"Clara's bringing it out on a pallet. She had to run this morning to grab your waders," Matt reports.

"Oh, great. Are you still keeping a low profile?"

"Of course. I have to. I don't want to get shot in the back because of whatever my idiot of a brother got himself into."

"Must suck to have the face of an idiot," Gregg chuckles to himself. "Clara, there you are."

"Let's get this pallet unloaded and get you back to your sweet lady. Less time you're in town, the better," Clara says.

Her petite frame moves quickly, assisting Gregg in loading the meat wagon. Her messy bun bounces up and down with her efforts.

When Gregg pulls in next to the cabin, hours later, he is surrounded by his loved ones.

"Look!" Christian runs over to him, holding up a piece of paper covered in the child's messy handwriting.

"Did you write me a letter?" Gregg asks.

"No… Look!"

"Okay, bud." Gregg studies the page and sees the months, weeks, and days of the year written in cursive.

"Nice. Did Miss Shea do this with you today?"

"Yup," he says, then turns and walks away, calling Diesel with him.

"Hey, John, let's get this unloaded. Oh, Matt says you have the face of an idiot."

"Yeah, cause it's his face!" John chuckles, shaking his head.

4 | Shea

Two months later

"Guys, we're gonna need more firewood, pronto. We're going through it too fast, it's cold as shit out!" Shea calls up the stairs to the sleeping quarters, where the men are currently caulking small gaps in the cabin walls.

"Need wood!" Christian calls, barreling down the stairs with Diesel nipping at his heels.

Shea jumps out of their way, almost avoiding them both. Christian barely grazes her arm.

"Careful guys, you're gonna hurt someone!"

Christian digs his heels into the wood floor, stopping dead in front of her. He stares at her with fear and sadness.

"What's wrong?" Shea asks. She approaches him, but he backs away from her.

"Gregg!" he screams up the stairs, his voice shaking in fear.

Shea and Diesel stand shock-still. Gregg's boots thunder down the stairs, deafening in Shea's ears. She can hear her pulse, and her hands begin to shake. She's never heard Christian's voice sound like that, and it makes fear turn to ice in her veins.

"What happened?! What is it?" Gregg demands as soon as he hits the bottom step.

Christian immediately holds his hand out to Gregg, desperation in his eyes.

Shea walks over to the couch to sit down, her knees feel like they're made of Jello. She watches as Gregg grabs Christian's hand. John stands on the step behind Gregg, watching the scene. Gregg's back goes stiff as a board. Diesel whines and plops down at Christian's feet.

What is happening?

Her hands and feet sweat as her stomach acid climbs up her throat. Fear of the unknown has her in a vice grip.

Finally, Gregg blinks in her direction. The look he gives her is one of unadulterated panic.

"What? What is it?" Shea asks, needing to know what the hell is going on. She clutches her crucifix in her hand, a habit she's never been able to kick.

Gregg turns to John on the stair behind him. "Code five. Get the bags, meet me downstairs."

The color drains from John's face. He stands on the stair, unmoving, unblinking, eyes locked on Shea.

I'm about to lose my shit!

"John! Now!" Gregg barks.

"Right." He steps off the stair and scoops Christian up with one arm. In just a couple of steps he has their 'go' bags in the other and is out the cabin door.

"Gregg, you're scaring me. What is going on?"

"Shea, go meet John downstairs. We need to get out of here now," he says, yanking open a kitchen drawer and pulling out a 'go' phone.

"Shea, please go. I need to make a call, and we need to get out of here. Now, Shea."

"Do not treat me like I don't know what our situation is. You keep doing this, even though I have my memories back! Tell me what's going on or I'm not moving."

"I will carry you out of here if I have to. GO!"

"You're my husband, and if you want to stay my husband you need to TELL. ME. WHAT'S. GOING. ON!"

Gregg takes a deep breath. "I love you, Shea. Please trust me, we don't have time for this."

"Then give me an earpiece and you can tell me on the way."

"Fine, they're in my pack. Grab two and I'll be right down."

Shea makes her way down to the snow machines Gregg had brought in after last month's grocery haul. She digs through Gregg's pack until she finds what she wants.

5 | GREGG

"Just meet us there. I'll pay for your flight if I need to, but we need you," Gregg says into the phone.

"No, no, it can't wait. We'll be there in like six hours. I need you to be there," desperation leaks into Gregg's voice.

"Alright. Call the sat phone if you run into any trouble," he says, hanging up the phone, then breaking it in two.

He heads out, locking the cabin behind him. The snow machines are already running. Everyone is loaded up, bundled in arctic gear and ready to go. As he lifts his leg to mount the snow machine in front of where Shea sits, she passes him an earpiece and microphone dot, which he places under his beanie.

"Alright, to town. As fast as possible," he says loudly over the engines to John. "You gonna let Diesel run?"

"Yeah, for a few miles at least. I'll load him up at our first break spot," he says, nodding toward the kennel strapped to the sled behind his snow machine.

"Alright, let's go!" Gregg hollers over the roar of the engines.

As they make their way through the bare, snow-covered trees, he's surprised she hasn't grilled him yet.

"You okay, beautiful?" he asks.

"No. I'm scared. What is it now? I thought we were safe."

"Take a deep breath. It's gonna be okay."

"Just tell me," she says, her voice pleading.

"Remember when I was doing different experiments in Ohio, with the chips?”

“Yeah, the patch, right?”

“That and the ingestible chip… remember?” he asks, hopeful she does.

“Oh, God.”

“Christian saw the moment the chip turned on this morning, when he brushed up against you. But the GPS isn’t active yet. So really, it’s lucky he touched you when he did.”

“So, what’s the plan?”

“Get outta dodge as fast as possible, for one. Once we get to the Jimmy, we’re going to head about a hundred miles north of here to the Denali Bluffs Hotel. We put this plan into place ahead of time, we already have a room. Dr. P is gonna meet us there. I talked to her this morning.”

“Then what?”

“Then she cuts it out. Shea, we can’t leave it in there. If we do and the GPS goes active, we’re all dead.”

“So his computers are back up?” Shea speculates.

“I’m assuming at least a few programs, yeah. I don’t see the time machine going up though.”

“Are we putting Dr. P at risk? This is all so messed up. Should John and Christian even be going with us?” Her voice shakes.

“We need Christian to monitor the implant. If it goes live, the two of them will leave immediately. Dr. P knows the risk, she’s been briefed. She seemed more excited about talking to you about your memory than worried, to be honest.”

“Oh, yeah. She promised I’d want to find out on my own. I forgot all about that.”

“Was she right?” Gregg inquires.

"I mean I might have been a little less appalled about my bathroom habits had I known, but yeah, it was better remembering on my own."

"It won't take long to get to town with all this snow. We don't have to weave around the foliage, we can cut a straighter path. So just try to relax. We're gonna stop near the train tracks so Christian can check you."

"Okay," she says, then rides quietly behind him.

Without the conversation distracting him, he notices the frozen snot under his nose and the numb, tingly feeling in his fingers.

6 | Shea

What the actual FUCK?

Shea rides behind Gregg, clutching his thick winter coat. She doesn't even have questions—a rare occurrence for her. She can only worry that everything they all went through to get here was for nothing—because of her. The thought that they're all in danger again because of her is eating her alive.

"Shea, we're about to take our break. Are you okay?" Gregg asks.

"No. I'm really not, but I'm powerless to do anything about it."

"We're not powerless. We're doing all we can. Put a brave face on for the kid, will ya? I'm sure the terrors of that glass cell are all Christian can think about."

"Gah! I'm so selfish. I'm sitting here thinking about how I've endangered you all, throwing myself a damn pity party. It never even occurred to me to think about what Christian must be feeling. I'm the worst!"

"No, you're just always so quick to take the blame. Here we are. Remember, brave face."

Gregg pulls the snow machine beside John's. They all turn toward each other in their seats, engines off. John breaks the snowy silence—handing each of them a small Ziploc bag of assorted dehydrated berries, mushrooms, and flowers.

"Figured we'd all be ready for a snack, so I got these from my bag," John says.

"Thanks, John. Good idea," Gregg says, grabbing a handful from the bag and tossing it into his mouth.

Shea watches Christian. He stares at the Ziploc bag in his hands. Diesel catches up to them and nudges Christian, hopeful he'll share his snack.

But he doesn't. He just continues to stare down at the bag in his hands.

Shea's chest tightens. He's already been through so much. She hates that she's adding to it.

"Christian?" she says gently.

He looks up at her through his thick lashes. As soon as his eyes meet hers, and sees that hers are filled with unshed tears, his eyes soften.

"I'm so sorry, bud. I didn't know. I would never put you in danger on purpose." Her voice verges on pleading.

"I know," he says. "No cry, please."

"I won't. I'm just sad that you're sad."

He shakes his head. "No sad… hate," he says. The T in the word hate cracks like a whip.

"Me?" she asks quietly.

Christian looks at her for a long second, then climbs off the snow machine and stands in front of her. He looks like he's working up the courage for something when he reaches out and brushes away her tears with his small fingers.

"No." Then, as if he had said it a million times, as if he'd practiced it, he says, "I love you, Shea."

Shea wraps her arms around him, and he clings to her. Over his shoulder Shea watches John and Gregg both suddenly get something in their eye.

Oh, my heart

She eases him away from her chest, makes sure she looks him in the eye, and says, "I love you, bud. Are we okay?"

He nods and backs away, chasing after Diesel.

She looks over at Gregg, tears still in her eyes.

7 | GREGG

Gregg's heart feels like it might explode as he watches her eyes fill with tears.

The sound of John clearing his throat kills the moment as both of their heads snap in his direction.

"Sorry," John says. "I just think we should have Christian do his thing so we can get moving. Time is of the essence, right?"

"Shit, right," Shea says, wiping away her tears.

"But he did already touch her. I think he would have alerted us if anything were amiss, right?" John asks.

"Yeah, but we need to make absolutely sure," Gregg says, then calls over to the kid currently chasing the dog through the snow.

"Hey, kid! Come here!"

"Okayyy," he hollers back, trudging over.

When he reaches them, he climbs onto John's snow machine, ready to go.

"Good job, bud, but has anything changed with her tracker?" John asks.

"No, same," Christian replies, his brow furrowed.

"Alright, that means we need to get moving so it stays that way," Gregg announces.

Making their way back onto the trail, Gregg softly says, "How you holding up, beautiful?"

"He said he loves me! He said it like it had been waiting to be said. He loves me, and I love him like he's my own, and now he's in danger because of me."

"Shea, of course he loves you. No one is in danger because of you. You did nothing to cause this. Todd did. He is the only one to blame."

"Don't even say his name."

Thirty-five minutes later, they pull the snow machines into the alleyway that Gregg uses to get their monthly delivery. They hand their keys off to Clara and Matt for safekeeping.

"Hey, uggo!" John calls out to his mirror image.

"Look who's talking. Your IQ's written all over your face," Matt retorts, then embraces his twin tightly. "Tell me the plan. Am I heading across the country?"

"No, not yet anyway. We're just heading to the hotel to get the tracker removed. I'll keep you posted if the plan changes though," Gregg answers.

"Okay, I'll keep my bug-out bag ready. Just in case."

Looking to Shea, he says, "Hey, boss. You gonna level a gun at me again? We were in this exact spot all those months ago when we first met." A shit-eating grin is plastered on his face.

Gregg watches the light bulb flick on in Shea's mind.

"You were? Oh my gosh, you were with us the whole way, right? You…I…I didn't realize who you so closely resembled when all of that happened. I'm so sorry!" Shea blushes and runs her hand over her hair.

"Hey, it's all good. I was really proud of you actually. Your reflexes were spot on! A strange man approaching your 'John Doe,' you did the right thing."

"Thanks," she replies, blushing.

Gregg smiles, remembering that day. He got his wife back that day.

"Okay, stooges, let's get to the Jimmy. Diesel and Christian in the back, please," Gregg calls.

John opens up the back for them and tosses all of their bags in behind them.

"John, you wanna drive? You're the only one who knows where we're going."

"Yeah, you wanna call Dr. P and ask her where she is?"

"Sure." Gregg walks a few feet away from the Jimmy and dials her number. He has been good about masking his anxiety for so long, but it is threatening to bubble over. He doesn't want anyone to know, so while the phone rings he takes deep breaths and focuses on the cold air burning his lungs. He flexes his hands in an attempt to stop them from shaking.

"Hello?" Dr. P answers.

"Hey, how's it going?"

"I'm set for 6 p.m."

"You bringing what you need?"

"Yes, Mr. Doe. I've got it covered. Don't stress. We've got this. See you soon."

The line clicks off and Gregg chuckles to himself, heading back to the Jimmy.

"What's so funny?" Shea asks.

"She gets me," he says, climbing in next to her.

"Who?" mock jealousy in the question.

"Dr. P, she's very intuitive."

"And smart. She figured out who you were in just a couple of days," Shea adds.

"Very true."

"I can't wait to meet her. Shea told me she's hot," John says, a large grin across his face and eyebrows raised.

John starts the Jimmy and adjusts the mirrors to reflect the ground, in an attempt to avoid his face reflecting to vehicles behind them.

"Everybody ready?" he asks the crew.

"Yeah, but maybe Christian should do one more check before we head out? So that we don't lead a psychopath to our next location?" Shea asks.

"Good idea," John agrees.

"Hey, bud, can you come give Shea a touch on her shoulder, see how we're doing?" Gregg asks, turning his body toward the back seat as he does.

"Yup," Christian says. He leans forward and softly rubs Shea's right shoulder, with his eyes closed. "Good," he says, leaning back in the seat to cuddle Diesel.

"Alright, let's go then! Next stop, a hotel with Dr. P," John calls out, pulling onto the road.

"Just like old times," Gregg says, smiling at Shea.

"My favorite protector—John Doe. I had such a crush on him," she teases.

"No kidding?" Gregg laughs, resting his hand on her knee.

"He was a little secretive, but I understand why now."

"Does anyone have any moose jerky left in their pack? I found a small scrap in mine. Man, I forgot how good that stuff was," John asks.

"I think I put a double ration in Christian's pack for Diesel. It was getting older, I didn't know you'd want to eat it," Shea confesses.

"Aw, man. That stuff is amazing, old or not," John says.

They hear a zipper and what sounds like rummaging, followed by, "Found it... here."

A small hand extends over the back of the seat, past John's right ear, holding three vacuum packs of moose jerky pouches. When John doesn't grab them right away, the small hand shakes them, arousing the napping pup. A wet nose and tongue then enter his ear.

Christian giggles and John snatches the packs before Christian decides to give them to the dog instead.

"You sure I can have all three of them?" he asks over his shoulder.

"Yup. Summore here."

"Sweet," John replies, opening one of the packs. Before diving in, he offers the open bag to Shea and Gregg.

"Aw, John, thanks, but I think I probably shouldn't eat, right? Procedure to remove a chip from my stomach an all," Shea says.

"Ah, yeah. My bad. Gregg?" he asks, shaking the bag under Gregg's nose.

"I should abstain, solidarity and all that."

"Good choice," Shea says, laying her head on Gregg's shoulder.

Over the next half hour, the radio—playing Shea's newest playlist called *Into the Woods*, goes from playing *Desperate* by Jamie Macdonald at maximum volume to *Behold the Lamb of God* by Hell's Enemy just barely above the threshold for hearing.

He grips the steering wheel tightly, eyes focused on the white landscape. The soft, even breathing and snores throughout the interior of the Jimmy make John feel important, like they all trust him with their lives. He will get them there safely, to fight another day.

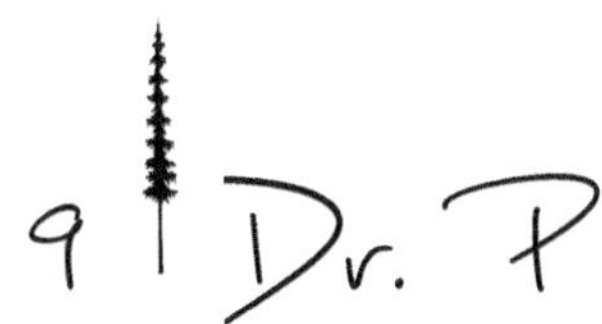

9 | Dr. P

Dr. P pulls into the hotel parking lot after engaging in some evasive maneuvers. No one was following her, but she needed to be sure. She parks, gets out and locks the doors immediately. She hopes her thousands of dollars' worth of equipment will be safe, while she checks into the Denali Bluffs Hotel.

"What am I getting myself into?" she mutters to herself.

She walks into the lobby, a large warm room with wood floors and drop ceilings with exposed wood beams, filled with different seating options. The trophy of the room is a taxidermy bear in a glass case, very Alaskan.

She approaches the front desk. The employee greets her, "Good evening. Welcome. How can I help you?"

"Hi, I believe my reservation is under the name John Doe?"

"Of course, that's been a long-standing reservation. It's nice to see it finally fulfilled."

"Great, do you need anything from me?"

"No ma'am. Everything is already taken care of. Here's your room key. You are booked in a deluxe room with a full river view," she says, sliding a key across the counter.

"Thank you. The rest of my party should be arriving soon. When they get here, could you send them my way?"

"Of course, ma'am."

She pulls her rental car around to the building their room is in and parks. Getting into the room, she drops her backpack and keys at the door, then gives the room a once over. Mr. Doe briefed her on security protocols, and she is trying to adhere to them. She walks back to the rental car and load after load, brings all her equipment into the room.

When she's done, she sits and waits. The TV on for background noise plays the news at a low volume. She has Gregg's satellite phone number but figures she'll give them a little while longer. She made better time than she thought she would.

At 5:49 p.m., she hears a key in the door. She reaches for her kit, pulls out a scalpel, and stands just inside the door in wait.

10 Shea

Shea wanted to be the one to unlock the hotel room door, but Gregg insisted, because of security protocols, she couldn't. So she's waiting in the Jimmy with Christian and Diesel, while the big strong men go unlock the door.

It's not like the tracker is live

She watches through the driver's side window as Gregg unlocks the door and then bends over laughing. John looks toward the Jimmy, grinning, and waves them over.

Shea jumps out. All three of them run toward Gregg. As Shea reaches the room, she peeks in the door to see what's so funny. She sees Dr. P standing just inside the door with a massive smile on her face, in a defensive stance, scalpel held out in front of her.

"Dr. P!" Shea exclaims softly.

She drops her scalpel. "Hey, L.T.! Looking good. How's your memory?"

"Fully loaded—and you can call me Shea. I think you've earned our trust."

"Well, thanks, Shea," she says, a knowing smile on her face.

"The name's Gregg," he announces, putting his hand out to shake.

Dr. P takes his hand in hers, and says, "I know, silly. And who might these three be?"

Christian looks to Gregg, who nods. Christian then points to the dog, and says, "Diesel, nice dog." Then points to himself, and says, "Christian, mam 'am."

"Well, hello you two. It's very nice to meet you."

Christian smiles, then darts by her into the room. He calls Diesel in after him and they choose one of the beds as theirs, promptly lying down.

John clears his throat. "It's a real honor to meet you, Doc. I've heard so much about you. I'm John—really," he says, his hand extended to her.

Shea and Gregg share a secret smile.

I knew he'd think she was hot

"John, so nice to meet you. Well, let's not loiter. We have business to attend to."

Stepping into the room, they're all amazed by the sheer volume of equipment Dr. P unloaded by herself.

"Wow, you've been busy," John says.

"Everything is ready to be set up. I didn't want to prep too much because it needs to stay sterile. So, John, Christian, and Diesel need to hang out on the veranda until we're finished."

"Veranda's a great idea, but why John and not Gregg?" Shea asks.

"Oh, just because I know Gregg's abilities and he's your husband, I just thought…" she trails off.

"I think John would be better suited for this actually," Gregg announces. "He was a field medic in the military. Everything I know, he taught me," Gregg admits.

"Oh, great. Then John can assist while you three enjoy the veranda."

"Sure thing," Gregg says, leaning over and kissing Shea on the forehead. "You'll do great. Just trust, okay?"

"Yeah."

Nerves, don't get me now

Dr. P carefully pulls on sterile gloves. "Okay, Shea. Hang tight. John, can you strip this bed? I have a sterile drape I'd like you to put down for her to lie on."

"Got it," John says, jumping into action. He strips the bed and places the drape with practiced precision.

"Great, can you just lift her onto it, so it stays flat?"

"Yes, ma'am." He looks to Shea. "Shea, you ready?"

"No… yes… yes, okay. I'm ready."

John carefully lifts her up and settles her on the draped mattress.

Dr. P checks out his handiwork. "Great job. Now can you start an IV?"

"Yes, ma'am."

"Shea, your head healed beautifully, considering. Any issues with it?"

Shea answers as John expertly inserts the needle into her vein. "No, it's been great. As soon as the IVs were finished, it sealed up."

"IV is in, ma'am," John says.

"Alright, Shea. There's no need to put you all the way under, but it'll be easier for both of us if you're unaware. I have plenty of drugs to knock you out but allow you to breathe on your own. I'm going to pass a scope through your esophagus to your stomach and into your small intestine, where the tracker should be. I'll excise it and then we'll be all set."

"Okay, will I remember any of it?"

"Not likely."

"Alright, well—let's get the beacon of doom out of me then."

"Here, lift up your head. I put a sterile drape on this pillow," John says, sliding the pillow under Shea's head. "Oh, your comms is still in, we should probably remove that."

"Good idea. Okay, it's time for the meds. It's going to take about thirty minutes for full effect, Shea. Just close your eyes and relax until it fully kicks in. Don't worry, you know we got you. You're safe."

"Right. I'm fine. I've gone through much worse."

As Dr. P pushes the meds through Shea's IV, John holds her hand. After thirty or so minutes, her body becomes fully relaxed. She feels weightless, like she's lying on a cloud. She lets go.

It only takes a few seconds for Shea to be completely out once the meds start to take effect.

"Alright, John. I'm gonna need you to roll her onto her left side and hold that tablet up while I guide the scope," Dr. P says.

"Yes, ma'am," he says, getting into position.

He watches her place the scope and advance it through Shea's stomach. Once it's in the small intestine, the small chip is identified immediately by a faint blinking light.

"It has a blinking light on it?" John questions.

"Appears that way," Dr. P says, carefully cutting the chip from Shea's intestinal wall.

The moment Dr. P pulls the chip from Shea's mouth, Gregg bursts in from the veranda—leaving Christian and Diesel outside. But it's not long before they follow him in.

"Gimme that," he says, taking the chip from Dr. P's gloved hand.

"Dang, man," John mutters. "It was out of her for like one second, dude."

"I know. I just want to block the GPS function for now, until we're ready."

"You can do that?" Dr. P asks.

"Of course I can. I designed the chip," Gregg replies, pulling a micro tool set out of his pocket—about the size of a wallet.

"Well, okay. I'll get all of this cleaned up and loaded back in the car. She shouldn't be out for long, that drug has a short half-life."

"Oh, don't worry about that, Doc. I'll get it all out to your rental car. No problem," John says.

"Oh, no, that's really not necessary. I got it all in here, I can bring it all out," Dr. P says.

"No, really. It's no problem. It would be my pleasure."

She hesitates for a moment, then smiles. "Well, I guess if you insist. That'd be great, thank you."

She turns to watch what Gregg is doing with the chip. Sensing her gaze, Gregg looks back at her, and says, "I've got the GPS blocked for now, but I'm not sure it will take effect immediately. We'll have to keep an eye on it."

Shea mumbles in her sleep, something about a goose and a berry. Dr. P walks over to the desk and inspects the chip herself. The light on it is now steady instead of blinking. "What does this light do? If you can't even see it inside of her intestines, why does it need to be there?"

"Well, it doesn't really. It wasn't part of my design. It was added on since my production of the chip. I'm not sure what its purpose is, but for our case it's helping me monitor whether or not the GPS snaps on."

"Oh, smart."

Christian looks over to Dr. P from the bed. "Pleasure? What's pleasure?"

Gregg stifles a laugh. "Buddy, it just means John was really happy to help Dr. P by carrying her stuff. As Shea would say, 'she needed a big strong man.'"

Dr. P laughs. "I've never needed a big strong man, but it is nice to have the help."

John comes back into the room and gets ready to carry a new load out. Hearing just the tail end of the conversation, he chuckles to himself, and says, "No? Well, I'll be your big, strong man anytime you need one."

12 | Shea

Shea hears voices and laughter surrounding her. She's stuck in a dream and can't find her way out. As time passes, she slowly floats to the top of her consciousness and opens her eyes. She looks around to see John and Dr. P sitting together on the other bed, Christian and Diesel sitting on the floor playing with something from his bag, and Gregg sitting at the desk, looking intently at the chip they pulled out of her.

"Well, I guess it's out then," she says, voice rough.

"Thank goodness you're awake. You slept longer than we thought you would. We were starting to worry," John says.

"Oh, you know me," Shea says, stretching. "Always last to join the party. At least I have my memories this time."

Dr. P looks over at her smiling. "Of course, you're not losing those again. Not on our watch."

Shea pushes herself into a sitting position and swings her legs over the side of the bed. She feels a little wobbly, like the medication still has some sort of effect on her body. She puts her hand up to her head and Gregg rushes to her side.

He takes her hand in his, and says, "Is everything okay?"

She looks at him and smiles. She sees love in his eyes and the tension inside her eases. Christian and Diesel barrel toward her, but Gregg puts out a stiff arm, and says, "Boys."

John chuckles at their excitement. "Hey, I saw a playground around the corner. Why don't we walk down there and play, give Shea a little time to wake up fully."

Dr. P agrees. "It would be good to give her some time to acclimate from the medication. I'll walk with you guys."

A huge smile settles on John's face. Shea can tell he's very excited by the news—to have a little alone-ish time with Dr. P.

As they parade out of the room, Gregg again holds Shea's hand, and says, "Really, are you okay?"

"Yeah, I'm just a little woozy. You know how it is. Well, maybe you don't know how it is. Have you ever gone under anesthesia or taken any meds—of any kind? I don't even know that about you and we're married. I should know these things about you. I feel like I don't know anything about your medical history. Do you even have your tonsils? I should know this!" she rambles, holding onto her crucifix.

Gregg chuckles. "I've never had anesthesia. I do still have my tonsils and… wait, where is this worry coming from?"

"I don't know, I just feel overwhelmed. We're married, and for most of that time I haven't had any of my memories, and now that I have them I don't remember anything about you. I remember you have a sibling, and I remember things about us, but I feel like we don't know that much about each other."

Gregg sighs, and says, "I know everything you've shared with me—about your parents, and your life at university. We know enough about each other to love one another, and that's what matters, right?"

"Well, yeah. Of course. I mean, I know I love you. I just feel this overwhelming sense of not knowing you."

"Where's this coming from?"

She sighs, wrapping her hand around her crucifix. "I don't know. I had a weird dream, and now I feel like everything's topsy-turvy, and something about a goose. I have no idea, okay."

He smiles. "Well, would it calm you down to hear some facts about me?"

"Maybe. I should know these things, you're my husband. Tell me everything."

"Alright," he says, leaning back. "Well, I don't know about everything. But let's start at the beginning. I have parents—obviously. They're both pretty laid back and hands off. Haven't had any surgeries. I haven't even skinned a knee. I was always the kid with the scientific calculator and the chemistry sets. I didn't really ride skateboards or bikes. I looked at ants under a magnifying glass and tried to burn them using the lens and the sun. I did weird nerdy stuff, and then I got obsessed with swords and fantasy, with living in a world that's not like ours and what I would do if I lived in a world like that. What could I accomplish? That and scientific advancement are all I've ever thought about... until I met you. And now all I think about is keeping you safe. That's all I want. I want your love, and I want to keep you safe."

She rests her head on his shoulder. "Well, we've accomplished that, so what's next?"

"I don't know where we go from here. We have to figure out if we're on the run or not. We don't really have time to think about our relationship that much or what we want next. We have to figure everything else out."

"I know, but think of it as one of your fantasy stories. What would you do? What would you want to do next in this story?"

"All I know is that I want to be with you and protect you from what evil and peril follows you around. Once we figure that out, we can think about our future and what we really want. Obviously, we want to provide a good life for Christian and Diesel—and John. You know we can't leave him out."

Shea giggles, "You're right, he's just a big lug."

"And after that... we can think about things we want for our future together. Maybe a mini nerd someday."

Shea leans over and kisses Gregg, muttering, "Someday," under her breath. She knows in her heart of hearts that he is the one. He is her forever. She just has no idea what forever is going to look like.

13 | JOHN

When they return from their trip to the park, John notices right away that both Gregg and Shea have wet hair. He flashes a sly, knowing smile in Gregg's direction.

"Nice, dude. Not even an hour post-op," John says.

"I feel fine, John!" Shea says indignantly, a blush creeping across her face.

"I bet you do."

Dr. P swats his arm. "Leave them alone, they're still in the honeymoon phase. Let them enjoy it."

"Fine, fine. How about you, Doc? Are you still in the honeymoon phase?" he asks with an eyebrow raised.

"Yes, I have been for many years." John deflates a little and Dr. P chuckles. "I've been married to my work, my one true love, for many years. Saving lives, truly helping people, never gets old."

"Yeah, I totally get that. So, no Mr. Doctor P?"

"Nope, just haven't found the right guy… yet."

Shea chuckles. "So, why don't we order in some room service and discuss what's going to happen next."

"Great idea. We should get those two to bed soon anyway, it's getting late," Gregg says, nodding to Christian and Diesel.

"Aw, Dad, come on, ten more minutes," John whines.

"Cut it out. Make an order and I'll run them a bath," Gregg orders.

"I love it when he takes charge," Shea says.

John makes gagging noises as they break apart to complete their tasks.

After dinner, Dr. P asks the million-dollar question. "If you don't want to be found, why not just leave the GPS function off?"

Gregg looks out into the distance, thinking. "In theory that sounds like the best option, but he will never stop. GPS or not, there will never be a day that we can sit back and enjoy life, not as long as he is free. We need a good plan, a way to draw him out but keep everyone safe. A way to get him locked up for the crimes he has committed."

Dr. P folds her arms. "Sorry if I sound crass, but why not put a bullet in him? Why not just end it?"

Gregg's jaw tightens. "Because we aren't him. We aren't murderers and we aren't going to let him change that about us."

"You're not wrong to think that. With my military training that makes the most sense to me, too. But Gregg's right, we shouldn't stoop to his level. And honestly, he isn't worth going to prison for," John says.

"So, am I allowed to ask? What's the plan?" Dr. P asks.

"Yeah, you are. I'd actually like to ask you to be part of it. I wouldn't put you in any danger, but it would be a big help if you could," Gregg says.

"I know you wouldn't do anything to endanger me, of course I'll help. I'd like to be able to spend time with all of you," she says, glancing to John, "and not always be treating one of you."

Shea grins. "You can be honest… treating me…"

"Well, if the badass hat fits, wear it," John says.

"Back on track, you two. My plan is to block the GPS and teach Dr. P how to unblock it. I'll have you take it with you and when your plane lands in Anchorage, you'll turn it on and leave it in a garbage can. The last he heard, we were in Anchorage, maybe he'll think we caught a flight. We'll stay here at the hotel for a few days, let them snoop around and leave with no leads. Then we'll head back to the cabin—once we receive the all clear from our contacts in Talkeetna and Anchorage."

"Wow, you really thought this through, huh?" Dr. P asks. "When would you want me to leave?"

"Probably first light—better to get it over with."

"Okay, wow. Sure," she nods.

That night the four adults sit around finalizing plans while the 'children' sleep. Later Shea and Gregg retreat to their bed, while John and Dr. P linger on the veranda talking. It feels like an endless night.

14 | GREGG

"Damn, just now getting up?" Gregg says to John. Looking at his watch, he notes it's 1:45 p.m.

"Man, you should've seen me. You would have been majorly impressed. I'm pretty sure Dr. P won't just be married to her work for much longer."

"Whoa, big boy! That good, huh? What'd you two talk about all night?" Gregg asks.

"Everything. I've never talked with a chick like that. I mean Shea—but she doesn't count."

"Hey! I count! Why don't I count?" Shea demands, standing from her spot on the floor.

"Where the frig did you just come from?" John asks, startled.

"Oh, I was lying on the floor next to the bed. My back has been a little crampy, probably due for my period."

"Okay, okay—TMI!" John groans. "I'm just saying, being able to talk to you until the early morning doesn't count. You're my main man's lady."

"Oh yeah. You're right. I don't count. Proceed—she's the future Mrs. Dr. Krieger?"

"Right, as I was saying. I'm not being a pig or full of myself, I really think there's a connection. I can understand her job and her passion because of my field medic history, and we like a lot of the same things, moi being one of them."

"Oh geez, all in one night you hooked her?" Shea asks, fists kneading her lower back.

"I mean… look at me, Shea. No, but seriously, there's a connection, you'll see. She said once the heat dies down she wants to come see my bunk at the cabin."

"She did not!" Shea says in mock outrage, giggling. "I'm sorry, babe, I completely hijacked your conversation, I'm the worst. I'm gonna go take a nice hot bath. Maybe that will calm my cramping down. Could you maybe order in a heating pad?" she asks Gregg.

"Sure thing, beautiful. Don't worry about it, he just likes to hear himself talk, anyway."

"I'm standing right here!" John exclaims.

"Oh, we know," Shea says, then turns on her heel and struts to the bathroom, fists still digging into her lower back.

"Is she okay?" John asks Gregg, brow creased.

"Yeah, she just hasn't had much of a period since her trauma. I think it's catching up to her," Gregg says, gently stroking Diesel's head while Christian naps.

"In other news, Dr. P got into Anchorage hours ago. She flipped on the GPS and dozens of suited guards were seen in the area. Nothing in Talkeetna according to Matt, but it's been radio silent for a few hours. I don't think they'd give up that easily, but maybe we really fooled them?"

"Or maybe this is the snake coiling before the attack," John says. He walks to his backpack and pulls out the case his handgun is locked in. Pulling out the coyote tan Sig Sauer M17X 9mm pistol, he puts it in the holster already attached to his belt.

"From here on out we need to be on high alert. No one alone, no one goes anywhere, and arm yourself, would you? Shea too, when she gets out."

"Right, you're right. I'm sitting here willing the sat phone to ring when I should be doing what I can to protect my family." He rises from his chair, and says, "But first I'm gonna go try to relieve some of my wife's pain with some pleasure, before we're on high alert for weeks."

"Rub it in, why don't you," John mumbles.

Twenty minutes later, Shea emerges from the bathroom in a plush bathrobe. Gregg trails behind her with a towel around his waist.

"How's your back?" John asks.

"I wish I could say it was better—but the pain relief only lasted, well, while…"

"Gross," John interrupts. "Well, since your husband bailed to go help his sore wife—I ordered your heating pad. It's already plugged in and under the covers on your side of the bed."

Shea sighs, delighted, and marches over to John, hugging him tightly around his hips. "My hero."

"Yeah, yeah. Just get dressed before you lounge, just in case. Have your gun handy too."

"Wait, did something happen?" Shea asks.

"No, I just want to be prepared," he says, then turns his attention to his half-naked best friend, "and you, get dressed pronto. We're going to split the watch. I'll go first since I slept so late."

"You gonna do a perimeter watch?" Gregg asks, a Q-tip deep in his ear.

"Yeah. I wish I could just hang on the veranda, but I doubt they'll come up the river."

"Move the Jimmy, just in case," Gregg says.

"Got it."

Shea comes back out of the bathroom in fuzzy pajamas.

"This is not what I meant, and you know it!" John exclaims.

"John, I am not in the mood. I'm wearing a fucking bra, thank you very much, so get off my back. I'm also wearing my tummy holster, so watch out I'm armed."

"Alright, fine. I'll be back. I'm going to move the Jimmy and walk the perimeter. I know it's early but get some sleep—especially while Christian is knocked out. I'm gonna take Diesel with me… for protection."

15 | Todd

"It's been six fucking months. Do I not employ the smartest people on the fucking planet?" Todd screams from behind his desk, at Tina who sits in one of his visitor chairs, laptop balanced on her knees.

"Toddy, baby, you have to calm down," she says gently. "I know you don't want to hear that, but they're working on it. It sounds like they're about to have a breakthrough, from what I hear in building 15."

"They've had six fucking months. It's one tracker!"

"Yes, but the multiple complex viruses that Gregg left in the system are incurable. Tech is having to rebuild from the ground up. That takes time."

Todd slams his hand on his desk. "I knew he was a genius I just didn't know he was a fucking evil genius."

"Right, but he did achieve a technological miracle. We're going to get him back and we'll be back up and running in no time."

"Tina, you need to take your feel-good attitude and get the fuck out of my office. Don't come back until there's news."

In his large office, Todd sits in his opulent chair. The phone on his desk rings. He reaches over to answer it, his ring prominent on his right ring finger. "What?" he barks into the receiver.

"Sir, we've made more progress on the computer system. The tracker went live two hours ago."

Todd's eyes sharpen. "Excellent. Send in a small team. I'm sure they think they're outsmarting us."

"Yessir. Anything else?"

"Update me with news."

Todd doesn't leave the office that night. He sits in front of the mission log unmoving, even though his team will be on his private jet for twelve hours.

As soon as he sees that Tina's phone is in the building—via location tracking—he presses the intercom button on his desk phone. "Tina, get your ass in here."

A few moments later, Tina enters the office, carrying her laptop on her hip like a toddler.

"What can I do for you, sir?" she asks, her expression neutral.

"Let's not throw a temper tantrum, dearest. Pull up the mission comms and listen with me. This might be over soon."

"Yes…dear."

Tina pulls up the mission. Todd is all but dancing in his seat, the anticipation is killing him.

A voice comes through the laptop, "Team A, head through baggage claim. Team B, perimeter. Team Charlie, we're going straight for the tracker location. Remember, we're just traveling businessmen, handle this like professionals. Quiet on the comms unless a target is spotted."

"There's no way they're at the airport," Todd muses.

"Just listen," Tina murmurs.

"This is Charlie, tracker is secured. It was in a trash can. Awaiting orders."

Todd exhales slowly. "Tell them to do a sweep and get Dom on the chip ASAP. He brought what he needs."

Tina relays the message, then the line goes quiet.

"Have the whole complex on alert. Any communication from Dom needs to be immediately routed to me."

"Yes, sir."

16 | Shea

Her sleep is rudely interrupted by the loudest, log-sawing snoring she has ever heard. Cracking one eye open, she looks to the body beside her. John is lying face down over the covers on Gregg's side of the bed.

My God, how is he even breathing? The pillowcase must be all the way up his nose

She smacks his shoulder, and loudly says, "John! Are you okay?"

"What, who?" he says, rolling onto his side and looking at her.

"John, you were face first in the pillow, sawing logs. I was worried for your health."

"Oh, shit. My bad, I was so tired. I literally passed out." He rubs his eyes.

"Where is everyone?" Shea asks, hanging her legs over the side of the bed, hands again at her back.

I wish my damn period would just start. These cramps are brutal

"Ah, Gregg was on watch when I went to sleep, so no idea. I guess I'll get up and see if he took the sat phone. Hopefully he has the dingleberries with him, otherwise we have a big problem."

"Okay, I'm gonna go to the bathroom, you look for the phone."

"Roger."

In the bathroom she pulls out her toiletry bag. Her pain isn't bad enough to reach for her not-so-secret tampon, but she has a bottle of ibuprofen in there too. She dry swallows three and plops herself onto the toilet. When she glances down, she sees a small spot of blood in her underwear and thanks God.

She pulls on new underwear, then dresses in leggings and a hoodie.

When she opens the door to head back into the room, she hears John talking. "A note would have been nice, man. Alright, we will see you in ten minutes then."

He looks over at Shea, and says, "They went to get ice cream. Apparently Christian had a hankering and he tracked Gregg down on his perimeter sweep. That kid can be relentless. I think I liked it better when he didn't talk."

"John! That's horrible! I mean, yes, he can be relentless, but he's a kid!"

"I know. Maybe I'm just jealous that he told you he loved you. What am I, chopped liver?"

"Aw, poor John. I love you!"

"Yeah, yeah."

Fifteen minutes later, they are all sitting on the veranda enjoying vanilla ice cream with sprinkles and whipped cream.

John suddenly stands—on high alert.

"What's up, man?" Gregg asks from his seat.

"Two blacked-out SUVs on the main road. Get inside, grab the bags, and get to the Jimmy. Just in case."

"You're not staying here. We're not splitting up again. John, grab the bags, the kid, and Diesel. I'll get the stuff we put in the safe and I'll be right behind you. Shea, go with John. This is not a drill. Move," Gregg demands.

17 | Todd

Todd's been patient. He hasn't yelled. He calmly waits for his phone to ring. Lucky for him, and everyone else, it only takes Dom a few hours to get what he needs from the chip. The second he hears Tina's voice over his intercom, his face lights up with joy, like a kid on Christmas morning.

"Sir, Dom is on line three."

He reaches for the receiver and brings it to his ear, pressing the button for line three.

"Dom, tell me you have good news."

"Hey, Boss. I have great news actually! So, you were right, they took the bait on the decoy. That light was a great idea. The GPS location we got was from that. Once I disassembled it though, the passive tracker on the inside had been recording for two days. We believe we have their exact location. Two teams were deployed from the satellite branch in Anchorage. They are at the target, awaiting your orders, sir."

"Excellent news! You'll have a promotion waiting for you when you get home."

"Thank you, sir. Orders?"

"Have the teams that are there watch and wait, corner them. I don't want them leaving wherever they are. Deploy the Black Hawks and at least fifteen additional men from the satellite office."

"Yes sir. Anything else?"

"Bring them in. Do not fail me. The child and Gregg must be brought in alive. The other two targets… dealer's choice."

"Yes sir, comms going live."

He hangs up the phone and before he can even press the intercom button, Tina comes barreling into his office, laptop in hand.

"I heard, pulling up the comms now," she says as she sits in one of his visitor chairs.

"Good. Very good."

18 | Shea

As they make their way to the Jimmy, John scans back and forth for any signs of danger. Shea tries to stay focused, but she's so sore, she just wants to curl into a ball on the pavement.

"Shit," she hears, and it pulls her out of her misery. When she looks up, John has stopped dead in his tracks, Christian beside him. Diesel stands at an angle in front of all of them, ever their protector.

"What is it?" she whispers.

"Those SUVs have blocked both of the exits we can get to from here." His voice drops low. "We're boxed in."

"So what do we do?"

"We'll have to leave on foot, through some brush, to try and stay undetected."

"Okay, so we'll just wait for Gregg and then head out on foot, right?"

John shakes his head. "We need to start heading that way. He'll see us. These SUVs might already have eyes on us. It's too dangerous to keep standing here like sitting ducks."

"So we double back. Go to the room, get him, and head out that way."

"Yeah, okay. Everyone turn around calmly, like we just forgot something and are going back to get it," John instructs.

They pivot together, except for Diesel, who remains planted in his position, watching their backs. When they get closer to the room, Shea starts to hear something in the distance. Her head snaps up. Two helicopters are heading in their direction, fast.

She immediately looks to John. "What now?"

"Same plan. Go!" He sends a whistle out for Diesel, who runs to catch up to them.

Shea runs out ahead, cramps be damned. She knows her husband, she knows he is going to try to sacrifice himself for them, and she is not having that shit.

When she gets closer to the room's slightly ajar door, she hears talking.

"Just come with me. I'll grab the kid and no one else gets hurt. Our orders are to bring you in alive. Put the gun down and we can do this the easy way."

"Shea, John, and Diesel get to just walk away?"

"Scot-free. A gift from Todd."

A thick muscular arm wraps around her midsection and lifts her feet off the ground. She flails, goes limp, beats at the arm, throws her head back to try to end the assault, but it's no use. She finally looks over her shoulder and sees that it's John who carries her with one arm. Christian dangles from the other. All of their bags are slung over his shoulders. He's running them toward the woods, away from their room.

"John, please. Please wait, we can get him out. Please, John!" she begs. Her heart is beginning to rip in two. Her crucifix digs into her palm.

This cannot be happening

Her pleas fall on deaf ears. John runs until they are about six feet deep into the tree line. Only then does he set them down, a single finger to his lips. Shea is handed a pair of binoculars. John lifts his shirt to take out his gun, the motion showing her that she should probably do the same. But she only has two hands, so she uses the binoculars first.

She places her eyes behind the eyepieces and turns the focus to make the image clearer. She can see their room door, still slightly ajar.

"Shea, we have to move. We can't stay here. Those helicopters are inbound, and we're fucked if we're still here when they arrive."

"There is only one guy on him, John. We can handle one guy and then Gregg can come with us. We don't have to leave him! This isn't right."

"He would not want you to put yourself in danger for him again, Shea. I promise you that. If I can get a clear shot and we can leave before the choppers get here, then okay. But all of that is a big if."

"It's something," she whispers.

Come on, Gregg, please

She continues watching through the binoculars. Her pulse is racing, her hands tremble so severely it's making it difficult to hold them steady. The distant thrum of two helicopters intensifies with every breath. She knows their time is drawing short, but she can't leave without him.

John's hand lands on her shoulder. "Shea, I'm sorry. We have to get out of here. There are more SUVs coming up the main road and those choppers will be here in less than a minute. We're cutting it way too close. He gave me a job, and I will carry you out of here if I have to."

"Wait, wait." Her breath catches. "He's coming out of the door."

She watches through the binoculars and John and Christian try to see through the leaves. Gregg is walked out by a man in a suit who holds a gun at Gregg's spine.

A small gasp leaves Shea.

John levels his pistol at the man, but Shea knows he won't make the shot from here. All it would do is give away their position.

Gregg looks straight ahead, unreadable, not looking for them at all.

The man yells at Gregg to stop where he is. He complies, turning toward the man.

The man demands he tell him where the child and the rest of the group are, but Gregg remains silent.

Tears slip down Shea's face. She will not leave him.

The man is screaming at Gregg now, with other men heading toward them. He gestures with his gun wildly, angrily.

Gregg remains silent.

A hand slaps over her mouth as she hears a gunshot and watches Gregg collapse to the pavement. Her scream is silenced. She can't breathe. The binoculars drop from her hands.

"I'm so sorry, Shea," John whispers in her ear, as he lifts her around her waist.

She watches as John nods to Christian, and he places his small hand on hers, turning her world to black.

19 | JOHN

John runs through the brush as fast as he can, carrying Shea over his shoulder in a fireman's carry. Blood drips down his cheek from tree branches slapping him in the face, but he can't feel it. He can't feel anything except the weight of Shea's unconscious body. He's in shock, and it's freezing cold, so that isn't helping either.

His senses are pushed to the max, listening for any signs of pursuit and keeping a three-sixty-degree watch. Christian keeps pace beside him, his hand steady on Shea's to keep her under, but he's breathing heavily. Diesel runs a protective perimeter around them, about twenty-five feet out from them.

He can't stop. He's trying to remember the plan, but all he can think about is the fact that he can't stop. He can't think about Gregg, and he can't let what happened be in vain. Every step farther away from that hotel is a step closer to freedom and safety. The loud whomp-whomp of two helicopters taking off stops him in his tracks.

"Hide in the deep brush. Get all the way on the ground," he orders Christian.

He gently places Shea on the ground and covers her with snow. Christian remains in contact with her, lying next to her. John buries him as well, then their bags. He looks around for Diesel, but he's nowhere to be seen. Hopefully he keeps his distance.

John sinks to his knees in his snow camo jacket. He buries his lower legs, pulls up his hood, puts his head down, and waits.

Spotlights illuminate the terrain around him. His heart races, hands shaking. He decides to take a page from Shea's book and sends up a near-silent plea. "I know you're there, please keep us safe."

Fifteen minutes that feel like hours later, he digs up his frozen friends and thinks he needs to change his underwear.

Diesel comes racing toward them through the woods, licking the snow off Christian's face.

"Good boy! That was the exact right thing! Good boy! I'll get you a treat in a minute. We need to get some warming packs in these guys' clothes."

Once they're out of the snow, John pulls out Gregg's plan. He needs to get them out of here, and fast. Their lips are blue and although they're no longer touching, they're both unconscious.

He's so cold. He held on as long as he could. He didn't mean to let go, he just couldn't stay awake any longer.

He's scared. He can't go back in that cell. He can't go back to that place, the one with all the torture and dead bodies.

He's worried for Diesel. He's a good boy but might do the wrong thing.

He's confused about Shea. The bad chip is gone, but something still feels off.

He wants to go home. He's never had a real home. Not before the cabin. The cabin made him happier than he'd ever been.

All of his new family have made him happier than he's ever been.

Is Gregg dead? He loves Gregg, just like Shea and John. And Diesel, of course.

Gregg can't be dead. But he saw him get shot.

Please. No.

21 | GREGG

Gregg's blood pools on the ground beneath him. He lies unmoving on the pavement where he landed. His eyes stare without focus.

He's really fucking pissed he got shot.

Men in suits swarm around him, jumping from helicopters on ropes. Someone slides him into a rescue basket and he's pulled upward toward the helicopter. He looks down at the ground below him. In the distance he watches John run through the brush with a lifeless Shea in his arms.

He feels his heartbeat and the burn of his blood freezing in the wound just under his collarbone on the right side of his chest, close to his armpit. It isn't a fatal wound, but he almost wishes it was. Whatever awaits him is bound to be worse than a gunshot wound.

Men in tactical gear pull him into the helicopter. They deposit him onto a bench built into the interior wall. They aggressively push gauze into the wound.

Gregg reacts violently. "Get the fuck off of me!"

"Sir, I know it hurts, but we need to stop the bleeding. Once I can start an IV, I'll get you something for the pain."

Gregg lies back. Considering they are currently trying to help him, he'll behave. An oxygen mask is placed over his face while one of the men places an IV in his forearm, a syringe in place ready to push pain medication.

"Wait. Please," Gregg says, pulling the mask off his face.

"Sir, you need to put that back on. I'm going to give you pain medication now."

"And I'm asking you to wait a sec, man. I need you to knock me out. Where we're going and what's going to happen, I need to be out, for now. Please, do this for me."

"Hold on."

The man pushes a button on his collar, and speaks, "Prisoner is requesting sedation until we arrive at the complex." The man's eyes rove over Gregg for a second while he listens to his earpiece. "Yes, sir. Affirmative." More listening. "Yessir, will do."

He looks back at Gregg's face, and says, "Todd thinks you should suffer. But because he wants your cooperation, he is willing to do this as an olive branch. I will give you a light sedation and maintain it until we are back at the compound."

"Thank God," Gregg says, under his breath.

"He prefers to be called Todd," the man says, depressing the plunger on the syringe and launching Gregg into a dreamless sleep.

22 | Todd

Todd stares at Tina, who sits across from him at their dinner table.

"I'm waiting."

"Todd, they were focused on Gregg. The others were able to get away while the team swarmed him."

"I can appreciate the situation, but then what happened? They just flew off? Drove away? Without the child?" His voice steadily rises through each question.

"They did sweeps over the area in concentric circles. They saw no movement, no traffic—nothing. It was twenty degrees, they weren't prepared to run, they might not have made it."

"So my team just gave up?" The veins in Todd's neck bulge.

"More agents are in the area now. No one is giving up. They left because they wanted to get Gregg on a plane and back here as soon as possible."

Todd exhales roughly through his nose. "Tina, I need you to give me a better play-by-play here. I could just listen to the recording, but I thought it would be nice to talk. If I didn't have to go to that other fucking meeting, I wouldn't need your report."

"I know, I tried to take it off the books," she says softly. "He refused."

"So they got Gregg and then they were in such a rush to get him back here, I didn't get my other trophy?"

"Todd..." she hesitates. "Agent Miller shot Gregg. It was unprovoked. Gregg wouldn't answer his question."

Todd's chair screeches back. "WHAT THE FUCK, TINA! Way to bury the fucking lead! What's the damage?"

"Through-and-through right shoulder. He'll need imaging to assess how much damage, but they've stopped the bleeding. He's stable and they think he'll do fine on the plane."

He rubs his temples. "That's what they called me about earlier. I thought he just wanted to be sedated because we took him away from his friends. Fuck, I hate being in the dark." He pulls out his cell phone and glances at a text. "Alright, one last thing, as soon as Miller is in the building, he's in my office. He disobeyed orders, and you know how much I hate that."

Tina swallows. "Yes, sir."

John rips open several packs of Hot Hands hand warmers at once. He shakes them and places them under Shea and Christian's clothes. Diesel whines beside him.

"I know, dude. We're gonna help them."

Shea's soaked hoodie and leggings do nothing to keep the cold out, as they cling to her body. He knows what he needs to do to help her, he's just pissed he has to.

"Why couldn't you just put on a bra and snow gear, Shea? Shit!"

He takes her snow gear out of her bag and quickly dresses her in dry leggings and snow pants, thanking the heavens she put on underwear. He saves the top for last. He finds one of Shea's neck gaiters, puts her legs through and pulls it all the way up to her waist. He then slides it under her wet hoodie and over her chest like a makeshift tube top.

"Look how smart I am, D," he says to the dog.

He strips off the hoodie and replaces it with a new one and a winter coat. He reapplies the Hot Hands to help warm her further. Next he assesses Christian, who is wearing full winter gear. John can feel the child's skin warming from the Hot Hands, but he needs to get them both out of the elements as soon as possible.

John lays Christian over one of the duffel bags and drops the strap across his body and onto his shoulder. Carefully he then he pulls Shea over his shoulder in a fireman's carry.

"Okay, D. You're on watch. It's just a couple of miles to the Jeep tour place. We need to be fast and quiet."

He braces himself and stands. He takes off (kind of) running parallel to the road within the cover of the brush. Periodically he stops to check on Shea and Christian. Their lips are no longer blue, but they're still asleep. With everything they're both going through emotionally, John sees it as a blessing.

His surroundings are now pitch dark. He's finding it hard to navigate without getting smacked in the face repeatedly. With no lights on the road to illuminate his way, he starts to fear he's walking in circles. He should have been at the Jeep tour place by now. He hears choppers in the distance and has seen vehicles traveling on the road, but it seems he's outside of their search radius for the moment. The search efforts seem pretty localized, they must not think John, Shea, and Christian made it out.

"Good, this is better for us."

He keeps moving, but at a slower pace, exhaustion making each limb feel like it weighs a thousand pounds.

From behind his back, he hears, "Put me down, John."

24 | Shea

Shea's head throbs from the pressure of her blood rushing to it. Her necklace swings and hits her in the nose with each step John takes. It takes her a second to figure out where she is and what's happening. She recognizes John's coat, and says, "Put me down, John."

"I'm glad you're awake," he says, sounding breathless, "but I can't put you down. I know you too well."

"I'm not going to run, please. My back was already killing me, this is making it a billion times worse."

"Alright," he says, gently depositing her feet onto the ground. He keeps his arm around her shoulder until she secures her footing.

"Thanks. Where are we?"

"I'm not completely sure, but I know we're heading the right way. We need to keep moving."

"Right. Just before we go…" She swallows hard. "Was he alive?"

He doesn't meet her eyes, his jaw tenses. "Shea, this is not a good idea right now, we have to ensure our safety first."

"John, just tell me."

"I don't know, Shea. A bunch of agents ran over to him so I couldn't see, but you know Todd wanted him alive. I'm going to say he's alive. He has to be."

She nods once. "Okay. What about Christian?"

"He's been out since I had to bury you in the snow. I think keeping you under took a lot out of him. That plus seeing what we all saw… I'm thinking he'll be out for a while."

Um, what am I wearing?

"One more thing, where'd my favorite hoodie go?"

"You were soaked. I had no choice. I didn't look at anything, you know I wouldn't do that."

"Alright, it's freezing. Let's get to where we're going."

Before they start again, Shea reaches in Gregg's bag. She pulls out a blanket that still smells like him—woodsy, clean and bright—and places it over Christian, on John's duffel bag. John takes out the binoculars and tries to see through the darkness, but it's too thick. He gives up, putting the binoculars away and pulling out smoked salmon instead. He cuts open three pouches and hands one to Shea.

"Eat something, it's been a long day."

"Thanks. I'm starving."

John uses a silent whistle to call for Diesel. The dog has been doing large laps all day, he has to be starving.

Once Diesel finishes his pack of smoked salmon—in about two seconds—they all take off at a jog in what John thinks is the right direction.

25 | GREGG

Somewhere over the Midwest, Gregg regains a fuzzy consciousness. His shoulder is throbbing and his mouth feels like the Sahara desert. He can hear men talking around him, they seem to not know he's awake yet. He keeps his eyelids gently closed in an attempt to not raise any suspicions.

"Bravo team hasn't had any luck?"

"No, nothing. Big man is pissed."

"At least we got one target, he can't be too mad at us."

"Not us, but Miller's a goner."

"No kidding."

Gregg's fuzzy mind feels slightly bad for Miller, but the man did shoot him after all. His attention shifts to his loved ones. It sounds like they weren't found. Gregg smiles on the inside. As long as they are safe, whatever awaits him, he can deal with it.

"You have any idea what's in store for this guy?"

"Todd's been pretty tight-lipped about the whole thing, but I know he wants him to rebuild the tech and possibly the time machine. It'll all have to wait until this guy's shoulder is looked at though."

"What makes Todd think the guy will cooperate?"

"I'm sure he'll play it like he has the other targets, threaten their lives, or something."

"Maybe. There have been some talks around medical, some compliance serum or something."

"I heard about that. They were testing it on that guy that dosed all the Directors last year."

"Yeah, have you seen him? His brain is like mush now."

"Yeah, last I saw he was strapped into a chair like a toddler, drool running from his mouth."

"Shit. Bad luck for this guy."

Gregg keeps his eyes and his mouth closed. If that is about to happen to him, he hopes Shea never has to see it.

26 | JOHN

John's snot is frozen to his mustache. His fingers ache inside his gloves. He puts one foot in front of the other, purposefully only thinking about the mission at hand. All other thoughts are shut down.

"Hey, I see lights," Shea's voice pierces through the silent woods like a bullet.

"Shit, you scared me!" he says, stopping to look around.

"Straight ahead, maybe a hundred feet or so."

He squints, trying to follow her raised arm with his eyes. "Oh, shit, okay. I know where we are! These cabins are behind the Jeep place. We'll have to go around but we're almost there!"

"Are you planning on stealing a Jeep?"

"Shea, you know us better than that, we can't have any heat. Gregg prearranged it, there will be a baby blue Jeep parked closest to the woods. The keys will be stuck to the left rear fender."

"Why doesn't anyone tell me anything?" she whines. "You guys have plans out your asses and I know nothing! What if you were both taken? I'd be screwed."

"Shea, take a breath. We wrote everything down. It's in your pack, in your little leather notebook. Gregg did everything the way he did because he didn't want to stress you out. He wanted you to heal, and to stop blaming yourself for everything. Shea, that man loved you more than the air he breathed, trust us."

"Loved? Breathed?" Shea pulls in a heavy gasp of air and holds it.

"Shea, breathe. He is fine. I don't know why I said it like that, okay? I'm sorry. We're so close, please hold it together a little while longer." He grabs her face and wipes his gloved fingers under her eyes. He can't feel the tears, but he knows they're there.

"Okay, let's just get out of here."

They move a little faster now, feeling rejuvenated by the sight of civilization. They move around the perimeter of the log cabins, quickly but quietly. John spots a blacked-out SUV on the far side of the parking lot.

"Okay, Shea. I need you to go get the Jeep. You need to play it cool. I will wait in the woods a little farther down and you'll pick me up there. You're wearing different clothes and they won't be expecting you to be alone. It'll be fine."

"Okay. I've got this. I can do this."

"Get your holster on, just in case."

"What do you mean? I am wearing it…" She smiles. "Wow, you really didn't look or feel at all. You're such a good man."

"Yeah, yeah. Let's do this."

27 | Shea

She strides confidently over to the Jeep Wrangler at the far end of the parking lot, carrying her bag over her shoulder, a beanie holding her long hair up off her back. The closer she gets to the vehicle, the more effort each step takes. Her body wants to break into a sprint.

She (very calmly) walks over to the rear of the vehicle, quickly sliding her hand against the fender until she feels the keys. She pulls, disengages the magnet, and the keys leave with her hand. She quickly hits the unlock button and throws her bag into the back.

Sitting in the driver's seat, she takes slow breaths. Her hands shake, making it hard to get the key into the ignition. Once she starts the Jeep, she blasts the heat and waits a minute to move. She wants it to be nice and warm for her friends when they get in.

Pulling about fifty feet away parallel to the woods, she spots her friends and puts the Jeep in park. John rushes over, standing with his back to the now faraway blacked out SUV. Diesel jumps in first and as soon as Christian is slid in next to him, he begins licking the boy's face. John stashes all of the bags, except for his backpack, in the back and drops himself into the passenger seat.

"Go, normal speeds, but get us out of here."

"Which way am I going?"

"North on the Parks Highway. They won't expect us to head that way, should be an easier trip. We have a pilot that will meet us at an airfield north of here. I need to make a bunch of calls, but we have some time. I'll stay on the lookout for a little while, but I need some sleep."

"I watch," a voice says from the backseat.

"BUD!" Shea exclaims. "Oh my gosh, are you okay? I've been worried sick."

"Hungry, but okay."

"The bags are behind you, little man. Take your pick, whatever you want," John instructs.

"I watch," he repeats, more firmly this time.

"You think you're up to it?" John asks, studying him.

"Yeah, you come here, I go there."

"Okay. Only for a few hours, then I need to make some calls. Make sure you wake me, Shea."

"No problem. I'll pull over so you can switch and so I can find my iPod."

"Okay, but be quick."

28 | Tina

Tina stares at her reflection in the mirror. Bruises mar her once perfect skin. It's not the first time he's taken his anger out on her, but it is the first time he's aimed for her face.

This morning though, he woke up in a great mood. Gregg is due to land in a few hours. She needs to make sure everything goes perfectly so he stays in that mood. She covers the bruises with makeup and plasters a smile onto her face.

Walking out to the kitchen in her six-inch heels, she slows as she gets to the bar. Todd stands in tailored slacks and a cobalt blue, long-sleeved button-down shirt. He pauses his shoveling of egg whites into his mouth and flashes her his megawatt smile.

"There's mon sweet petit. Want some eggs?"

"Good morning," she says cautiously. "I think I'll fast today. I have a figure to maintain for my sexy husband."

"Oh, stop it, you! Well, let me finish this then and we'll hit the road, okay?"

"Yeah, I'm gonna go feed Ren and Stimpy and then I'll meet you out front."

"Ah, yes, the rats." He waves her off. "Well, get the lead out, I already placed the order for the car."

"Ferrets, my love. Not rats."

Tina's true loves are her ferrets. They have their own room in the Donoghue mansion. It's filled with tunnels, ball pits, and all the toys they could ever want. She refreshes their food and water and picks them up for kisses. She leaves their room, closing the door behind her.

When she gets out front, Todd is already in the town car. She holds her tongue as she sits down beside him.

"Now you have rat fur all over your lovely black blouse," he says without even looking at her.

"Thank you for telling me, I have a lint roller in my purse," she says as sweetly as she can manage.

As she lint-rolls herself, she watches Todd's face—mesmerized by his phone—light up with joy. She waits for him to share, afraid asking will lead to another dark mood.

"Look at this," he says, turning the phone toward her.

She leans in. "A deed to a cabin?"

"Yes! This was apparently on Gregg when he was shot. So it's safe to assume that it's where they've been."

"Do you think they'll go back?" she asks, knowing Gregg is too smart for that, but is John?

He laughs softly, delighted. "No, but we might find some clues there. Like where the others have gone."

29 | Shea

Shea's been driving for hours. Christian has been a great co-captain, pointing out moose, feeding her snacks and headbanging when appropriate.

"Alright, wake the human chainsaw. I think my ears have started to bleed," Shea says.

Christian giggles, turns in his seat and pokes John with a single outstretched finger.

Christian shrieks when John grabs his wrist and twists. The sound wakes John fully. He immediately releases Christian's wrist. Shea glances in the rearview and sees John's face is stricken. Shea can tell he feels terrible.

"Oh dammit bud, I'm so sorry. It was a reflex. Are you okay?"

"I okay," Christian says, holding his wrist to his chest.

"Remember when I punched you in the throat?" Shea asks John, trying to distract Christian.

"Yeah, our training might have been a little too good. Pull over, I gotta pee and I'm sure little man does too."

"Yup."

"I need to pee too," Shea admits.

"Okay, Christian and I will go, then you and Diesel."

"Alright."

She pulls over and as John and Christian do their business, Shea digs in her bag for a regular tampon and her special tampon. Her cramps are shitty, but she's leaning on the Percocet more for her emotional pain. John will be driving now, so she's going to kill the pain while she can.

When they come bounding back to the Jeep, she grabs her toilet paper and tampon, calling Diesel to her. A few feet into the woods, she relieves herself. Though her cramps are bad, her tampon is dry.

What the hell

Diesel sticks to her like glue the whole way back to the Jeep. She jumps in the passenger seat, ready for a nap, but hears John already on the phone.

"It's time for the plan. Head over to the Alcan. Remember only let yourself be seen every few days, then immediately go back underground. Gather as many of our old buddies as you can along the way. Get in touch with Captain Charlie, okay?"

John is quiet for a moment, then she hears, "Yeah, you too, fuck face." She chuckles to herself, knowing he must have been talking to Matt.

As soon as that call ends, another begins.

"Hey, it's me. They found us. I wanted to let you know so you wouldn't think I ghosted you or something."

Is he talking to Dr. P?

"I can't put you in danger and we won't be in Alaska for much longer. When this all calms down, can I give you a call?" He pauses for a moment, then adds, "Oh also, my twin brother Matt is trying to make a case. He might give you a call. Talk soon."

Shea pulls on her seat belt and slightly reclines in her seat, ready for her nap.

"Hey, any news?"

Who is he talking to now?

"Okay, I'll call in a few days."

She hears him break the phone and throw it in the woods.

When he slides into the driver's seat, Shea asks, "Who was that?"

"Well, I called our pilot while you were peeing to make sure he's ready. Then Matt. He will be traveling across the country on a different path than us to throw Todd off of our scent. Then I called Dr. P to give her the heads up that she wouldn't be hearing from me. And last but not least, I called one of my buddies who still works as a guard in Todd's compound. Gregg is inbound. He's alive, Shea."

Oh God

30 | Todd

Todd watches Tina scramble, getting everything ready for Gregg's arrival. Her heels click against the tile as she wipes invisible dust from every surface.

He smiles. This is going to be the best freaking day.

Tina's cell phone rings. "Hello, go for Tina."

He waits as patiently as possible for her to be done. As soon as she hangs up, he asks, "Who was it, love?"

"Alpha team just landed on our private runway. They're loading Gregg into a private ambulance. They will be en route shortly."

"Fantastic! Why don't you order in some Chinese? It'll be just like old times."

"Yes, sir. Right away."

Todd looks around at the room's sterile decor. A medical chair sits in the middle, complete with leather and metal straps. A table with instruments lined up on it sits to the right of the chair. Several pairs of sterile gloves, some sterile gauze, and sutures line the counter.

Todd's body thrums with excitement. Gregg has no idea what's in store for him.

John puts the Jeep into drive, feeling the weight of Shea's stare. He keeps his eyes on the snowy road ahead.

"Breathe, Shea. This is good news. Todd isn't going to kill him, he needs him."

"I'm… I don't know what to say. I hadn't let myself really think about it yet. Now everything's hitting me all at once," she says, wiping tears from her cheeks.

"Take your nap. You've got time, we've got miles to go. Get your sleep while you can."

Almost as soon as she lies back, she begins snoring.

He remains focused on the road, the cabin filled with quiet snores. A small voice breaks through the silence. "Gregg, okay?"

"Yeah, bud," he says, eyes flicking to the rearview mirror. "He's on his way to Todd's compound, but he's alive."

"But…prisoner?"

"Yeah, bud. Don't worry, we're working on getting him out. It's just going to take some time."

"Have to hurry!" Christian exclaims.

"I know, Christian. But we have to be very careful. We can't let Todd get ahold of you or Shea. Gregg would kill me if Todd got either of you. You're my priority."

The Jeep goes quiet and stays that way for a while. John thinks Christian has fallen asleep. He's now alone with his thoughts, without immediate danger, for the first time in a couple of days. There's a clear plan he needs to follow, and he will do everything in his power to keep his people safe.

"John?" he hears from the backseat.

"Yeah?"

"And Diesel?"

"And Diesel what, bud?"

"Priority?"

"Ah, yes. Of course. Diesel is also my backup in protecting you two. He does a great job."

"Yup."

"You feeling okay about everything?"

"Worried."

"I know, bud."

"John?"

"Yeah?"

"Thank you."

32 | GREGG

Gregg is fully awake by the time the plane touches down on Todd's private landing strip. Todd's team has stopped talking, so Gregg passes the time by fantasizing about all the ways he plans to sabotage Todd's tech.

When the door to the plane opens, the men accompanying Gregg carefully lift his gurney down the stairs and onto the tarmac.

The humid air makes Gregg take a gasping breath. He closes his eyes and breathes deeply. The more anxious he gets, the faster his heart beats. He begins to feel blood dripping down his arm, but before he can alert someone, one of Todd's goons walks over and shoves a gloved finger into his gunshot wound.

"FUCK!" he screams, bolting upright.

The same goon plants his large hand on Gregg's chest and shoves him back down onto the gurney. Gregg realizes in this moment how weakened he truly is. His body protests, begging for him to pass out for a while, but sheer willpower shuts that shit down.

He's alert enough to notice they're wheeling him into building 32. He's never been this far back in the compound, so he has no idea what happens on the other side of this door. The jolt of the gurney being pushed over the threshold brings back the argument in favor of unconsciousness. His ears suddenly forget how to hear, and spots flood his vision.

He's pretty sure he's about to lose the battle, when he hears, "Gregg, my man! Welcome home!"

"I'm sorry, Clara. It's too dangerous. It would be like putting a target on your back." There's no way in hell he's allowing that.

"I want to help!" she argues, hands on her hips.

"And you are," he says, softening. "By staying here and letting us know when Todd's goons are in the area."

"Matt, Betty down at the bead store can do that—she's trustworthy."

"Clara, we're not having this discussion. I don't even want to go." He's only going because he shares a face with an idiot.

"What are your plans after all this is over? When you can go back to doing whatever you want?" she asks softly.

"Is that what this is about? Shit, girl, you know you got me on lock. I'll call you whenever I can. You're stuck with me forever." He wraps his arms around her petite frame and nuzzles his face into the side of her neck.

"Stttaaaahhhppppp, you know I'm ticklish!" she squeals.

"Will you still be my lady when I get back?" he asks, earnest.

"Of course," she says, a smile lighting up her face. "I hid your favorite hat in the couch. I know that's what you're looking for."

"You thought I wouldn't leave without it?" he asks. She knows him so well.

"Of course not. It's lucky—you need it."

"Be safe while I'm gone, please. Will you carry that smaller bag out for me? I really need to get going."

"Alright, fine."

A few miles before the Alaska-Canadian border, he stops at The Old Border City Lodge. He makes sure he talks to as many people as possible and books a room for several weeks.

He crosses the border sometime in the middle of the night in a new (to him) car.

34 | JOHN

The sat phone rings in the middle of the night. Shea, Christian, and Diesel startle awake. John continues driving, hearing the scrambling of a child digging through a backpack.

A frustrated, "Gah, who's?" comes from the backseat.

"I thought mine, but it might be Gregg's. Hurry up, would ya!" John says, a smile in his voice.

"I YAM!"

John hears the phone break free from the backpack and the volume of its annoying ringtone increases. Christian's small hand delivers the phone into John's. He accepts the call as soon as he can reach the button, and says, "Code?"

"A/C twenty minutes ago. All's well."

"Okay. Keep going—and hey, thanks."

"Yeah, fuck off. Love ya!"

As soon as he ends the call, Shea says, "Okay, a few things. One, I need more ibuprofen. Two, what and who was that? I need the deets. Three, I need some real food, a real bed and a playlist ASAP!"

John chuckles and Christian shakes a bottle of pills from the backseat.

"Ask and ye shall receive. That was Matt. He crossed the border from Alaska into Canada twenty minutes ago. We can eat, sleep, and jam out in luxury soon. The airfield isn't far."

Shea dry swallows her pills. "How are we paying? There's no bag of cash."

"Yeah, all of this was preauthorized using untraceable methods that Gregg set up. Between all our savings, you guys' relocation bonuses, and what we saved while working in hell, we don't have to worry too much about money."

"Right, but what about stuff we'll need along the way? Gas, food, toiletries—we need cash, right?"

"Yeah, smarty-pants. We overpaid for the plane, kind of like cash back. We're fine. I got us covered."

"Okay, well how long till we're there?"

He side-eyes her. "Did you just 'are we there yet' me?"

"Ha, I guess I did."

"See that tower ahead? Up on the right, with the blinking light?" John asks.

"Yeah?"

"That's our airfield. We should be there in five."

The ache in his chest grows. Gregg injured and captured. Matt running from dangerous people for him. Shea and Christian depending on him to keep them all alive. He's got to stay strong for all of them… and himself.

35 | GREGG

Gregg feels about as vulnerable as a man can get. His archenemy stands over him as he lies bleeding on a gurney—looking up at said nemesis from his position on his back.

"Oh, hey…man," he gets out from his place at the edge of consciousness.

"You in pain, Greggy?" Todds face is a mask of concern.

"Only when I breathe."

"That's a bummer, man. I never meant for any of that to happen. You have my apologies."

Gregg blinks up at him, dazed. "Thanks—uh, so, what's next, Todd? Torture? You gonna dig around in my wound to make me talk? I'll never tell you where they are. You might as well kill me now."

"Gregg, take a breath. I'm not going to torture or kill you! We're friends!"

Gregg decides to hold his tongue. In lieu of a response, he grunts and closes his eyes.

"Alright, I get it. Long day. Our medical team is going to take great care of you. Our head of radiology, Donna, is going to grab some X-rays and the surgical team is already prepped and ready to repair the gunshot wound. We'll talk more once you're in recovery, okay?"

With that, Todd pats him on the shoulder, then turns and leaves the room. Leaving Gregg in Donna's hands.

After several minutes of Donna manhandling him into different painful positions, she wheels him into the surgical suite.

"Here you go. Good luck, Mr. Marsh," she says, then leaves the room.

Laying on the gurney, looking around, he thinks he recognizes the doctor reading his X-rays. He's in a room that looks like a surgical suite from TV, with big lights overhead and stainless-steel surfaces.

"Gregg! Long time no see. I'm Dr. Hughes. We met at orientation. Anyway, there are no bullet or bone fragments on the image, but there are some muscles, tendons and ligaments that need to be repaired. So, out you go!"

A man pushes a mask that smells of plastic over his mouth and nose as he pushes a milky white medication through his IV. On his way into unconsciousness, he hears the man say, "Milk of Amnesia…"

36 | Shea

Settling Christian and Diesel into their own room on the luxurious private jet that Gregg arranged for them, Shea takes a deep breath.

He's alive.

"Shea, you okay?" Christian asks.

She sits on the bed next to him and runs her hands through his hair. "I'm alright. Relieved and stressed. And we all need showers. We stink! Pee-yew."

Christian giggles for a moment, then stares at her with unshed tears in his eyes.

"Oh, bud. It's okay. We'll rescue him and we will all be together again. Those cabin bees aren't going to chase themselves, are they?"

He smiles and shakes his head, tears escaping from the corners of his eyes. Diesel whines and cuddles in closer to Christian.

"What is it, bud? Are you worried?"

"Yeah. But…ugh, something else… happy."

Her hand stills in his hair. "Happy? To be with us?"

He shakes his head again. "No."

"Use your words, okay? I'm starving, and I need a shower—seriously."

"Not sure, yet. Later."

"Are you sure?" she asks.

"Yeah—all good!"

Shea sighs. "You spend too much time with John. Alright, get some sleep. When you wake up, straight to the shower, understand?"

"Yes, ma 'aam," he says, tears still sliding from his eyes.

"Christian, I don't feel right leaving you upset like this," she says, genuinely concerned.

"I'm not. Happy tears."

"Okay. If you need us, we're one door down, got it?"

"Got it."

She leaves the room, pulling the door closed behind her.

Kids are weird

She walks out to the main area, where John sits with a burger and fries in front of him.

"I waited! I'd like the jury to know, I waited!" he exclaims.

"Shut up. I'm starved." She sits beside him and takes in the amazing aroma coming off her burger. Her mouth fills with saliva, and she's pretty sure John is talking to her, but she's too focused on getting that burger in her mouth.

"…really there's no reason for us to be uncomfortable. What do you think?"

Beef juices run down her chin. She gives him a hold on finger while she chews her exceptionally large bite and swallows. "What? I wasn't listening. You never stop talking, so I tune you out."

"Rude! I was saying—we know each other well and Gregg's our dude. So, can I sleep in the room with you? I'm too tall for this couch," he asks, with a half-chewed bite of burger rolling around in his mouth.

"Oh. I don't care. Although I thought about smothering you a couple of times the other day when you slept next to me."

"Good to know," he says, then takes another large bite of his burger.

"I'm having horrible déjà vu," she says, a hand on her stomach.

"Why? I mean, how so?"

"When Gregg brought me on a private plane, I got super nauseated and puked. I mean, I was kind of dying at the time, but I'm feeling a little nauseated now."

"Shit. Maybe try to eat more. Maybe it's because you're like overly hungry?" he suggests.

"I think I'll let this settle while I shower. Then I'll finish the rest."

"Okay, I'll be here. I don't want to get in that bed until I'm clean."

About midway up her thigh with a washcloth, the urgent need to puke all over the shower floor washes over Shea. Not wanting to puke in the shower, she steps out, drops to her knees, and crawls to the toilet.

Oh, Lord. This feels like it's going to be violent

When her body is empty and only dry heaves wrack her body, a knock echoes off the walls of the small lavatory.

"What?" she says weakly from her spot on the floor.

"Shea, you've been in there for like an hour. Are you okay?"

"No. I'm sick. Motion sickness or something."

"Well, hurry up. I need a shower and Christian is up. He says he can't sleep and refuses to lie down until he shows you something."

"Okay…gimmie a minute."

Mustering all the strength she has left, she stands and gets back in the shower. Though she continues to dry heave, she finishes washing up quickly. Dressed in fluffy pajamas, she exits the bathroom with a towel atop her head.

"Man, I feel like garbage," she says, plopping into a seat next to Christian.

His small hand waits impatiently on the armrest. Looking over, she sees his other hand is out to John.

"What's up, bud?" John asks.

"It's time," he responds.

"Ominous, considering you have no idea what day or time it is," John retorts.

Christian's answer is to wiggle his hands impatiently.

"Alright," Shea says as she takes his hand.

Her world goes black, and she knows her spine is inhumanly straight in her seat. Slowly, a soft light fills her vision, illuminating a downed tree next to the cabin. Then she sees him. Her heart, sitting on the tree.

The soft focus sharpens, and he says, "This is not goodbye."

37 | GReGG

As soon as Gregg cracks an eyelid, Todd jumps up and sits on the edge of his bed.

"Welcome back, Greggy! Shoulder should heal up just fine," Todd says from his perched position. "Dr. Hughes did a bang-up job. You don't even need to be immobilized. How's it feel?"

"Good as new," Gregg retorts. His mouth feels like he licked a fuzzy creature and his tongue is now coated in fur. But his shoulder really doesn't hurt at all.

"Excellent! I was going to wait to get you to work, but I think I'm too excited to wait."

He walks over to the doorway and sticks his head out. "I need a wheelchair and an assist. Now!"

A woman…no—the woman…the woman that was in charge of Christian before Gregg got to Crown. The woman that kept him in that cage 24/7, walks in pushing a wheelchair. Gregg can feel the hatred change his facial expression.

"Prefect," Todd purrs.

Although he's still a bit groggy, Gregg sits up and swings his legs over the bed. The woman steps to his side to 'help' him. He looks at her with all the venom bubbling under the surface. She backs off.

"Gregg, you'll probably need help. I don't want you to fall," Todd muses.

"I'm fine. I just need a second to get my bearings."

Ten minutes later, the woman pushes his wheelchair down a long hallway, bright with harsh fluorescent light.

"Ah, here we are. Room 32-9," Todd says, opening the door with a swipe of his keycard and leading them inside.

This room is very dim compared to the hallway. Gregg notes how odd the room is, with a medical table with restraints right in the middle. A military-looking man in fatigues stands next to it, a metal tray on the other side of him. But the oddest thing of all is that the entire ceiling is made up of twelve-by-twelve square LED screens.

His gaze returns to Todd, who has a large, manic looking grin on his face. "Gregg, I have so much to share. R and D really knocked it out of the park. You're going to love this." He looks to the military man. "Get him strapped in. I'll let the video we made explain more."

"Yes, sir."

Gregg is filled with the ominous feeling of foreboding. He tries to stand from the wheelchair and make a break for it, but a large hand lands on each of his shoulders, holding him down.

"Mr. Time will help you up this time. Just to be cautious."

Gregg remains silent as Mr. Time pulls him from the wheelchair and deposits him onto the table. Leather restraints are clasped over his wrists, ankles and pelvis. Mr. Time places a metal brace over his forehead and secures it to the table, forcing Gregg to look up at the screens.

The lights dim even further, and the screens come to life, playing as a single unit.

"A Crowned Skull Laboratories production," a voice says over the Crown logo that now covers the ceiling.

Todd appears on the screen in a mauve three-piece suit. The Todd standing in the room applauds.

"What the fuck?" Gregg mutters.

On screen, Todd continues, "Gregg, I want to say it is a pleasure having you back with us. I look forward to all we can do together. I have taken the last six months to move on from our last interaction, and I hope you have too"

"But you know I can't take that chance, right? Bygones—will—be bygones," he says, his tone sharpening. "That brings me to this moment. While you were gone and things were tech-free around here, the boys in the lab really outdid themselves!"

The screen shifts to a vial of medication labeled EBW-∞. Todd's voice is played over the image. "Meet EBW-infinity, an amazing drug. With a dose of just five milliliters intravenously, it gives the subject an interesting effect—only lasting five minutes."

Todd reappears on the screen next to a man strapped to the very table Gregg is strapped to at this moment.

"This is Neal, the man who overdosed Shea. I lied. He didn't get arrested. He's been here, in a cell, for about a year now."

Mr. Time walks over to Neal and pushes the drug through his IV. Neal shrieks and thrashes against the restraints. As soon as the syringe detaches, he seems to go into a catatonic state.

The screen cuts to Todd again.

"EBW-infinity, also known as eternity-brainwash-infinity, really is an amazing innovation with great results in just five minutes. Quick—for us, but for the subject, those five minutes stretch into an eternity. It works by making your brain process external stimuli a million times more efficiently, turning each second into over a decade. It's extremely effective in brainwashing. Though when used more than once, the effects are varied."

The scene shifts to Neal strapped into a wheelchair. Drool pours from his mouth. His gaze unfocused, stares off screen, but it looks like his eyes no longer see. The video ends and the lights go up.

Todd bends over into Gregg's line of sight. "You ready? I know I am."

38 | Dr. P

Dr. P's laptop screen shifts from loading to a Zoom meeting with a face she doesn't recognize.

"Dr. P! It's great to meet you. I looked over your paperwork and research articles. I have to say, your discussion on wound healing innovations had me captivated."

"Oh, wow. Thanks so much. It really is a passion of mine. I worked in a lab for a bit, but it was small, and I didn't really have the backing I needed."

"Well, lucky for us, then! We have been looking for someone with your experience to make some real innovations here."

"Really?"

"Absolutely. I emailed you all of the information right before I got on here, so review that. If you have any questions, just shoot me a text. Otherwise, just send the paperwork back when you're ready."

"Okay! Thank you so much for the opportunity. I'm sorry, I don't think I got your name. The email didn't have one."

"Ah, yes. I'm Tina, Director of Services here at Crowned Skull Labs. Your meeting was originally arranged with our CEO, Todd Donoghue. However, due to extenuating circumstances, he was unable to get away. So you got me instead."

"Oh, no problem. Thanks, Tina."

"Talk soon." Tina says.

The screen returns to her desktop picture.

"Holy shit."

She pulls up her email and signs the agreement. She's very unsure about any of it, but she feels compelled to help the good guys. She stands from her desk, takes a deep breath, then faxes the forms to Tina.

She grabs her phone and dials Matt's sat phone number. He answers on the second ring.

"Hey!"

"Hey, Matt. Side quest number one is in effect."

"Hell yeah! I knew you could do it. Remember, if you talk to John, don't mention it."

"I know. Remind me why that is again?" she asks, curious.

"He's in protector-hero mode. Plus, I heard he's keen on you. He's already stressed out protecting his present party. We can't distract him from that."

"Right. Don't want to put them in danger," Dr. P agrees.

"Exactly. Update me with details. I'll be meeting with Captain Charlie in a few days. He might want to get your statement about everything. Will it be cool to call?"

"Yeah, call whenever. I have double encryption and route the calls to my cell. Gregg set it up, actually… Any news on him?"

"He's alive and at the compound, that's all we know."

"So the sooner I get down there, the better?"
"Yeah."

John watches Shea take Christian's hand, then looks at Christian, who smiles at him with tears in his eyes and urgently shakes his hand at him.

"Alright," he says, and grasps Christian's small hand.

Immediately, his vision is filled with a scene at the cabin. Gregg stands at the railing, looking down. John's point of view is from the ground. Christian was given Gregg's thoughts, from whenever this was, to create a vision for John.

"Hey, man. You know me, always prepared for every possibility." Gregg's voice is steady. "I know no matter what happens, Shea and Christian are in great hands. Protect them with your life, John. Be there for them, they'll need you." Gregg pauses, visibly swallowing the lump in his throat.

"Man, there is no one else I would trust with this. You're my best friend and my brother. I know you won't like this, but I have something I need from you." Gregg's gaze sharpens, pleading. "John, this is not a request. Do. Not. Come. For. Me."

John's pulse hammers. Gregg's words cut him deeply.

"I know it goes against everything you are, but don't. You'd be putting Shea and Christian in unfathomable danger. I'm not worth it. Shea got out, and I can too. I'm not playing around. Keep them safe and far away from Crown. Leave the country. I'll find you when I get out. If I see you anywhere around Crown, I'll never forgive you."

"Please don't come for me. I love you, man. See you soon."

The vision goes black. Tears stream down John's face, but Christian doesn't let go.

40 | Shea

"This is not goodbye."

Shea immediately starts sobbing, her body folding in on itself.

"You know I wouldn't leave you without telling you how much I love you." Gregg's voice thick with unshed tears.

He laughs once through his nose. "I know it sounds nuts with everything we've gone through, but my life has been infinitely better since I met you."

Yeah right

"Shea," he continues, "you are my heart, the other half of my soul, my everything. I love you so utterly and completely that it almost destroys me on a daily basis. I can't wait to see what the future has in store for us." He sniffles.

My heart

"Shea, I'm begging you, leave me here. I know you're digging your heels in even as I say this—but Shea... you gotta leave it alone. Think of Christian. Don't put yourself or him in danger. Please, if you love me at all, I'm begging you. I will get free. You did it. Trust that I am just as capable. Please, beautiful."

He pauses and stands.

"So this is not goodbye. It's see you soon, beautiful."

The vision fades to black. Tears stream down Shea's face. She feels like she can't breathe. Her heart is shattering.

A small light appears and then Christian stands in front of her. John stands beside her, and reaches out a hand, taking hers in his, he squeezes once.

"Why are we still in here? If it's just the three of us?" Shea asks.

"It's easier for me to speak to you this way," Christian says softly. "A lot needs to be said."

"Christian, my man! Let's hear it," John encourages.

"Gregg made it clear to both of you. He doesn't want you to search for him or trying to rescue him. He wanted to make sure that was understood."

"Yeah, and it's bullshit!" John says.

"But it's not. Gregg is just as capable as Shea, and you trusted her to get out. It's not my decision, but I'd rather not go anywhere near that place. And this is his choice," Christian urges.

"I understand, bud," Shea whispers. "But—I can't." Her voice breaks with a sob.

"I know, Shea. I just wanted to show you that and something else before you decide."

He smiles lovingly at her, but nothing happens.

"I don't see anything, except you two."

"Listen…" Christian whispers.

She closes her eyes and hears nothing at first. Then she hears her breathing and her heartbeat. Then a second heartbeat, much faster than the first.

Her eyes spring open to see Christian crying in front of her. Before she can ask anything, her vision fills with a plum-sized fetus twitching in its amniotic sac.

Her vision goes black, this time, as she is falling from consciousness.

41 | GREGG

Gregg thrashes against his bindings, but it's no use. Todd lets him continue long after his limbs start to bleed. He fights until he exhausts himself, at which point he goes limp. Before accepting his fate, he decides to try one more time.

"Todd, please don't do this! I'll cooperate! Bygones and everything!"

"Gregg," Todd says, standing over him. "That's great to hear—but no. I need you at peak performance. I need my buddy back. We can never be buddies now that I tortured your precious wife. It is what it is, Gregg. But you're in luck—Neal taught us a lot, before the drool…"

"Please, Todd!" he yells over Todd's speech.

"Patience, Gregg. As I was saying, we learned that we can actually erase memories with a specific brainwashing technique. We're just gonna take you back to pre-Crown Gregg. You'll get an offer to come to Crown, alone. Which you will eagerly accept, because—well—brainwash. Then you'll start fresh and we can try again. I might not have my time machine, but I can still make things go my way, Gregg," he says, like the mastermind of evil he is.

"So you're taking me back to Ohio? What the fuck, man."

"No, Gregg. Well, mentally, yes. Physically, you'll be in this building. We built an exact replica of your old Salt and Vinegar stomping grounds. It's gonna be great. I can't wait. Matter of fact, I'm done waiting. Mr. Time, let's begin."

"Todd, I swear! We can be friends. Please don't erase her! Please!" His voice thick with desperation.

"I can't, man. I'll see you after. In Ohio. We're going to be fast friends!"

With that the lights dim into nothingness. Mr. Time approaches him with a syringe. Gregg is completely terrified. His body shakes, his mind races, bile rises in his throat and he thinks he might actually shit his pants.

"Mr. Marsh. We'll see you on the other side," Mr. Time sneers. "But it'll be like a year ago for you."

He leans in over Gregg, getting uncomfortably close to hook the syringe to his IV.

"Man, I have some money, please! What do you want? I'll do it!" he pleads.

"Forget, Mr. Marsh… forget," he says in a hushed, melodic tone.

Time slows for Gregg during the administration of the medication. He forces himself to think of only her. The curve of her face. The tenderness in her kiss. The loving way she teaches Christian. Her smart mouth. Their first kiss and every kiss since.

"Her face, her smile, her hair, her face, her smile, her smell, her love…"

42 | JOHN

The vision dissolves and John rushes to Shea's side. She's slumped over in her seat and Christian is rocking her shoulder with his small hand, trying to rouse her. Tears stream down her face.

"She's okay, bud. That was a lot to take in, that's all. Plus, she barely ate. Can you find an attendant and ask them for some ginger ale and crackers?"

"Yup," he says, without his usual enthusiasm.

"Shea. Shea, come on!" John says loudly.

Nothing.

"Alright," he mutters, more to himself than her. "This is going to hurt me more than it hurts you."

He draws back his hand but drops it before it reaches her face. He can't slap a pregnant woman. He's not a monster.

Instead, he slides an arm under her neck and the other under her knees, lifting her gently. He carries her to the bedroom and lays her on the bed. He tucks her under the covers and brushes her hair back from her face. Before he leaves, he kisses her forehead, places a hand on her stomach, and whispers, "I got you too, little one."

When he's back in the common area, a flight attendant and Christian stand waiting.

"Sir, he seemed to need something but couldn't quite get the words out."

"That's okay. Hey, Big C, go get Diesel and head to Shea's room. Keep her company and get some sleep, okay?"

"Okay!" he says, a little pep back in his step.

Once Christian leaves the area, John turns to the attendant. "How much longer?" he asks, running a hand down his face.

"About five hours left in this flight plan. We're stopping in Millinocket, Maine. A small town, for safety. Is there something I can do for you?"

He pulls a folded piece of paper from his pocket. "Yes, I made a list." He hands it to her, then adds, "Can you add prenatal vitamins and lots of spinach to the list?"

"Of course. For your woman friend?"

"Yeah. She's in shock at the moment. I think I might be too—but a good shock."

"I'll grab some other stuff too. Things I wanted when I was pregnant."

"That's great. I really only know about the vitamins and need for folic acid."

"You're doing great. Are you planning to wait on board when we stop?"

"Yes, ma'am."

 43 | Christian

Christian snuggles close to Shea, his hand resting on her tummy as he talks to her baby. Diesel curls against him on the other side.

"We be best friends. Or brothers maybe," he whispers.

He closes his eyes and focuses on the fetus. He watches the tiny thing wiggle around. It's so small, barely anything. But it's alive. He can hear its heartbeat.

Diesel nudges him, and he can tell the dog needs to poop—really bad!

"Ugh, come on, D," he sighs, carefully sliding out of bed so he doesn't disturb Shea.

He walks back into the common area and sees John sitting with his head in his hands.

"You okay?"

"Ah, yeah, bud. Right as rain," John says, quickly wiping tears from his face.

"Bullshit."

Christian has never seen John cry before. It makes him want to cry too.

"Whoa. C. You can't say that!"

"Tell me," he pushes, unable to let it go.

"I'm okay," John says. Then seeing Christians no nonsense face, he changes his tune. "Okay. I'm so happy for them, but it kills me that Gregg isn't the first person she told. Being able to watch his face light up and all the dumb dad jokes he'd come up with. It sucks."

"Yup."

"How'd you know?"

"Extra heartbeat when I touched her," Christian says carefully, working to get all the words out.

Diesel whines again.

"Oh, yeah—poop."

"D's gotta poop?"

"Yup."

"Okay. I'll show you how to take him potty. It'll be your responsibility, okay?"

"Yeah, fine."

John shows him that within the closet in the smaller bedroom there is a two-by-three feet piece of AstroTurf on the floor.

"You can pull it out…"

Diesel is already pooping.

"Well, in the future, if he doesn't go into the closet, just pull it out."

"What about poop?" Christian asks, wrinkling his nose.

"Get some toilet paper, pick it up, then flush it."

"Ew!"

John smirks. "Well, he's technically Shea's dog. Do you want her to do it when she gets up?"

"NO! No—I do it."

44 | Todd

Todd watches through a special glass barrier that blocks whatever the screen is showing Gregg. Reprogramming his brain to not only forget the last year, but to also hate Shea. To believe she treated him like a number and never really saw him, of course.

Tina stands beside him, curious.

It's been two minutes for them, but centuries for Gregg. During the first thirty seconds, he howled and cried, trying to refuse to watch the screen. But that turned quickly into pleading, and now—silent staring.

Todd watches closely, hoping they will get the results he wants in just one round. He'd hate to turn Gregg into a drooling Neanderthal.

Mr. Time exits the room and removes his glasses, made from the same special glass. "Just a minute and a half to go. You want me to put him under right at five minutes?"

"Yes. Then we'll move him over to the mock-up and see if he remembers me."

"Alright. Something short-acting, or maybe something with a reversal agent, then?"

"I think Dr. Hughes made a recommendation. Just call him. Better hurry, we're almost there!"

45 | GREGG

Gregg feels the serum burn its way through his veins. He tries to fight the restraints, but the leather is thick and eats into his skin. The metal brace across his forehead leaves no room to thrash. As the burning slows, so does time. Suddenly he is stuck in the place between breaths and heartbeats.

The screens on the ceiling come alive. Images flash across the screen, too fast for the human eye to see. To him, they stretch on forever. He focuses on thinking only of her.

Her face fills the screen. A friendly smile. Her head tilted back in a laugh. Her hand reaching out for him. He's happy. He spends what feels like years watching her smile.

Then the image flickers and her smile twists. She rolls her eyes in annoyance.

"No. I love Shea. I love Shea. I love…"

She looks at him without warmth, without love. She turns and walks away from him. With another flicker she sneers at him. Shoves past him. Ignores him when he speaks. She walks away from him, always walking away.

He tries to cling to the truth, but it's like trying to hold mist. Moments blur, melt, and reform. From one blink to another, laughter and love… gone. All the good memories vanish and only the memories they plant remain.

46 | Todd

Todd watches Gregg sleep at his desk, head resting on his folded arms. After a moment, Gregg stirs, sits up and rubs his eyes, looking mildly confused. He reaches for his mouse and shakes it to wake-up his computer.

"Cue Todd," Todd murmurs to himself.

He enters the scene and walks straight up to Gregg's desk.

"Mr. Marsh?" he says with a megawatt smile.

Gregg looks up, blinking. "Yes, hello. How can I help you?"

"I'm Todd Donoghue, CEO at Crowned Skull Labs."

"Mr. Donoghue, amazing to meet you. I've heard a lot of great things." Gregg sits up a little straighter.

"Please, call me Todd." Todd pauses, watching closely for any signs of recognition. There is none.

"Okay, Todd. I'm Greggory." Extending his hand out to shake.

"Well, Gregg…" he starts, accepting Gregg's outstretched hand.

"No, Greggory—sorry. I knew someone who called me Gregg, and, well, it's a long story, but I'd like to be called Greggory."

Another test passed.

"Alright, Greggory—I'm pretty good friends with Dax, and he's been bragging about your skills."

Greggory brightens. "Really? Wow!"

Todd lightly slaps his hand down on the top of Greggory's shoulder. "I'd like to discuss an opportunity with you."

47 | Shea

Shea wakes with a full bladder and a back soaked in sweat.

Why is it so hot?

She starts to fling the covers off but pauses when she realizes Christian is clinging to her, with an arm over her abdomen and a leg draped over her thighs. She gently slides out from under him and rushes to the bathroom.

As she sits, the events of the day before come rushing back to her. She drops her head into her hands and prepares for tears—but they don't come. Instead, a wide smile spreads across her face. She places a hand on her stomach.

"Hello, baby."

Her mind races with thoughts about the baby and what it might look like. Will it have her brown eyes or Gregg's seafoam? Would it be as sweet and loving as Gregg is? Have his curls or her waves?

A knock at the door startles her.

"Yes?"

"Hey. You okay?" John's voice filters through the door.

"Surprisingly, yeah. Like Christian said—happy."

"That's great. We've got a couple of hours before we take off again, and I have a few things on the list that we need to get done. So when you're done, meet me in the main area."

"Okay. Be right there."

She walks out to find John sitting at the table with a plethora of items spread out in front of him. Her eyes rove over hair scissors, an electric hair trimmer, hair bleach, spinach, and prenatal vitamins.

"Are we dying your beard?" she asks.

An attendant approaches her with crackers and ginger ale. "Miss, how's your nausea?"

"Um, not horrible. I think I'll stick with the crackers, though. Thank you."

She sits next to John, awaiting an explanation.

"Shea, we all need to change how we look—in case we need or want to get off the plane."

"What do you mean? Where's our destination?"

"We don't have one. We'll be staying in the air until the time is right. We'll stop for fuel and supplies, and we'll also need to get Diesel out for exercise. One of the attendants took him on her run about an hour ago. But you can't just stay on this plane until—God knows when."

"So you want what to happen?"

"We'll buzz all my long, luxurious beard locks, buzz Christian's hair and cut yours short—and bleach it," he says, his hand instinctively covering his crotch.

"No way. My hair is down to my ass—do you know how long that took to grow?"

"Shea, my beard is thirteen inches long. This isn't something I say lightly— we have to."

"Okay. I'll cut some off, but you can't bleach it. Sorry."

"It would be better…"

She cuts him off. "John, I'm pregnant. I can't."

"Oh. That's a thing?" he asks, blinking at her.

"Yes, it's a thing. We could use lemon juice and sit me in the sun for a few hours."

"Okay. We'll figure that out later. We're currently in Maine, so Alaska 2.0."

"Oh. Where to next?"

"California. We're gonna zig-zag across the US."

"Fun."

48 | Dr. P

Dr. P sits in the all-white waiting area, uncrossing and recrossing her legs. The environment is cold and sterile, perfect for her field of study. Her nerves are causing a feeling like there's some sort of battle happening in her stomach. She pulls out her phone and opens an app to secretly record—just in case.

She hears the confident stride of a woman in heels heading her way. She slips her phone into her purse and stands when she sees that it's Tina.

"Dr. P." Tina offers her hand. "Such a pleasure. Your CV is quite impressive, as well as your published works."

Dr. P shakes Tina's hand. "The pleasure is mine. Talk about impressive. I've fit many patients with the state-of-the-art prosthetics coming out of here."

"Of course. It's a bit of a passion project for Mr. T. If you'll follow me, he has a narrow window to meet with you before I give you the tour of your building."

She follows Tina's short strides to an elevator. They exit on the second floor, walk down a long hallway, and finally stop at an office.

Tina knocks once, then opens the door. "Mr. T, Dr. P is here," she announces into the room, then steps aside and ushers Dr. P inside.

Todd stands and walks out from behind a massive, elegant desk and walks toward her.

"So great to meet you. Please, sit." He waves a hand toward a couch against one wall of the room. She walks over and sits.

He stalks over and sits next to her, a little too close for her comfort. She smiles at him and fights the urge to fidget. He's strikingly handsome, which is slightly off putting. He's dressed in a beautifully tailored suit, complete with a matching pocket square. A dashing smile is smeared across his face, but most notably is his smell. She could never describe it accurately, but it's rich, woodsy, manly and intoxicating.

"So," he says, eyes glinting. "I knew you were incredibly smart and talented. But beauty as well? Total package."

Intoxication gone. Her body threatens to vomit in her mouth. "You flatter me, sir."

"Quite the contrary. Your experience speaks for itself. I will mainly have you on wound innovations, but we're also restarting work on our neural implant project. I may have you help out there as well. Their lab is connected to yours, so it won't be too much of an inconvenience."

"Sounds interesting. I'll go wherever I'm needed. Thank you for the opportunity."

"My pleasure. I'll be seeing you around. Do you mind if I call you by your first name? I like to keep things casual."

"No problem," she says lightly. "Though I might not answer. I've been Dr. P for so long."

He laughs. "Fair enough. Alright, Dr. P it is."

As soon as he stops talking, with almost creepy timing, Tina walks in and smiles. The smile on her face seems sad. Dr. P hopes she doesn't think she picked this seating arrangement.

"I'll take you over to Building 4, if you're ready," Tina says to Dr. P, then turning to Todd, asks, "is that all?"

"For now." Turning to Dr. P, he says, "Have a great first day."

49 | GREGGORY

He packs up his desk slowly, feeling a bit lost. That nap really did a number on him. As he logs out of his computer, his lady friend Lydia walks over.

Without looking up, he says, "Hey, Lyd. I'm not flying out until tomorrow, if you want to come over tonight."

"I can't. I have plans. I just wanted to say, good luck at your new job."

He looks up and notices her eyes are red-rimmed, her face puffy and splotchy, and there's a bruise on her cheek. "Lydia, what happened? Are you okay?" he asks, worried about her.

"Oh, yeah. You know me, clumsy. I got frustrated and had a good cry about it, but I'm fine."

"Okay… well, I guess I'll call you sometime then?" he says, trying to figure out where she stands on a long-distance relationship.

"Gregg, I think…"

He cuts her off. "Greggory, please."

"Right. Greggory. I think it's best for both of us to just have a clean break. You're gonna be in Florida, and I think it's better if you just meet someone new. Forget about me and have a great life." She turns and walks away before he can respond.

"That was weird," he mutters.

Considering they weren't that serious, he agrees with her evaluation. Grabbing his things, he heads for the exit. The place looks like a ghost town compared to the usual hustle and bustle.

Just as he's about to step into the elevator, something sharp stings him in the side of his neck.

50 | Todd

The team pushes a wheelchair under Greggory, just as he's about to pass out.

"He's out. Get him to the jet. It's time to fly."

Todd glances back and watches two of his men grab Lydia.

"As promised," Todd says smoothly, "you'll be returned to your home, and twenty thousand dollars will be deposited into your account. You will be watched. If you decide to tell anyone about this, your memory will be next to go. Got it?"

She sobs, huge hiccupping, hyperventilating sobs. She works hard to get out, "…Yes…sir…"

"Good girl. Get her home," he orders his lackies. As they turn to leave, Todd gives them a look that tells them what they should actually do with her.

He strides confidently toward the jet that waits on his private runway. Greggory is pushed to the plane, then carried onboard. Todd settles into the seat next to Greggory's sleeping form and pops a bottle of champagne.

As the plane takes off, Greggory begins to stir. As soon as the plane is fully in the air and he's halfway awake, Todd smiles. "Hey man. You've been asleep most of the flight. You okay?"

Greggory blinks, disoriented. "Oh man, I don't even remember getting to the airport."

"Well," Todd chuckles. "I had my private town car bring you down to the airstrip I use in Ohio. You must have dozed off. Happens to the best of us."

Greggory rubs the back of his neck. "What about all my stuff? I didn't pack up my house or anything. I know I didn't sell it. I didn't prepare for this at all, man."

"Listen, Greggory, you'll come to learn that working for me means things get handled. The money from the sale of your house is already in your account. We got a pretty good deal on it. The moving company I hired packed everything up, per your specifications, of course. Your swords were all carefully packaged with foam to keep them safe, and they were all shipped out to my place in Florida."

Todd leans back. "I figured since you don't really know anyone there yet and don't have anything lined up, you could stay with me and my wife, until you get something for yourself."

"Wow, man. That's really nice of you. Are you sure?"

"Absolutely. I have a feeling you and I are going to be fast friends. I've got plenty of space, so there's no need for you to stress about any of that."

"Okay, man. That's awesome. And everything from my house will be there when I arrive?"

"Yes. The moving team is probably already unpacking and setting up your room."

"Wow. That's really unexpected. Thanks, man."

Todd notices Greggory's pinched expression. "Listen, man, I'm not trying to be overbearing. I just want to make this transition as easy as possible for you. I want you to get focused on work straight away, not worrying about buying a car, finding a house, and everything else that comes with relocation. I want you to be fully immersed in the work. I just hired another new employee, she's a doctor. She'll be helping you with the neural implants. I think you two will make a really great team."

Greggory looks over at him and nods. "Wow, that's really thoughtful of you. Thank you, boss."

51 | Shea

"Would you just sit still? I can't cut your hair straight if you keep moving," John protests.

"Do you know how hard this is for me, John? I've been growing my hair for years. I don't want it that short, I need to be able to put it in a ponytail," she says, swatting his hand away from the base of her neck.

"Fine, but I'm only giving you a few extra inches. I'm cutting it. Sit still."

"Fine," she says, forcing her hands under her thighs. "What am I going to do without my long hair?"

Christian sits nearby, rubbing the fuzzy stubble on his head. John buzzed his hair off first. It makes the boy look so much older. She pouts a little at the thought.

"Christian, you're looking like a little preteen now," she says.

Christian smiles and winks.

Diesel slumps at Christian's feet, probably glad he doesn't have to get a haircut.

"Shea, I have to cut my beard off after this. Do you know how hard that's gonna be for me? I completely understand what you're saying, but we can't be recognized, and we can't stay on this plane for who knows how long."

"Yeah, who does know how long, John? You make all these plans, but we're just sitting around waiting. Why aren't we flying to Florida right now?"

Christian clears his throat.

She looks at him and takes a deep breath. "I know. I know his wishes, and what he wants, and I don't care. Here's the difference between him and me. I don't always listen to what people tell me, okay? I do what I know is right for me. And I am glad none of you came after me, because it worked out. But I also couldn't remember any of you. I didn't know anything. What if Gregg hadn't been there? What if the timing wasn't right? I would've been all on my own, knowing no one and they would have snatched me right back up. They could be doing the same thing to Gregg. They could be torturing him! They could be doing anything! And we're gonna, what—sit around and let all that happen?"

John lays his hand on her shoulder. "Shea, you need to calm down."

"Don't tell me to calm down," she seethes.

"Shea, just listen, okay. It's not good for you or the baby to be this stressed. You need to take a deep breath and remember that we are doing something. We're getting ready to do something. We have a man on the inside and we're waiting for information. We can't go in there halfcocked, not knowing what's meeting us on the other side."

"We need to go in there. We need to get him back. He is the father of my unborn child. I will not stand by while we just fly around the United States, and he sits in a cell somewhere and rots. I won't do it."

"First of all, you know Gregg is not rotting in a cell. You know damn well, just as well as I do, that Todd has put him to work to get the systems back up and who knows what else. But you know he's working. We know Todd, he wouldn't just throw him in a cell. He's too valuable. We are going to go. We just need a plan, and we're gonna work that out while we fly around the United States. We're going to get it figured out. Matt has already been spotted a couple of times, on purpose. Once at the Alaska-Canadian border and again at Haines Junction, so we're in the clear right now. But if we step off this plane and your hair's still down to your ass, they're going to recognize you."

She swallows. "Fine. Just cut it."

She sits, silent in the seat, seething with anger. It fills her veins, and she wants to explode. When she thinks about it, she's sure it's probably the pregnancy hormones that have her over the top today. But it's also all too much, and when she hears those scissors and the sound they make slicing through her long, thick, luscious locks, she loses it a little. She doesn't cry. She doesn't scream. She doesn't fight.

She just sits silent. Not knowing what tomorrow will bring or when she'll see Gregg again. And John's cutting off all her hair. Yes, she's stuck on that, okay.

Christian walks over and places his hand on hers, and she can't help but soften.

This kid and what he does to me.

She can only imagine what her future child might do to her emotionally. And then she knows it's worth cutting her hair. It's worth cutting her hair and changing her appearance, so that she can see Gregg again. Worth it, so he can be there when their baby is born. She'll go with the plan. She'll go with the flow. She'll do what she has to, in order to see him again.

"You know I'm pissed, right?" she says.

"I know. Now will you help me with my beard? Your hair is done."

He hands her a small mirror and at first she refuses to look. She doesn't want to see the damage that he's done to her. But he hasn't done any damage, this is just what they have to do. She's placing the blame on John, but really, she should be thanking him. She holds the mirror up and inspects her hair, which is just barely brushing her shoulders. Her waves are a little less impressive, with the shortness of her hair.

"Thanks, John," she says quietly. "I appreciate you looking out for us and trying to make some sort of plan. I'm sorry for my outbursts."

"It's alright." He waves the electric trimmer next to her face. "Do you want to do the honors?"

She turns in her seat and grins. "Really?

"Well, somebody's got to do it. And I'd rather not watch it fall from my face.”

"Alright. Gimmie.”

52 | JOHN

John listens to the buzz of the electric trimmer and watches chunks of hair fall. He hasn't been freshly shaven since he was in the military. He can't even remember what the bottom of his face looks like. Matt has a full beard too—so there's no help from that idiot.

He appreciates how gentle she is. She doesn't rush. She isn't pulling or snagging the hair. She's moving slowly. She looks almost like she's in a trance.

"You okay?" he asks.

"Yeah. I'm just remembering when Gregg and I first became friends with you," she says softly. "How much I admired your beard. It made Gregg want to grow one, and he's had a beard ever since. I wonder if he'll shave it. Not knowing what's going on is really killing me."

"I know, Shea. But he's alive, and he's okay. We know that much. We have to stay the course. The best thing for us and for Gregg is for us to be out of the public eye so that we don't get snatched up too. We can't put Christian at risk and now with you being pregnant, we really can't be putting you at risk."

"I know it complicates things," she says.

"It doesn't complicate things, Shea. It illuminates things, makes things clear. You and Christian are precious to Gregg. You're precious to me too. Keeping you safe is the most important thing I can do. And if I can do that for Gregg, then I'm doing something right."

She tilts her head. "Aw, you think I'm precious?"

"Why are you like this, Shea?"

They burst into laughter.

She sets down the trimmer. "Wow. I didn't realize how ugly you were before, but I'm really seeing a new angle now."

"Shut up! I am not ugly!"

"Your butt-chin says otherwise," she says with a sly smile.

"My butt-chin?

 "Yeah. You have a butt-chin."

"It's a cleft, Shea. Some people find it distinguished."

"People find it what it is… a butt-chin."

"Whatever."

He storms to the bathroom like he's mad. At the sink with his head still down, he braces himself, grabbing the edge of the counter. Then he looks in the mirror. She actually did a really great job. It's not shaved down to the skin, still a little bit of stubble. Just enough to hold back the baby-faced look like he knew he would with a clean shave.

He washes his face and feels the stubble beneath his fingers. "This is different," he mutters.

When he returns to the main area, the table is cleared of all hair removing devices. An attendant is sweeping up the fallen hair from the floor.

"Thank you. I was going to clean it up. I really appreciate it," he says.

"No problem. My pleasure." She gives him a soft smile and walks away with a dustpan full of hair.

Shea watches the interaction. "That flight attendant better watch out. I'm gonna tell Dr. P."

He groans. "Would you cut it out?"

He barely hears Christian softly say, "Pleaaasuureeee."

"I'm just saying, you're kind of spoken for. And the woman who has spoken for you is kind of the best. So that flight attendant better watch out.”

He points at her stomach. “Your pregnancy hormones have you all over the place. Go lie down or something.”

“I can't. I'm too wound up. Want to play a game or something?”

Christian pops up from his seat, grinning.

“You know what game he wants to play, right?” John asks.

“No?”

“What? You haven't noticed him obsessing over Connect Four? He beats the pants off Gregg.”

“Well, I bet I could beat you,” Shea challenges, eyes narrowed at Christian.

Christian grabs the game from his bag and brings it over to the table, dumping all the contents. The little plastic pieces clink on and off the table. After he gathers them all, he sits down and crosses his arms. Giving the eyes of a challenge to Shea.

53 | GREGGORY

Greggory looks out the plane window at the complex sprawling below them. "Wow. How many acres do you have here?" he asks Todd.

"In this compound, over a hundred. With forty-six buildings, including a medical complex and an Olympic sized swimming pool," Todd answers, prideful.

Greggory whistles. "Wow. That's insanely awesome."

"Would you prefer to see your new lab first, or head to the house and check out your living quarters? Your new counterpart is having her orientation as we speak. Might be a good chance to get to know each other."

"Sure. I'm feeling energized. Must be that nap I took. Let's see the lab."

"Fantastic!

The plane touches down on Todd's private airstrip. When Greggory descends the plane's stairs, his eyes go wide with wonder.

"Come on, buddy. There's so much more to see," Todd says, standing beside a golf cart parked at the bottom of the stairs.

"I can't believe this is real life."

"Well, believe it! Hop in, let's go see your lab," Todd says, gesturing to the golf cart.

On the way to building 4, Todd outlines some of Greggory's new job duties.

Greggory is practically vibrating with excitement.

"It'll all be up to you, Greggory. This is your baby. Some of the researchers have had ideas—but nothing cohesive."

"I already have some ideas," Greggory says, grinning. "I'm ready."

"Excellent. This new doctor is working in innovative wound healing. I think that knowledge will be a great addition, to fully integrating the chip."

"Oh yeah. That's awesome."

Pulling in front of building 4 and stepping from the golf cart, Todd accesses the building with his key card. He opens the door and ushers Greggory inside.

"Oh, here," Todd says, handing Greggory a card attached to a lanyard. "Your keycard. It gives you access to every door in your building, the pool, gym, and the firing range."

"Thanks, man. I was wondering where I was gonna work out."

Todd chuckles. "There's a huge gym here on campus. But you're in luck, we have a full-size gym at home, too. It has a sauna, steam room, and jacuzzi."

"Did I win some kind of lottery?" Greggory asks, chuckling.

Todd laughs once through his nose. "You could say that."

Greggory scans the lobby. It's white and sterile, with glass walls dividing the interior. He can see into one of the hallways and spots two women approaching. One a petite blond woman and the other a tall curvaceous woman with dark hair.

"Oh, look at this," Todd says.

"Good afternoon, Mr. T. Hello, Greggory. My name's Tina, and this," she says, gesturing to the dark-haired woman, "is our other new hire, Dr. P."

Greggory notes to himself how beautiful Dr. P is, reaching out his hand to take hers.

"Pleasure to meet you, Dr. P. I'm technically Dr. Marsh, though a different kind than you, I suppose. You can call me Greggory. No need for the formality with me."

She shakes his hand firmly, and says, "The pleasure is mine. I've heard so many great things."

The four of them walk back down the hallway and up to the lab.

Greggory is intrigued to see that Dr. P's workstation sits right beside his.

"Well, we'll leave you two to R and D it up. I'll come get you when it's time to head out, Greggory. We'll ride home together," Todd says.

Then he turns to Dr. P. "I'd like to invite you to our house for dinner tomorrow, with my wife and I, and Greggory here."

"Oh, that would be great. I don't know anyone here yet, so that's very kind of you. Thank you."

"Perfect. I'll leave you two to it then!" Todd says, leaving with Tina.

Dr. P stands beside Greggory, watching that vile man leave her area and disappear into the elevator.

"So, Greggory," she says carefully. "You think maybe a couple of days of brainstorming independently, then having a meeting of the minds to collaborate is the best plan of action?"

Greggory looks at her with kind eyes. "Yeah, a couple of days sounds great. Since we'll be working so closely together, maybe we can loop each other in whenever a great idea sparks to life?"

"Yes! I'd love that!" she says, smiling at his thoughtful approach.

"Okay! I'm gonna dive in right now. I can't wait another second," he says, with childlike excitement.

"Awesome."

She turns and walks the few steps to her workstation. The moment she reaches her chair, she sits. Her legs were threatening to give out on her. He looks at her like he has no idea who she is, like they had never met.

She pulls out her phone and opens her encrypted texting app.

Text to Matt at 1315

« Gregg has no memory

« They have us working together

« He's living with Todd!

« You need to tell John.

« Have him text me!

« ASAP!

Text from Matt at 1317

» Wow, ok. That's a lot

» I'll text him now

She takes a deep breath through her nose and blows it out through pursed lips, putting her phone away. Looking over at Gregg, she can see he's already ordering the techs around and has drawn and written several things on a nearby whiteboard.

She takes out her own research and boots up her computer. They work separately for the rest of the day.

Todd and Tina walk into the lab at 4:30 p.m., hand in hand.

"Alright, folks. Let's call it a day. You've both had a very productive first day," Todd announces.

"Already?" Greggory asks from behind his thick lenses. His hair is sticking up in all different directions, like he's been running his hands through it all day.

55 | JOHN

After what felt like a thousand rounds of Connect Four with Christian, Shea yawns, stretches and takes her pregnant ass to bed for a nap.

John got Christian and Diesel some food and got everything ready for takeoff. They are now, however many feet safely in the air, and everyone except John is napping. He tried to lie down, but his racing thoughts kept him awake.

Almost a whole episode of *Forged in Fire* later, his sat phone rings. He checks the display—it's his inside man.

"Hello?" John answers.

"Hey, really quick. He's here, working. And he's living with Todd. Also—some lady doctor just started too. They put her with him. He doesn't seem to have any memories."

John nods. "Okay. Has Captain Charlie been in contact yet?"

"No. I haven't heard from Matt in a while either," he says.

"Same. Okay, I'll check in with Matt. Keep an eye on our boy, alright?"

After he hangs up, he goes into Shea's room to make sure she's still asleep. Her loud snoring confirms that she is. He heads back to the table and dials Matt's number. It rings twice, before he hears, "Hey, fugly!"

"Matt, tell me what's going on. Why have you been radio silent?"

"Nothing's going on, man. Calm down. I have to sleep sometime."

John rolls his eyes. "Nice try. Remember we grew up together, enlisted together and got deployed together. This is Stephanie Helm all over again."
Matt laughs once. "Oh, come on! She totally liked me first."

"For the last time, you ignoramus, she thought you were me and you took advantage!"

"Either way, that's ancient history. Why are you bringing it up now?" Matt asks with a smile in his voice.

"Get it through your Neanderthal skull, I know you. Now. Tell. Me. I just talked to our mole."

"Shit. Okay. What'd he say?"

"Nope. Spill it. NOW!" he orders.

"It was Dr. P's idea. She wanted to help. I couldn't stop her."

"What was her idea?" John asks in a clipped manner.

"She got a job at Crown."

"I'll kill you," John promises.

"John, calm down. There's nothing either of us could've done and you know it."

"Well, we'll never know now, will we?"

"She has an encrypted texting app. She wants you to text her."

"Give it." He writes her number on the grocery list he was making. Sighing, he says goodbye to his idiot brother and drops his head into his hands.

"That bad?" he hears Shea ask.

Looking up, he sees she's leaning against the bar, pickle in hand.

He nods. "It's bad."

56 | Todd

Todd lounges in the back of the town car beside Greggory. Tina rides shotgun, unhappily.

"So, since it's a bit early, I thought I'd show you the gym when we get home—if you're up for it," Todd says.

"Yeah, absolutely," Greggory agrees. "I feel like I haven't worked out in forever. I'm losing definition."

"Oh, we'll fix that real quick," Todd says chuckling.

A few minutes of comfortable silence later, the town car pulls into the covered, wraparound driveway. Todd glances over and watches Greggory's face light up, eyes wide.

The house has thirty-two bedrooms, including a gym room and Greggory's mother-in-law suite. Which boasts its own bathroom, kitchen, living room and balcony, overlooking a large natural lake.

Todd swells with pride at Greggory's reaction—all but drooling over his new surroundings.

"Let's go look at your suite and get changed," Todd says, stepping out as the driver opens his door. "Then we'll hit up the gym."

"Lead the way, man. I really appreciate you letting me stay here."

Todd hears Tina jogging in her heels to catch up with them. When she reaches them, they stop and turn toward her.

"Sorry, guys, I didn't get towels into the bathroom yet. I wanted to give you these." She holds out a stack of sage green oversized towels, hand towels and washcloths.

When Greggory reaches for them, Todd clears his throat and shakes his head.

"Tina, you're already holding them. Can't you just take them?" Todd asks sweetly.

"Of course. I just thought because…" She trails off. He knows she's scared of him.

He smiles, savoring her fear.

"It's no big deal. Here," Greggory says, taking the towels from her.

"Our guests do not carry their own towels to their suite," Todd seethes through clenched teeth.

"Good thing I'm not a guest then," Greggory says, in true Gregg fashion. "Don't worry about it. Thanks, Tina," he says, winking at her.

"Oh, I see how it's going to be—gang up on Todd," he says playfully.

Tina turns and walks away. Todd leads Greggory to his new living quarters.

57 | GREGGORY

Walking through the long halls of Todd's mansion, Greggory's head turns back and forth. One wall displays framed news articles about Crown's innovations. Another showcases art pieces from the Renaissance period, which Greggory could only guess at artist and authenticity.

Todd stops in front of a door with a fingerprint padlock.

"I know it's a little weird," Todd says lightly, "but this way you'll feel like you have privacy and security. Your door only opens with your thumbprint."

"Oh yeah, that's pretty secure. Where'd you get my print, though?" Greggory asks, genuinely curious.

"Your background check," Todd replies smoothly. "Go on, try it out."

Greggory balances the towels in his left arm and presses his right thumb to the scanner pad. A small green light rolls from the top of the pad to the bottom. The door to his suite not only unlocks but pops open.

Todd pushes the door open the rest of the way and walks in first, then turns to Greggory.

The door opens into the living room. Decorated in dark phthalo green and copper, Greggory thinks he's died and gone to heaven.

Todd chuckles. "I thought you'd love it, look closer."

Greggory steps further into the room and sees his swords have all been mounted on deep green velvet, matching the walls they hang from.

"Wow. This is insane!" he breathes. "Thank you so much!"

He walks around the room, taking it all in. Then he notices a couple of swords are missing.

"Hey, not to be that guy—but a couple are missing. Are they in another room?"

"Oh, really? I…" Todd seems to stumble over his words. "Sorry, man. A couple got damaged in transit. I was hoping you wouldn't notice, but I should've known better." He grins. "I'll pay for replacements, if you want to order new ones."

Greggory nods, satisfied.

"Alright, go put those damn towels away and get changed. We've got iron to pump!" Todd redirects.

"Yes, sir!" Greggory laughs, heading into the bathroom.

58 | Todd

As soon as Greggory disappears into the bathroom, Todd pulls out his phone and dials Tina.

"Yes?" Her voice trembles slightly.

"What the actual fuck, Tina? With the towels?" His voice is low, tone venomous.

"I forgot. I'm sorry. I didn't think…"

He cuts her off. "No, you didn't think at all! And there are swords missing from his collection. Where the fuck are they, Tina?"

"How am I supposed to know his entire collection? You're the one who spent all your time over there!"

"Watch it!" he snaps.

"Yes, sir."

The line goes silent. When he looks at it, Tina has already hung up. His jaw tightens. She'll pay for that later.

Greggory reappears in basketball shorts and a plain white tee. "I'm ready, man. How 'bout you?"

"I have a locker at the gym with my gym clothes in it. I just wanted to show you something first."

Todd leads him into the bedroom and throws open the door to his walk-in closet. Greggory peeks around Todd's broad frame.

"Holy shit, man. Whose clothes are these?" he asks, stunned.

"Yours, my man! We have a high standard at Crown, I thought I'd help you meet it. We'll send your laundry out every Saturday morning. Throughout the week, just toss it down the chute," he says, walking to the back of the closet and opening a well-hidden hatch. "And it'll be hung outside your main door every Sunday."

"You're gonna spoil me, bro!" Greggory says, staring at the hatch in wonder.

"That's the point," Todd says, clapping a hand on his upper back. "Let's hit the gym before dinner."

They lift weights, then run. Now they are sitting in the sauna, sweat pouring down their bodies, towels wrapped around their waists.

"I didn't realize you were that ripped. You hide behind those loose clothes you wear," Todd comments.

Greggory blushes. "I don't hide. I just like being comfortable and kind of invisible. It's easier that way."

Todd tilts his head. "What's easier?"

He shrugs. "I dunno, life? I care more about my work than meeting people, I guess. Being invisible is just easier."

"You're an attractive guy—you could have any lady you want."

"Nah. Honestly that's all just background noise anyway. I want to make a name for myself in scientific history. I'll worry about the other stuff later."

"Alright. That benefits me, so I'll leave it alone."

59 | Dr. P

Dr. P sits in her small apartment in a secondhand Lay-Z-Boy, eating Chinese takeout straight from the carton. Her laptop rests on a milk crate, streaming the latest episode of *Resident Alien.*

Her phone dings—a notification from her encrypted texting app. She checks it immediately, using her fingerprint to unlock it.

Text from John at 1830

» What were you thinking?

She rolls her eyes, but she can't help herself, she smiles.

Text to John at 1830

« Hello, John. I was thinking I was in a unique position to help.

« Was I wrong?

Text from John at 1835

» Yes, you were wrong. You have no training and have put yourself in danger! I have enough to worry about! Seriously, what were you thinking?

Text to John at 1836

« This isn't about you. I'm helping my friends. You don't like it- just stay out of it!

She tosses the phone into her lap and turns back to her show, pouting. Of course he's mad, she would be too. But she's not going to tell him that.

Her phone rings.

Looking at the display, she sees his name. Again, that stupid smile.

"What?" she answers, leaning over and pausing her show.

"Don't do that. Don't try to make me feel bad for caring, it's not fair," he says, serious.

"I know. But it's happening, so…"

"I know. Tell me everything."

"We started today. They put us in the same lab. We're all having dinner together tomorrow."

"You get a plus one?"

"No, it felt like a set up—with Gregg."

"Shit."

"I know. And he doesn't seem to know me. I don't know what to do," she admits.

"Shit."

"John. Be more helpful, please!"

"I'm saying shit—you're gonna have to date him if he asks you out. Keep him from cheating on Shea."

"Shit," she mirrors his sentiment.

"Please be careful, P."

"I am. Don't worry."

"That's not happening. I told you I wanted to sweep you off your feet—not you do the sweeping."

"How am I doing the sweeping?" she asks.

"Because not only are you smart as hell, beautiful as hell and cool as hell—you're also brave as hell. I might have to make good on a promise I made to Gregg."

"What promise?"

"You'll see," he says mischievously.

"Oh? Also, he goes by Greggory now. It's weird."

"That is weird. Guess it's better than John Doe."

"Yeah. There's only one true John."

"I'm glad we're on the same page about that."

She laughs softly. "Alright. I'm gonna go finish my dinner and do some research before bed. Text me sometime, okay?"

"Like regular text or naughty text?" he says, completely serious.

"Good night, John."

"Good night, boo."

She chuckles, ending the call. He makes her feel sixteen again.

There's that smile again.

60 | Shea

"The promise you made to Gregg is that you're gonna marry her, right?" Shea asks between bites of ice cream.

"Yup," John says lightheartedly.

"So she's on the inside? Isn't that dangerous?" she asks, nervous.

"I don't want to think about it," he admits. "She got hired though, and she's working with Gregg. Memory or not, he's not going to let anything happen to her."

Her heart catches. "He's working, then?"

"Yeah, in neural implants," he says, with a short laugh through his nose.

She sighs. "Well, I would never want Dr. P to put herself in danger, but I'm honestly kind of relieved. I was afraid we wouldn't know what's going on, but this way we will."

"That's one way to look at it."

"What? What did I miss?"

"Todd's trying to set her up with Gregg."

"So… your girl is gonna date my husband?"

"Yyyyeeeeeaaaahhhhhhhh," he draws out.

"He's never been anything but a gentleman. They'll be fine," she says, hopeful.

"I'll take your word for it. We do have her number now though."

"Awesome. I'd like to ask her some questions," she says, genuinely glad.

"About what?" John inquires, curious.

"Hello! I'm pregnant with no doctor! I want to make sure I'm doing everything right."

My priorities need to change a little…

"Oh, you know she's not a lady doctor though, right?"

"Duh—but she has a medical degree, which is more than you or I have."

"Oh, yeah. Fair point."

Shea finishes her ice cream and places the bowl in the sink. She downloads the encrypted app John told her about and opens a new chat to Dr. P.

Text to Dr. P at 2100

« Hey! Tell me what to do!

Text from Dr. P at 2100

» Hey you! I feel like I should be asking you the same thing!

Text to Dr. P at 2101

« Well. You just need to be yourself and keep Gregg loyal to his wife. That's my advice.

Text from Dr. P at 2101

» You know I will. What do you need?

Text to Dr. P at 2103

« I'm pregnant! With no physician! Help me!

Text from Dr. P at 2103

» Pregnant??!!!! Oh my gosh! Congrats, Shea!

Text to Dr. P at 2105

« Thanks, but seriously, tell me!

Text from Dr. P at 2106

» Okay. No alcohol or drugs-duh

» No deli meat or sushi

» Limit caffeine, to one cup a day…I know that'll be hard for you!

» Exercise regularly and trust me—we're getting Gregg out of here! Don't stress!

Text to Dr. P at 2110

« Text me anytime. I know I'll be asking you lots of things.

Shea sets her phone down, her face becoming a mask of contemplation. In her mind, Gregg could only love her and be with her. But this feels like a different reality, one where Dr. P and John Doe get together in the end. Her heart breaks a little.

Chrisitan must be able to see the pain on her face, because he walks over and offers her his hand.

A vision Gregg had arranged with Chrisitan before everything happened plays in her mind. Gregg sits with her by the river, slowly casting for fish.

"Beautiful, no matter what, I love you so much. More than anything. I'll only ever love you." He casts and leaves her with the most loving smile, her heart warms.

The vision shifts to her tiny fetus. Its head is a little large for its body, and it floats in what appears to be space—but she knows it's inside of her. It twitches and sloshes around. The vision fades and Christian sits in front of her, empathy and compassion shining in his smile.

"I call it Rhaego," he announces.

"John…" she calls across the plane.

He jogs to where she is. "What?"

"What did I tell you about *Game of Thrones*?"

"Yeah, okay… but all he has to do is brush past me, Shea!" he argues.

"Point taken." She eyes Christian. "And you—you know better!"

He gives her his most innocent smile, and says, "I'm almost nine! Been prisoner! Know things!"

"I know—we'll argue about it later. Get ready for bed and take Diesel to the AstroTurf."

"Fine…" he sighs, dragging his feet as he walks away.

Later that night, she lies in bed with Christian tucked against her side and Diesel snoring next to him. She pictures Gregg's face. She remembers what he said, that he will only ever love her.

You just wait, Gregg

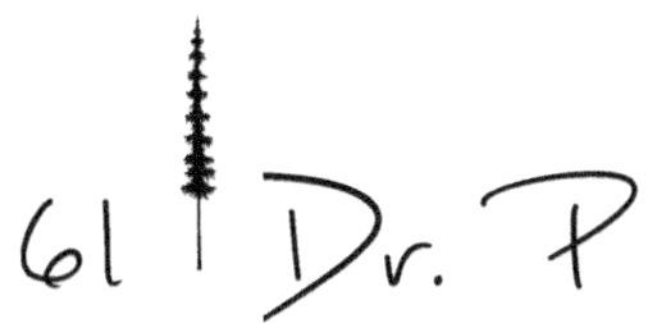

61 | Dr. P

Dr. P's first full day in the lab with Greggory goes amazingly. He includes her several times in his brainstorming sessions and makes her feel like they're really a team. They get so deep into the zone that she 'forgets' for a few hours. When the Donoghues arrive to retrieve them at five o'clock on the dot, reality snaps back into place.

"Hey, you two," Todd says, walking through the lab's glass doors. "You guys killed it today. I love to see how cohesive this lab has become! Who's ready for dinner? I hired a private chef—he's been at the house all day!"

"Great timing," Greggory says, smiling. "I think we're at a good stopping point, don't you agree?" he asks, turning to Dr. P.

"Actually, yes. I need to do some more research before the next hurdle anyway."

"Great! I've called for a limo. The driver can bring you back to your car after dinner," Todd announces.

"That's fine," Dr. P agrees.

Talk about awkward. Sitting next to Greggory in the limo, she tries to observe as much as she can about her surroundings. Tina seems to be trying to take up as little space as possible, a smile plastered across her face. Todd sits beside her in the widest manspread she's ever seen, with his head down. He stares at his phone, his finger swiftly scrolling over and over. Small short smiles or flashes of disgust cross his face.

Then there's Greggory, in beautifully tailored slacks and a long-sleeved button down. His hair is a slightly gelled mess of curls. He's handsome, and childlike, looking out the limo window like a kid on a field trip—if he only knew.

At dinner, her seat is across from Greggory's. A massive dining table sits pushed off to the side, unused. Instead, they sit at a small square table. Small meals that could barely feed a mouse are served on comically large plates. Though, the wine freely flows.

Dr. P enjoys Greggory's reactions to each course more than the actual food.

"Let's not talk about work." Tina says. "Any news from home, Dr. P?"

"My family says they miss me, of course," she says. Then she decides to press her luck. "I did hear from my sister last night though. She's expecting."

"How wonderful! You'll be an aunt. Have you ever thought about children yourself?" Todd asks.

"I'm not opposed to the idea. I just wanted children the more traditional way. Ideally a husband first. But because I'm kind of married to my work, that's tricky. What about you, Greggory?" she asks.

He quickly chews and swallows the tiny caprese salad. "Uh, yeah, same. I think. I think I'd be a fun dad. I'm just focused on my career right now. I'm in my prime. I'll meet someone eventually."

"Of course you will. A handsome guy like you, any woman would be stupid to turn you down," Tina says sweetly, flicking her eyes from Greggory to Dr. P as she says it.

Greggory coughs, nearly choking on his itty-bitty salad, at the remark.

"That's quite enough, Tina," Todd says, with a wink. "They're adults. They'll figure it out."

Tina winces, then quickly schools her features. "Ugh, fine. They're just both so beautiful. I can't help myself."

Dr. P chuckles and glances up at Greggory through her lashes. He sits with his mouth slightly agape, staring at her.

After a few bottles of wine between the four of them, Todd convinces Greggory to show Dr. P his swords. Todd and Tina exchange a quiet snicker as Greggory leads her up the stairs.

62 | MATT

Matt has switched vehicles three times already and is currently trying to stay off the radar in a region of British Columbia the map calls Coal River. He continued to follow the Alaska Highway, and it led him here.

Hat pulled low on his head, he checks into Coal River Services RV Park and Lodge using his real ID. He's on the run as his brother, not as himself.

Letting himself into the small room, he pulls off his boots and collapses into bed. He's cold, exhausted and has needed sleep for something like twenty hours.

"Better text fuck-face," he mutters, pulling his phone out of his pocket, from under the covers.

Text to Fuck-boi at 0246

« Hey. I'm safe. How's everything?

Text from Fuck-boi at 0246

» Good. Keep it on ice for a few days. Relax.

Text to Fuck-boi at 0330

« Ok, easy! Sorry I fell asleep. Going back to bed. Love ya!

The phone drops onto the mattress beside him. He is out instantly.

He wakes, eighteen hours later because his phone won't shut the fuck up!

"Holy fuck!"

Looking at his phone screen, he sees that there are five texts and three missed calls. All from Clara.

"Shit."

Text from Mine at 0510

» Hey. It's been a few hours since I heard anything. I know you need sleep, but I'm worried. Text me, please.

At 0730

» Matt, please tell me you're ok.

At 0810

» Suits have been in the area all morning. They tossed our apartment. They found a picture of you and John.

At 0900

» Matt, please. I'm scared!

At 1700

» Mr. Krieger, I regret to inform you that your lack of response caused Miss Clara a great deal of distress. She has suffered a mild heart attack. She was evaluated at the community health center, then airlifted and admitted to Mat-Su Regional Medical Center. Please return our call at this number.

"What the fuck!" he whisper-screams at the screen.

Not knowing what else to do, he dials his brother's number.

John answers, "Miss me, Fuggo?"

Matt takes a second, at a loss for words. He can't say it, because as soon as he does he'll lose it. He takes deep breaths, but it's no use. He's stuck—stuck in this time where only he knows what's happened. If he says it, it'll be real.

"Matt?" John asks, voice panicky.

"…I…" he tries.

"Are you okay?"

"Yes."

"Is Clara okay?"

He sobs—it just rips out of him without his consent.

"Shit," John breathes.

There's a long pause, where Matt hears his brother sniffle. John never could handle hearing his twin cry.

"Um," John says, obviously trying to compose himself. "Taken?"

"I…"

"Not sure?"

"Yeah."

"You get a call?"

"Text."

"Send it to me. I'll call you right back. I love you, Matt. Be strong. Get to Captain Charlie and get there like yesterday."

"Okay. Love you, bro."

The line goes dead.

Matt screenshots the messages and sends them to John right away. Shoving his feet into his boots, he grabs his keys from the nightstand and heads out the door.

63 | GREGGORY

Greggory uses his thumbprint to open his door and ushers Dr. P inside. He can still hear the tittering of schoolchildren at the bottom of the stairs. He flips the light switch and stands beside Dr. P.

"Welp, this is where the magic happens." He chuckles, then follows that with, "I don't know why I just said that—it was very early 2000s MTV Cribs." He laughs awkwardly.

She laughs—warm, rich and real. "That was very early 2000s MTV Cribs," she says between gasps and laughs.

She moseys around the room, admiring the décor. He feels nervous she'll think he's a giant nerd. She stops at his Lego Mjölnir. "Wow. This must have taken a long time."

He steps up beside her. "Yeah, it did. Especially because I superglued each piece. I didn't want to chance it breaking apart."

She looks at him and he feels that she is genuine, when she says, "That's smart!"

He blushes and turns his face away. When he looks back, he sees a knowing smile spread across her face.

"Well, unless you want to see my laundry chute—this's pretty much it."

"I think I'm good. Unless I can fit in there and slide down to escape whatever they think is happening up here."

"Yeah, that was kind of weird, huh?"

"You can say that again."

Greggory musters up some courage, and says, "Listen, I think you're really great, and to be honest it feels like I've known you forever. Maybe in another life. But I'm not really looking for anything romantic right now. I'd like to spend more time with you, just not in the way they," he gestures toward the floor, "are encouraging."

She cocks her head to the side and watches him for a minute. Then walks over to the bed, sits down, and pats the spot on the bed next to her.

He walks over, heat creeping up his ears, and sits. Before he can even turn to look at her, she says softly, "Can you keep a secret?"

He looks at her, and says earnestly, "Of course. Scout's honor." He holds up three fingers.

"I'm really glad you said that. I met someone right before relocating, and I think he might be…" She trails off.

"Oh. Like the one? The guy for you?" he asks.

Now she blushes—not as noticeable on her lightly tanned skin, but it's there.

"Maybe," she admits.

"I won't tell anyone. I promise."

"Now I have a favor to ask. And you won't understand why, but I need it." She sounds nervous.

"Okay. Whatever I can do."

She hesitates. Seemingly unable to find the words she wants to use.

"Hey, it's okay—whatever it is," he encourages gently.

"Ugh… I don't know how to ask this, and it has to stay between us… and I don't know if I trust you that much yet."

"Wow. Okay. Well, I don't know how to convince you, but I'm very trustworthy."

She laughs softly. "You do seem to be. I just don't want anyone knowing my private business. And since you don't really want a relationship right now anyway, I just thought… maybe we could pretend to be dating?"

She rushes on. "It sounds stupid when I say it out loud. I just figured we could kill two birds with one stone. We'd get to hang out as friends and not get hounded to date at the same time…"

He stops her. "Sure. That actually sounds great. You'd be willing to do that?"

"Well. It benefits both of us, right? I'd just rather be friends and focus on the work."

"Yeah, me too," he agrees quickly.

He watches her unzip her purse and pull out pajamas and a toiletry bag. She stands and tosses her purse onto a nearby chair.

"I came prepared. I trust we can stay in the same room, as friends?"

"Oh, yeah. I can sleep on the couch. The bathroom is around that corner, there," he says, pointing to the left.

He watches her retreating form, thinking he really must have won the lottery.

64 | Dr. P

When Dr. P closes the bathroom door, she smiles. Some things just work out.

She pulls her phone from her pocket and sees several notifications stacked on the lock screen.

1 missed call from John.

3 missed texts from John.

She clicks on the text thread.

Text from John at 2139

» Hey, I wanted to see how your day was.

Text at 2202

» I need to talk to you. Call me

Text at 2230

» Are you okay?! Call me!

She looks at the notification bar across the top of her screen to check the time. It's 2306.

"Shit, where'd the night go?" she mutters, while hitting the call icon next to John's picture on her phone.

Half a ring later, she hears, "Are you okay?" His voice tightly laced with fear.

"Yeah, I'm fine. I had that dinner I told you about," she answers in hushed tones.

"Oh. I forgot. Shit. Sorry for blowing you up."

"No big deal. My phone was on silent. I had a good talk with Greggory tonight. We're going to pretend to be in a relationship. Helps us both out."

"Why are you whispering?"

"I'm in his bathroom. I'm going to sleep over to really sell it."

"Um…"

"John, trust me. He's going to sleep on the couch."

"Okay. I trust you." He exhales. "I needed to talk because some shit went down. I need your help."

"Let's hear it," she says, bracing the phone to her ear with her shoulder while she changes.

"I'm pretty sure Crown got Clara." He drops the bomb conversationally.

The phone slips, falling to the floor. So does her stomach.

She scrambles to pick it up. "Shit, shit, sorry. I dropped the phone. How are you pretty sure?"

"She texted Matt that suits were in the area and that they tossed their apartment. The next text he got was supposedly from a hospital, saying she had a heart attack," John reports.

"No way, they definitely took her," she says, plopping down onto the closed toilet.

"Smart lady. Now I just need confirmation. Matt is biting at the bit to go in guns blazing. I talked him down for now, but I need answers."

"I don't know how I can help. My badge only works for my building," her tone fearful and apologetic.

"I know. But you're good with computers and so is Gregg. Make it a game. Find something. Anything. Please, boo?" She can hear the hurt in his voice as he pleads with her.

"I'll try. No promises," she says, unsure what she'll be able to do.

"That's all I ask. Thank you. Sweet dreams."

"Night."

She hangs up the phone and rushes through her skin care routine, hands shaking the entire time.

When she steps out of the bathroom, she sees Greggory curled up with a book, on the couch—as promised.

She swallows her feelings, not wanting to give anything away yet. "What 'cha reading?"

"Ah, the latest book in Brandon Sanderson's *Stormlight Archive*," he says, hefting up the heavy tome, so she can see it.

"It's… large," she says.

"Yeah, it is—and awesome!"

"I'll take your word for it." She chuckles to herself and walks over to the bed. She smiles. He turned down the covers for her. His bed is huge and beautiful, with black silk sheets and a dark green velvet comforter.

"Well, good night, Greggory. And thank you, again—for everything," she says, slipping beneath the unbelievably soft covers.

"We're in this together. If you get hungry or thirsty, the kitchen is down the hall. It's fully stocked."

"Thank you."

She settles down, shuffling her body deeper into the bed. She thinks behind closed eyes about ways to address the Clara issue with Greggory without raising suspicion, until sleep takes her.

65 | Shea

It's the middle of the freaking night!

Shea harrumphs and rolls out of bed. She tiptoes over to the bathroom and empties her bladder.

When she leaves the bathroom to return to her warm bed, she hears John softly 'screaming', "Fuck, fuck, fuck! Why? What the fuck am I gonna do now? FUCK!"

She opens the bedroom door and finds him sitting at the table, with his head face down on the table. His fist rests next to his head, clenched around a bottle of Crown Royal whiskey.

"It's the middle of the night. What's gotten into you?" she asks barely above a whisper.

"Shea, I'm sorry…" he slurs.

"Wow. Drunk John—this is new," she observes.

"Shea… everything is fucked. I dunno what we're gonna do."

"What do you mean? Is it Gregg? Oh God," she says, pressing a hand to her lower abdomen. Her pulse bounds in her temples, and even though she just emptied her bladder, it threatens to let go.

"Shit. No. Sorry. He's fine. Fake dating P."

"You'll have to explain that one later. What's fucked?" she asks, sitting beside him. She takes the bottle from him and places it just out of reach.

"Hey… ugh, never mind. This hangover is gonna suuuuccckkkk," he mumbles.

"John, focus! What is fucked?"

He spends the next half hour explaining everything that has happened and letting her read the texts. He tried to read them to her himself, but the alcohol made all the words run together, apparently.

"So, Crown has Clara? We're sure?" she asks, when he completed his explanation.

"Well, I mean pretty-fucking-sure, Shea. This is Crown we're talking about."

She nods slowly. "Right. Maybe there's a way to get her back. Has Matt called her phone?"

"Hell no. They'd ask him where we are. I love Matt, probably more than myself. I know him better than anyone… It'd be like Gregg turning himself in to save you. He might not sell us out, but he might turn himself in as me. They'd never know the difference. And I know what they would do to him. I've seen it before, you know."

She goes still and holds her breath.

"I know what they did to you, too. I'm so sorry, Shea. I should've never involved them." He begins to sob.

She's never seen him like this. And because her pregnancy hormones have her in a choke hold, she cries right along with him.

Before long, Christian exits the bedroom with Diesel. He takes one look at the two of them and his eyes fill with tears.

That kid is such a little empath

"Diesel's gotta poop," he says, quietly leading the dog into the second room.

"Shit. Pull it together. We're not going to get anywhere blubbering away like this," she says, wiping her face.

He sniffles a few times and clears his throat. "I honestly don't know what to do, Shea. I asked P to look around and see what she can find, but she doesn't have much access."

"Yeah, I doubt she finds anything. What about your inside man? Seems like he has more clearance," she suggests.

"He does. But I don't want to pull him off Gregg duty either."

"It sounds like Gregg's doing fine. Like you said before, Todd needs him. Plus, we have Dr. P now. It sounds like she'll be spending more time with him. We can afford to move the inside man."

He exhales slowly. "I know you're right. I'll call him in the morning, when I've sobered up. What do I tell Matt? He's barely holding it together."

"Tell him the truth. And tell him to enact whatever plan you guys have worked out." She squeezes his hand. "The plan is Captain Charlie, right? He has to keep going. For all of our sakes."

66 | MATT

Matt drives the speed limit, constantly checking his mirrors for any signs of trouble or a tail. He's gotten off the Al-Can Highway and is now driving toward Washington state. He's been driving since he talked to John—twenty hours ago, give or take. He refuses to stop until he reaches Oregon and Captain Charlie.

So far, his travels have been incident free. He's stopped for gas, snacks and the occasional poo. Otherwise, he stays laser focused with only one thing on his mind—Clara.

It had been a year since he moved to Alaska to help John and his friends, but it feels like yesterday. He was in Talkeetna for only two weeks, walking every day, trying to get to know people—when he saw her.

She was working at her family's store, helping an elderly woman lift something heavy. He can't even remember what the heavy thing was, now—he only sees her face.

High cheekbones, pale blue eyes, full lips and a beautiful Greek nose. Her long dirty-blonde hair was in a high, ridiculously messy bun that flopped around as she moved. She was wearing jeans tucked into XtraTuf boots, a shirt with 'Yo-Mama' printed on the front, and a belt made from a seatbelt. She could've been wearing couture or a burlap sack, she was beautiful—pure and simple.

He couldn't help himself—he was drawn to her. He walked over to her store and bee-lined it straight for her. Getting into her orbit, he smelled lavender and citrus, it was intoxicating.

He remembers asking her for her name and the rest is history. Once they started talking they didn't stop. In the months since, he has thought about proposing at least a thousand times.

"Why didn't I just do it? Fucking coward!" he yells into the car's dark interior, lit only by the speedometer and radio display.

He knows she would have said yes. He should've asked her when she hid his hat—he knew then that she was his for sure.

He smacks the steering wheel several times, takes a deep breath and re-focuses. It's late and dark and he'd hate to have an accident.

"Focus. Only nine hours to go."

67 | Todd

"Well, good morning, you two lovebirds," Todd coos as Greggory and Dr. P walk into the kitchen.

Blush rises in Greggory's face, making Todd's grin stretch even wider.

"We fell asleep talking, that's all," Dr. P says, though Todd doesn't hear any conviction in the words.

"Well, either way, Tina and I made some quiche. Sit, sit. Enjoy some breakfast with us."

Todd watches Greggory place his hand at the small of Dr. P's back. She turns her head to him, smiling.

Giddy is the only word to explain how this simple interaction makes him feel. This is just perfect. If Greggory moves on, it will cement all the work they did with the EBW-∞.

They all sit at the usual, much larger table. Greggory chooses the seat next to Dr. P instead of across from her.

"Excellent. I'm glad you stayed, Dr. P," Todd says brightly.

"Well, I'm never one to turn down quiche," she replies, smiling first at Todd then at Greggory.

"Tina and I were thinking about maybe having a beach day. If you two are interested in going," Todd offers casually.

He notices Tina trying to hide her surprise.

"Oh. Well, Greggory and I already made plans. He's going to buy me the Milky Way Galaxy Lego set and help me put it together. Add a little art to my new apartment," Dr. P says.

"Aw, that's so… wholesome. I love it!" Todd announces his approval.

"It's really cool. A layered art style Lego. It has over three thousand pieces, so it should take a while," Greggory adds.

"I'll call a town car to take you guys to Dr. P's car after breakfast. I'll send you the app link Greggory—in case you need a ride back later."

"Thanks, boss."

Crossing into Oregon, he wipes his eyes and yawns so hard his jaw pops. Not much longer now. He's struggling to keep his eyes open when his phone rings.

He answers immediately. "Go for Matt."

He pulls over to the shoulder to talk, steps out of the vehicle and paces along the side of the road.

"Bro, it's me. I don't have any news yet, but I wanted to update you on what I have done," John's voice comes through the phone.

"Okay." He kicks small pebbles as he paces.

"I asked Dr. P to do what she can. We probably won't hear anything from her for a few days. I also talked to our inside man, who has more access to the kinds of places they take prisoners. He's gonna poke around, but again, that could take a couple of days—because it's the weekend. So stay calm. We're working on it."

"Thanks, bro. So… be patient? That's what you're telling me?" Feeling like patience has never been a strong suit of his.

"I'm telling you that you have other shit to worry about. Let me handle this," John persists.

"You have five days to give me a real update. After that—no promises." He refuses to let Clara rot in some Crown prison.

"Cool it, Jason Statham," John mutters. "Don't do anything without talking to me first. Okay?"

"Whatever."

"Where are you now?"

"I just entered Portland, Oregon. I'll be at Captain Charlie's in about an hour and a half," Matt answers.

"Have you talked to him at all?"

Matt snorts. "No, John. I'm headed to a retired military captain's private residence with no notice," he says dryly.

"I know you're being sarcastic. But seriously, he's a private contractor now. His place is probably crawling with ex-military," John warns.

"I know, fuck face. I talked to him. No specifics, just that I needed help. He's expecting me."

"Alright. Update me later then, fuggo."

Matt hangs up, gets back in the car, and pulls back onto the highway, feeling a little more awake after the call.

69 | GREGGORY

The town car pulls into the parking lot in front of their work building, next to Dr. P's Mercedes.

"Thanks, man," Greggory says to the driver as he steps out.

He walks with Dr. P to her car and pauses before getting in. "You don't really have to do this, if you're not into it. Friends should be honest with each other."

She unlocks the car with her fob, and says, "I wouldn't have agreed if I wasn't interested. Fair warning though, my apartment is like a third the size of your suite."

"Oh, I don't care about that. Should we grab some food while we're at Walmart?" he asks.

"Great idea. Make a list on your phone, so we're not in there forever."

"It is an easy place to get lost in," he says.

Twenty-two minutes later, she parks in the farthest recess of the Walmart parking lot.

Inside they peruse the Lego aisle. She even spots a few other Lego's she'd like to do in the future. They grab premade subs and head to self-checkout.

At checkout, Greggory steps in front of her. "I've got it. It'd be an honor for me to buy your first Lego."

"So chivalrous," Dr. P says, smiling.

They spend the whole afternoon building the set while watching *Severance*. They laugh and enjoy each other's company. He says he likes the show and wonders out loud how strange it would be to live a life without access to some of your memories. Dr. P quickly changes the subject.

70 | Shea

Shea sits at the table, using her tablet to Google. They are in the air again, having quickly touched down in Boone, North Carolina.

"Hey, Christian, can you show me the baby?"

"Yeah!" he says excitedly and abandons his sandwich to sit beside her. He places his small hand on her abdomen, and her world goes black.

The baby appears. It's more developed now—its head doesn't look as large as last time, or maybe it's that the baby's body has caught up. Christian maintains contact and gently presses on her abdomen, making ripples in the amniotic fluid. The small thing twitches and adjusts itself. He allows her to hear its beating heart.

Taking his hand away, he smiles at her. "Looks like you."

"You saying I have a huge forehead?" she asks with mock outrage. "Just kidding. Thank you, Christian."

He beams.

"John," she calls through the plane.

"One sec!" she hears him holler.

She returns to Googling.

"Alright, sorry. What's up?" he asks, plopping down next to her.

"I've been doing some research on the Google. I think, I mean—it's hard to know exactly when I got pregnant, because I haven't really had a period. TMI, I know. Quit looking at me like that," she says, shoving his shoulder.

"Sorry. Continue."

"So based on the way the baby looks and my symptoms of nausea and a bladder the size of a pea, I think I'm about fourteen weeks pregnant."

He chuckles. "You have been in the bathroom a lot. It's coming out of every orifice."

"Well, I'm just letting you know. That's probably why my boobs have been—different."

He immediately stands from the table. "Okay. Well, my turn for news."

He walks to the fridge and pulls out a Coke. He pops it open and takes a sip.

"Out with it!" she orders.

"Matt just made it to Captain Charlie's compound. We're rerouting our flight to land there. We're going to hire Captain Charlie to put an end to all of this. Once and for all. We'll continue our travels with him and his men."

"We're making a plan?" Shea asks, excitement lighting her face.

"We're making a plan!" he confirms.

71 | Tina

Tina has been sitting in their master suite for a couple of hours now. It started with her skincare routine, including lymphatic massage and waxing. Then it turned into reading, curled onto her side in bed. Now she scrolls through the endless, mindless internet.

She's bored. She hates Todd… half the time, but he is entertaining. She thought that they might actually go to the beach after his announcement at breakfast, but once Greggory and Dr. P left, so did he—into his home office.

Looking at her alarm clock, she sees that it's 1:10 a.m. Instead of lying there bored, she decides to seek him out. She tiptoes down the stairs, unsure where he might be. He's usually in bed by now.

Halfway down the stairs, she spots him at the front window, peeking through the blinds like a nosy neighbor. She can't help herself, she feels a giggle bubbling up. She quickly clamps both hands over her mouth to stifle it.

She just can't believe what she is seeing.

He's wearing his gym clothes, barefoot, hair a mess. His six-foot-five muscular frame is hunched over to about Tina's height (just under five feet). One finger barely parts the blinds, while his eyes peer through the gap. He's so close, his nose almost touches the blinds. That's not even the funniest thing to Tina. The funniest part is how antsy he looks, shifting from the ball of one foot to the other.

She decides to make herself known, while also acting like she doesn't see him. She yawns loudly and turns for the kitchen, keeping her eyes down cast.

"Tina! You scared the shit out of me!" he reprimands, walking to meet her.

"Oh, sorry. I forgot my water bottle down here and I was thirsty," she replies.

"Well, hurry up! Greggory could be home any minute. I wanna liquor him up with some hundred-year-old Scotch and find out what happened between him and Dr. P."

"That's why you're up so late? What if he stays the night at her place?" she asks.

"I didn't ask for your opinion. Get your water bottle and get your ass back to bed. I don't want him feeling pressured. It might scare him off her."

"Yes sir, Mr. T," she says snarkily, upset by his reprimanding.

"Don't start." His face darkens. The look screams 'Don't fuck with me.'

She quickly back peddles. "Sorry, babe. I'm just tired and it's hard to fall asleep when you're not next to me," she says sweetly, unwilling to be his punching bag tonight.

"Aw. Sorry, babe. I gotta take care of business. You know this."

He checks his phone and when he looks back at her, she can't read his face. It unnerves her.

"He just ordered a car. Get. To. Bed," he enunciates and snaps each word.

"On second thought, I think my water bottle is in the room," she says, turning and quickly running up the stairs before he can react.

72 | Todd

Todd lets Tina get away with her childish behavior. This time.

He can feel excitement tickling his nerves. He walks to one of the many liquor cabinets in the house and grabs a bottle of hundred-year-old Scotch and two glasses. He carries them to the front sitting room and sets them on the low coffee table. He leaves the lights off and sits down in one of the armchairs.

He begins talking to himself.

"You just wait, Shea. Greggory is going to build a full life without you and never even mourn your loss. When I eventually get my hands on you and the child subject, I'll drag you out in front of the child and Greggory and gut you. The only reaction you might get from Greggory is a smile."

He sits in the silence of his statement until headlights illuminate his surroundings. The shadows of the large trees out front grow and stretch across the walls. A minute later, Greggory unlocks the front door and quietly steps inside.

"Greggory! My man. I was just about to open this expensive bottle of Scotch. Join me, won't you?" Todd calls into the dark, silent entry way.

Greggory shrieks, "Holy shit! Why are you sitting in the dark?"

"I was on my phone, I didn't notice," he says, standing and flipping on the light.

Greggory walks into the sitting room and plops down in the armchair opposite Todd.

"SoooOoo…" Todd says, pouring two fingers of Scotch and handing it to Greggory.

"So?" Greggory parrots back at him.

"C'mon. Tell me how it went!" Todd encourages, on the edge of his seat.

"She's great. I mean, you've seen her and man is she smart and fun. Easy to be around. I totally lost track of time today."

Todd screams internally like a teenage girl. He keeps his cool on the outside, though.

"What'd you guys get up to today? Just the Lego?" he pries.

"Well, it did take a while—but no. We spent the last few hours finishing the first season of a show and tossing popcorn into each other's mouths. We even came up with a point system. It was pretty fun."

"Greggory, fun is great and everything, but I mean…" Todd trails off, hoping he gets the hint. Anticipation dances along his body, hopeful Dr. P has hooked her claws in him.

Greggory downs his Scotch in one swallow, places the glass on the table and stands. "Todd, I really like being friends with you, and I appreciate the Scotch. But Dr. P and I are taking things slow. And either way, I don't kiss and tell. Night, man."

Greggory ascends the stairs, and Todd watches him until he is out of sight.

Todd chuckles to himself, and says, "Well, shit."

73 | Shea

As they get closer to their destination, Shea busies herself ensuring all their bags are packed and that they leave nothing behind.

"Christian," she hollers, "why am I looking at your dry toothbrush—still in the bathroom?"

"Sorry. Forgot."

"Well, come do it now, please. And pack it when you're done!"

"Yes ma 'am."

"Yay! Big C—you said it right!" Shea coos.

"I did it!" he says proudly.

John walks through the cabin and stops in front of Shea—who is currently on her hands and knees, looking under his bed.

"Shea, get up and sit down. That sounded weird, but you know what I mean. We're about forty-five minutes out. We're gonna start our decent soon."

"Okay," a muffled voice comes from under the bed. She pops her head up, and says, "Sorry, I can't find a sock. It's not under there, but I did find the other half of the PB and J Christian lost a few days ago." She holds up a smushed half of a sandwich.

"I'm surprised Diesel didn't get it," John says. Then seeing her change in demeanor, says, "Aw, shit, Shea. Run. Go!"

She slaps her hand over her mouth and bolts for the bathroom, still holding the sandwich. When she leans over to—well—be sick, she plops the PB and J into the toilet too.

Why not. It all goes to the same place

She looks at her face in the mirror as she scoops water into her mouth from the faucet and swishes. She's looking a bit puffy, and the dark circles of exhaustion stain the skin under her eyes. She decides, since she'll be meeting a bunch of new people, she should put on some makeup.

When she opens the bathroom door, John is leaning on the doorframe just outside.

"You okay, Shea?" he asks, face strained with worry.

"Yeah, right as rain. If the rain was pickle flavored. It's morning sickness. Or afternoon, in this case. It's normal. It sucks, but it's normal," she says, putting a hand on his shoulder as she walks past him.

He's so sweet, when he wants to be

"I'm just grabbing some make-up. I look like death."

"Ah, stop it. You're beautiful and you have that pregnancy glow."

"I'm pretty sure that's just grease. I just don't feel very confident. Maybe it's the pregnancy or maybe it has to do with my hair," she says, feeling vulnerable.

"I'm glad I'm not the only one. I'm mentally preparing for the razzing I'm about to get from my old military buddies. I can hear it now. Baby face and probably a spin on your favorite, Sergeant First Class butt chin," he says, hanging his head dramatically.

She laughs, then feels bad. "I'm sorry, John. I didn't mean…"

He waves her off. "All good. It was nice to hear you laugh."

"Okay, time is running out. I need to fix my face and hair."

Nothing much. A little concealer, mascara, and Carmex to make her look more alive. Then she wets her hair to tame the frizz and coax out her waves. She's glad she usually wears leggings, because although she doesn't feel like she's gained any weight, she does feel very sensitive, sensory wise to fabrics and tight clothes. She picks black leggings and one of Gregg's old hoodies, camo with an Under Armor logo on the front.

While she digs through Gregg's bag for the hoodie, she feels tears prickle her eyes. She misses him so much. When she gets to the bottom of the bag, she laughs, one single laugh, punctuated by tears.

"You okay?" John asks, rushing into the room.

She turns and holds up what she found.

He laughs as well. His face full of joy. "Which ones are they?" he asks.

She pulls off the thick leather covers. "This one is Needle and the other is Longclaw. They're both from *Game of Thrones*. They're my favorites of his collection. I had no idea he brought them."

"He didn't know what would happen to all the stuff we had to leave at that house. When we first went out to the cabin without you, he kept talking about how upset he was that he couldn't take any of them. He must've risked going back to that house when he was back in Florida to get you."

"He risked that for swords? That was stupid," Shea says.

"No," John says gently. "That's love, Shea. Out of all his swords, you think these two, your favorites, just happen to be the ones he grabbed?"

"I mean…"

"No. He grabbed your favorites, not his. I know for a fact his *He-Man* sword and *Aragorn's* sword, *Andúril* were his favorites. That man loves you so much, Shea."

She sniffs. "Well, he did."

74 | MATT

Matt's been pacing for hours. He can't sit or relax, there's too much going on. He's currently in Captain Charlie's living room. It has tall, vaulted ceilings and enough seating for like twenty people. The place smells faintly of coffee, gun oil, and leather. He continues pacing, wearing a path into the expensive looking area rug.

A whistle sounds behind him, and he turns.

A huge grin spreads across his face. "Duce! You ugly bastard! Damn, it's been too long, brotha."

He walks over and pulls the man who is several inches shorter into a hug slapping his back. Duce wears a black baseball cap over his high and tight haircut, black fatigues, and a short beard.

"Thing Two! Who else is here? Cap sent me straight in, but I haven't seen anyone else," Duce says.

"I don't know to be honest. He probably sent you in for comedic relief," Matt says, laughing through his nose.

"Well, once you shit your pants on an op—it's pretty much all uphill from there," Duce replies.

"You would know." Matt smirks.

Duce drops into a chair and promptly props his feet up on a nearby table. "So what's the mission? Cap didn't tell me anything. Just booked me a ticket."

"Search and rescue. Let's wait until everyone shows up to talk about it. I don't want to have to repeat myself a bunch of times."

They sit together, talking about old times. For a few minutes, Matt forgets just a little bit.

Twenty minutes later the front door bursts open and all hell breaks loose.

Matt stands there, confused watching a man in a baseball cap with his head down, stride straight toward him. Shea, Christian, and Diesel trail behind.

The man pulls Matt into a loving hug.

Matt knows exactly who it is when the man whispers in his ear, "Hey, fuggo."

75 | Shea

Shea stands in a crowd of military men, with Christian and Diesel. She watches John hold his brother like he's afraid Matt will disappear if he lets go. She wipes the tears as they appear.

Stupid hormones

"Alright, men, find a seat. Uh… lady also, please," Captain Charlie announces.

He stands with his back to a large wall with a framed photo of a young man and woman, who look like younger versions of him and his wife. Cap is a muscular older man now, with more white hairs than red. He's clean shaven and wears a baseball cap, that says, 'Get in Line'. He looks like the fun uncle.

Shea moves to the couch that Matt and John are standing in front of and pulls Christian along behind her. She makes sure he does not touch anyone, and no one touches him. She says, "Hi," to Matt and they all sit on the couch together. Diesel settles down at their feet, his nose twitching in all directions.

"This will not be actionable until further notice," Cap begins. "This meeting is to get everyone on the same page and assign bunks. For the benefit of our new friends let's do some… uh… appropriate introductions." He eyeballs the men then points to the man on his left. "You start. Then you. And so on."

"Hey, everybody. My name's Tank, and I'm an alcoholic."

A voice calls from the chair next to Shea, "Wrong meeting, brotha!"

The room erupts in laughter.

Tank grins. "I kid! Ya'll know I've never been to AA. I'm not a quitter."

More laughter follows. Shea can't help but smile.

"Let's go, keep it together or we'll be here all night! My smoker only has three hours left. I'd like to be done before it is!" Captain Charlie says, trying to get them back on track.

The man next to Tank goes by Gas.

"Tell me why they have the nicknames when they say them, I'm so lost," Shea whispers to John.

He winks and leans in close. "Okay, Tank can drink anyone under the table and still run an op. Gas is always missing when you need him, like a fart in the wind. Teddy is a softie, like a big teddy bear. Ghost is a sniper, it's a common sniper nickname. DD is Dirty Doug, he's a mechanic and he's literally always dirty. Hoover will eat any and all snacks left unattended for even a nano-second. Cap or Captain Charlie was our Captain. Terry is just a big, bald, dude and someone said he looked like Terry Crews. Innie, well it doesn't make much sense but it's short for numb nuts, he once sat on one of his testicles and it went numb for hours. Thing Two for Matt because we're twins. I'm Thing One," he explains.

"Oh. Okay." She nods.

He elbows her gently.

"Ow, what the shit?" she blurts out.

The room laughs.

"It's your turn," John urges.

"Oh, sorry!" she announces. "I'm Shea. I just want to say, I'm so grateful you all answered Captain Charlie's call."

She turns to Christian and nods.

"I'm Christian. This Diesel," he says, patting the dog on the head. "He nice boy," he finishes, smiling.

Shea pipes back up, "Also, please do not touch Christian. He has a very rare condition and just… please don't."

"Everybody got that?" Captain Charlie asks.

The room speaks as one, "Yes, sir!"

Monday morning, Dr. P makes sure she styles her hair and does her make-up to the best of her ability. She also applies her favorite perfume, Lancôme's *La Vie Est Belle.*

When she arrives at her desk, Greggory's already hard at work.

"Hey, Greggory! Good morning. I saw that there's coffee and Danishes in the kitchen. Want to walk with me?"

He looks up from his work, smiles at her, and says, "Hey, you look really nice today. Sure, a little breakfast sounds great."

In the kitchen, Greggory grabs an apple Danish and a coffee. He walks over to where Dr. P is perusing the selection, and cryptically says, "Oh, I accidentally went home with one of your blankets yesterday. It's in my car, if you wanna take a slightly longer walk."

"Sure…" she drags out, grabbing a cherry cheese Danish and a coffee for herself. She follows him out of the building.

Once they make it to the asphalt of the parking lot, he presses unlock on the key fob in his hand.

"I thought you didn't have a car?" Dr. P asks.

"I didn't. But it seemed like more independence was needed, especially if we'll be hanging out more," he says, blushing.

She smiles. "It's nice!"

"It's older, but the engine was rebuilt. I got a great deal on it," he says, slapping the roof of the dark blue, 2005 Cadillac CTS. "It's fully loaded and everything," he adds.

Dr. P smiles. "It's really great! Is this why you invited me out here? I know you don't have one of my blankets. You left them all attached to the fort we built."

He chuckles. "Yes and no. I don't want to get into details on company property, but the plan we came up with is looking more and more like the best idea we've ever had."

"Really?" she asks, her voice light but her mind racing. "Okay well, you want to do something with me after work? I'm thinking about taking up crocheting, to make a blanket for my sister's baby."

"Sure. Maybe I'll try too! You did a Lego with me, so it's only fair," Greggory says.

"That sounds great!" she says.

They head back inside.

Back at their desks, they work out some kinks they had been dealing with and finalize their chip design. As soon as they send their report, Todd makes an appearance in their building. Greggory and Dr. P see him enter through the glass walls of their enclosed space and exchange knowing smiles.

He enters their space with flair. "Lady, gentleman. Great news today, huh?"

"Yes, sir," Greggory admits.

"Well, now is when the two of you split. Greggory, I want you running diagnostics on our main computer systems. We caught a nasty bug a while back and haven't been able to come back from it. They're bringing you a console connected to that network to work from."

"What about the next steps on the chip?" Greggory inquires.

"Dr. P will design the chip and do the mock implantations. We're sending up cases of gel brains now. Then she'll begin animal trials, which you will help her with. Because of the complexity of the human brain and the various uses we want for this chip, we chose ravens. We have an aviary for them and will bring them up only for the procedure. All observations will be conducted in the aviary."

"Ravens, wow. They are super intelligent, so I guess that makes sense," Dr. P observes, hoping they escape this hell hole before it gets that far.

"Those are your assignments. Dr. P if you need or want Greggory's help, he'll still be right next to you, so don't hesitate to ask him." He smiles wide and sickly sweet, then says, "Any questions?"

"How long has this virus had free rein in your old system?" Greggory asks.

"About seven months. That system has been shut down for two, though. My guys gave it all they had and thought it best to quit before they caused more damage."

"Okay. I'll give it everything I've got, boss."

"Great! Ah, here comes Tina leading the charge!" Todd announces.

Dr. P and Greggory step aside allowing their new additions to be set up for them. Once the space is theirs again, Dr. P looks over at Greggory, who shrugs and gets to work.

Remembering John's request, Dr. P clears her throat. "Hey, when we leave, you want to ride together to Michaels? I need to talk to you about something."

"Yeah, sure. Wanna ride in the Caddi?" he asks with a big grin.

"Sure. The Caddi it is."

They spend the rest of the day working diligently on their new assignments. Dr. P wrestles with herself all day about how much she should tell Greggory and how quickly she should further their research in the neural chip technology.

77 | Christian

Christian sits on the couch with Diesel at his feet, gently stroking the dog's head. He was very anxious when they arrived, but since Shea's announcement, all the adults have kept their distance. They talk to him but haven't touched.

He watches the man they call Duce clear a path through all the other men, Shea close behind her hand over her mouth. Duce gets her to the bathroom in no time. As he walks away from the bathroom, he eyes Christian sitting alone and heads over.

"Hey, kid. I'm Duce. You alright? Can I sit? I'll keep my distance."

"Okay!" he says enthusiastically.

Duce lowers himself into the seat beside him. Diesel turns to him, sniffing his legs. Once satisfied, he lies on the ground between them, tail wagging.

"He likes you," Christian offers.

"He seems like a chill buddy to have. While we're here training for the mission, I'm gonna work with you and Diesel. I'll teach him some commands and how to truly protect you. I trained a lot of the dogs that got deployed."

"He is. He listens good," Christian says defending the pup.

"Oh, no doubt. I've been watching him. He's stuck to you like glue. But Shea is vulnerable too, right?"

"Oh, yes," he says.

"She's expecting?" Duce asks.

"Yes," he says, a smile spreading across his face as he thinks about his little alien friend.

"Ey, Tank… Preggers," Duce calls over his shoulder.

"YES!" Tank shouts back.

Christian sits confused until Shea exits the bathroom and the entire unit hollers, "Preggers!"

She smiles. "Did I just get my very own nickname?"

"Yup!" Tank answers proudly.

Christian smiles again. He loves seeing her look so happy.

Duce catches his attention again, when he says, "You're a man of few words, aren't you, kid?"

"Yup."

"Hey, Tank," he again calls over his shoulder.

"Yeah, man?"

"Gather the unit around this young man."

The men walk over, getting close, but keeping a healthy distance. Diesel jumps up and gives everyone a turn at being sniffed. When he's done, he sits on Christian's feet, looking out at everyone assembled, on full alert.

"That's a good-ass dog, Duce. Training will be easy," DD observes.

"Hell yeah, man," Duce responds. "Alright, are you all listening?"

"Yes," the room responds, then softly Christian says the same.

Duce stands and holds out his closed pocketknife. "For our resident little quiet dude, I do dub thee SBD!" Duce says, landing the closed knife just above each of Christian's shoulders, careful to not touch.

A couple of the men chuckle, then as one they chant, "SBD! SBD! SBD!"

Shea walks over and rests her hand on Christian's shoulder. Leaning in close, she says, "We're part of the unit now, bud!"

He smiles, but it falls quickly. He looks at Duce, and asks, "What's SBD mean?"

"Oh. Well, you ever heard somebody say their fart is silent but deadly?"

"Oh. Yes," he says, his face giving away his confusion and disappointment.

"Christian, this is a super badass name! It's not about the farts. It's because you don't talk much. A silent killer!" John explains.

Christian perks up hearing that and smiles at the assembled unit. "Yeah, SBD!" he declares.

78 | Clara

Clara knows it's been days, but has it been weeks?

When the men in suits grabbed her, they put a bag over her head. It's been dark ever since. She runs through the events in her mind again, she has nothing better to do.

They grabbed her, immediately putting the bag over her head and loaded her into a vehicle she had to step up into. She started counting as soon as they loaded her but lost count several times and fell asleep. When she woke, she was in a different place. She thinks it was a plane, because of the sounds. She tried to focus, but after being awake only a few minutes she fell asleep again.

The next time she woke up, she was here. Wherever here is. She can tell she isn't wearing her clothes, though she has no idea what's in their place. There are some medical devices managing her waste and she knows she has an IV, because they've changed it a few times. She felt around and also figured out that they sewed her eyelids closed.

A man with a deep, soothing voice comes in once a day and asks her where John is. She tells the truth, she has no idea. She doesn't even know where Matt is. She hopes he's okay. After that they shock her or hit her, then ask where Shea is. She tells them the truth.

He doesn't believe her anyway, so she stopped answering. He really doesn't like that. However it goes, she promptly falls asleep when he leaves until her visit the next day.

She has tried to force her eyelids open, but she can't. She tried using her fingers, but again silent hands stopped her.

She has lost hope.

Until they're ready to rescue Gregg, which could be months from now, she's stuck and there's nothing she can do about it. This is some damsel in distress bullshit!

Before sleep takes her again, she sends up a silent plea to anyone who will listen, "Please let their training go quickly. Please. I need a rescue… Please!"

79 | Todd

Todd sits at his desk, reviewing the informatics Greggory and Dr. P sent him. Tina sits across from him in a visitor chair, reading through the same document on her laptop.

"What part are you on?" he asks, leaning toward her.

"Appendix B," she says, not looking up.

"Dr. P has been a great influence, making the chip even more potent. Did you read the potential use list Greggory drafted?"

"Yes," she answers.

"This is certainly more developed than the version you have implanted. He really killed it. After animal testing, I might be able to involve the US military in human trials. I'm sure they would be first in line to invest. I can see it now. Legions of soldiers only able to follow orders, with no memory of their mission afterward. Perfect," he says, glassy eyed.

Coming back down to reality, he says, "This will give a huge influx of funding. Maybe make it possible to fix the time machine next."

"You think he can crack it?" Tina asks.

"He caused it. If anyone can, it's him."

The intercom on Todd's desk buzzes to life. "Mr. Donoghue, Dr. Hughes is here to see you."

Todd shoos Tina out, who ushers Dr. Hughes in as she leaves.

Todd stands behind his desk. "Dr. Hughes, how are things in 25 these days?"

"Eventful, with our new arrival. Our daily visits continue to produce no new information. Is there another tactic you would like us to implement?"

"She probably doesn't know anything. Keep up the routine. John will want to protect his brother. He'll end up leading Shea and the boy straight to me."

"Clever plan, boss."

"Thank you, Dr. Hughes," he says, genuinely.

"I was thinking, maybe I could text them from her phone. Tell them how badly she's being treated. Add some fuel to the fire?"

Todd smiles broadly. "I don't say this often, but you're an evil genius. I love it. Implement this immediately. Can you blind copy me on the text? Either way, send me screen shots or something."

"I'll get right on this, boss," Dr. Hughes says, vacating the room quickly.

80 Shea

It feels great to be around these guys. They have only been here one day, and they already felt like family. Since dinner, they've been sitting around swapping all their funny stories, like when Duce shit his pants during an op.

Shea snuggles into the corner of a couch on her side with her legs up and tucked up close to her body. Christian cuddles with her legs, his head resting on her bum. She stifles another yawn, but Cap sees it. He walks over and kneels in front of her.

"I set up a room for you, SBD, and Diesel. It's down the same hallway as the bathroom, second door on the right. Whenever you're ready."

"Thanks so much, Cap. What about the boys?"

"I have a separate barrack house they'll stay in with the unit. It's good for them to get in sync before an op," he explains.

"Okay. Thanks again."

As she starts to rouse Christian, she hears her regular text tone, encrypted but not from the secure app they like to use. A second later she hears John's and Matt's phones chime too.

Aw shit. What now

She pulls out her phone and sees a group text to her, John, and Matt.

Group Message from Clara at 1859

» Guys, I'm in Todd's compound. I was able to subdue one of my captors and get my phone. They torture me every day. I've got all kinds of tubes in me. Help me!

She looks up just in time to see Matt hurl his phone at Cap's oven, shattering the glass door. She watches as he storms out of the house. Front door slamming.

"Sorry, Cap. I'll pay for that," John says. He meets Shea's eyes and gives a subtle nod toward the door.

She quickly and carefully slides out from under Christian. She looks at Duce and mouths, "Watch him, please." He nods.

As soon as she opens the door, she hears screaming and slapping.

SLAP. "Get your mind right. That is not her!" John yells.

SLAP. "But they're probably telling the truth, fuck face!" Matt screams.

"BOYS!" Shea shouts, her voice cracking through the night like a whip. She stands with her hands planted on her hips. They stop and look at her.

"Take a deep breath," she orders. "This changes nothing. We already have a plan. This is what they want. They want your emotions ruling you so that you charge in there halfcocked and get yourself killed!"

John nods.

"That is not going to happen. My baby needs its uncles—intact and alive! Go to the barracks and Go. To. Sleep. Cap says we're getting the plan started tomorrow at 0800. Don't make me bring this to him! Please, be smarter than this!"

She looks specifically at Matt. "Okay?"

"Yes, ma'am," Matt says, dejected.

She eyes John.

"Yes ma'am!" he says, full of pride and respect.

81 | GREGGORY

Greggory's been looking at the virus code all day, line after line. It's more like one of the four horsemen of the apocalypse. The code is beautifully written, intricate and ouroboros like. One move to change it causes a cascade of other system locks and failures.

As he works, a strange sense of déjà vu creeps in. There's something familiar about it. Dr. P pulls him from his intense focus.

"It's 5:10, my friend. Let's blow this popsicle stand," she says, with a hand on his shoulder.

"Oh, good. My eyes were starting to bug out." He stands from his desk, removes his glasses, and pinches the bridge of his nose.

"Wow. Your eyes are intense. Have you ever thought about contacts?" Dr. P asks.

"No. My prescription is pretty bad. I never wanted to mess with it, I guess."

"You should," she says, walking out of the office ahead of him.

He blushes and hurries to catch up to her. Outside, they climb into his new car and head for Michaels.

Reaching for the radio volume knob, he turns it all the way down. He clears his throat and glances at her quickly, then back at the road. "You said there was something you needed to talk to me about?" he asks gently.

"Yeah, um… There are some things I know, and I can't tell you all of them. You wouldn't believe me anyway. This is really delicate and I'm feeling really nervous," she says, her fingers fussing with the ends of her cardigan.

He doesn't understand what she's talking about. So instead of prying, he says, "Last night when I got home, Todd was waiting up for me, with Scotch. He asked how our day went, so I told him the truth. He insinuated he didn't want to hear about that." He clears his throat, blushing. "He wanted… um, sexual details. I told him that we decided to take it slow and that either way I don't kiss and tell. I walked away and went to bed."

He chances a glance at her again. She looks torn.

"I realize something isn't right here. I recognize the code I'm working on," he adds.

"What do you mean, recognize it?" she asks, angling her body toward him.

"Just like an artist signs their paintings, a coder can add lines of code that have nothing to do with the virus, a signature of sorts. This code tells a story of a life I never lived," he says, voice cracking.

"What do you mean?"

"I don't know what you need to tell me, but I'll believe you," he says, pulling into the Michaels parking lot.

She stares at him, speechless. "Who wrote the code?" she finally asks.

"Only one option makes sense but also makes no sense. Me."

"You left yourself messages in the code?"

"Someone did. Yes."

"Holy shit. Okay. I think it best that we don't get into that yet."

"Yeah, agreed," he says.

She takes a breath. "But I do need your help. A man that helped some enemies of Todd's, well, it pissed Todd off. So he kidnapped the man's girlfriend. They're probably torturing her somewhere on campus. I don't know if you can access that information on their network, but I said I would ask," she rambles.

"My laptop is in the back seat. I already hacked his network. We can look when we get to your place."

"Holy shit. I'll text him. Thank you, Greggory." Her shoulders sag with relief.

82 | JOHN

John's unit has been training all morning. They still don't have a concrete plan, but they know there are three targets, one potentially hostile. So they're training in teams of four.

Team Alpha includes Matt, Innie, Duce, Tank and Diesel.

Team Bravo includes John, Gas, Ghost and Hoover.

Team Charlie is Cap, DD, Teddy and Terry.

Shea plans on joining Team Bravo, Gregg's search team. Christian will go with Diesel as one of his handlers.

John takes a break to drink some water and watch Duce run drills with Diesel, weaving in and out of his legs. Christian cheers him on nearby. John laughs through his nose and picks up his phone. He has one text.

Text from Dr. P at 1330

» I need to talk to you. ASAP. Call me when you get this.

He immediately whistles and waves a hand toward himself for Matt, who runs over panting.

"What, shitbag—I'm busy."

"Now, that's just lazy—shitbag? Dr. P texted me to call her. Figured you might wanna be present."

"Oh, shit. Yeah. Put it on speaker."

"Hold your horses. I need to greet my lady first."

"Do your nonsense after we get the intel," Matt urges, then whistles for the rest of the unit to come listen.

Once they're all assembled, John taps her name.

She answers on the first ring. "John?!"

"Yeah, boo. I'm here with the whole unit."

The men hoot and holler their hellos. Tank mocks John in a singsong voice, "Heyyyyy bbbOOOOoooo."

John shoots him a look that could kill.

"Hey, everybody!" her lovely voice comes through the speaker.

"What was so urgent?" John asks.

"You might want to sit down," she starts, voice excited. "They started Gregg on the virus today. He told me that a virus code is like a painting. Coders leave signatures on their work. He said there's a story in this code and he can't explain it but he thinks he wrote it!"

"He did," John replies.

"I know that! But now so does he!"

"Oh, shit."

"I asked him, without telling him much, to look for Clara. He said he already hacked their system and had it downloaded to his laptop! As soon as we get to my apartment, he's gonna look!"

"No shit?" Matt asks.

"Yeah. So as soon as there is an update I'll text you. We're at Michaels now, but we're going straight to my place after."

"Michaels?" John asks.

"Yeah. I'm trying a new hobby. I want to crochet Shea a baby blanket."

"You okay? Just throwing her name out like that?"

"I'm in the bathroom, silly."

He holds a hand over the mic. "Go train," he says to the unit. They walk away whistling and making kissy noises.

He uncovers his phone. "Thank you for doing this. It was a risk for you and I'm sorry for asking you to do it."

"No problem. Your Gregg is still in there, he's just… finding himself again."

"I'm glad you're there to help guide him. You're an angel."

She chuckles. "Funny, that's not the first time I've heard that. Give Shea, Matt, Christian, and Diesel my love. Talk soon, okay?"

"Be safe, boo."

He ends the call and puts his phone back on the chair. When he looks up, Shea stands nearby, tears streaming down her face. Her lip quivers.

"He… he knows it was his code?" she forces out.

"Well, I don't know yet if it's a girl or a boy," Dr. P says, walking up and down the yarn aisle with Greggory.

"Then pick a neutral color, like green. Everybody loves green," Greggory says confidently.

"Everybody does not love green. What are you talking about?"

"Well, I get a lot of compliments on my eyes. They're green."

"They're a color I've never seen before. But I guess you have a point," she says, thinking he actually has a really good point—considering who the blanket is for. "Here, take off your glasses."

When he does, she holds a few different shades of green next to his face. None are just right, but maybe if she mixes a few, she could get close. She chooses three colors and tosses them into their basket.

"See. Everybody loves green!"

"Yeah, yeah. What about you? What color are you picking?"

"Hmm. Well, you took my favorite. So maybe yellow? That's a neutral one too, right?"

"Yeah. What kind of yellow?"

He grabs a marshmallow Peep shade of yellow and tosses several skeins into the basket. "Look. It says pattern included. What's next?" he asks.

"We need crochet hooks, right? And something called a stitch marker."

"Like a sharpie?"

"I don't know. Let's ask for help," she says.

The employee at Michaels laughs when they ask if they can use a sharpie as a stitch marker, then points them in the right direction. A stitch marker is a little plastic safety pin looking clip, so no to the sharpie.

Dr. P pays this time, $82.25. It is her craft after all. They climb back into the Caddi and head to her apartment. She's hopeful they'll actually be able to make blankets, and that Shea understands why she picked the colors she did.

Back at her apartment, they get distracted by their new craft and completely forget about Greggory's laptop. The first few attempts go horribly for both of them. Knots, tangles, and mess is all they have to show for an hour of work. They don't give up. Even pausing the second season of their show to watch YouTube tutorials. By the end of the night, they both have a few rows started. It actually looks like the beginning of blankets.

At around midnight, Greggory decides he should head home. Instead of taking her to her car, he promises to pick her up in the morning before work. He leaves his work in progress at her place to avoid questions.

84 | Todd

Todd sits alone in his home office. He sent Tina to visit her sister so he could handle some 'home renovations.'

Now he sits in front of a wall of monitors showing more than fifty views of the interior of his house, including Greggory's suite. He sneers.

This will be better. Now Greggory won't know he's checking up on him. Todd needs a little more control over the situation, especially now that Greggory is digging into his own code. His technicians never found anything, but they only went a couple levels deep before admitting they were in over their heads.

He sips his drink and yawns. Today has been a busy day. All the cameras were placed inconspicuously, and covertly. Greggory and Tina should never notice. He can watch till he drops. He chuckles to himself.

When Greggory walks in at 12:20 a.m. Todd scoots to the edge of his seat. Greggory's tailored long-sleeved button down is untucked from his slacks. His hair looks disheveled and his face tired. He appears contemplative, not happy or sad. Todd doesn't know what to make of this. He watches closely.

Greggory goes straight to the shower. A few minutes later he emerges from the bathroom in just his boxers. He rubs his chest with his right hand, then face plants onto the bed.

Todd is confused at first, then a huge smile spreads across his face. He's figured it out. Greggory is rubbing his chest, over his heart, because he's in love!

He sits back in the chair and laughs maniacally.

85 | Clara

The voice sounds different today—a little deranged.

"Well, Clara," his deep timbre breaks through the silence. "You did it. Broke your binds, found your phone, and texted all your traitorous friends. Begging them to come to your rescue. This deserves punishment don't you think?"

"How?" Her voice raspy from disuse. "I mean, you're off your rocker. But how exactly would I accomplish that? I'm watched twenty-four seven and my freaking eyes are sewn shut. Not to mention all these tubes coming out of me, that I have no idea where they're connected!" she exclaims.

Her head feels foggy enough that she wonders if maybe she did do what he said.

"But you did," he insists. "How resourceful of you. Unfortunately, that's not a quality we reward in our prisoners."

"I haven't moved in… however long I've been here. And you know it," she says, knowing it's just whatever drug they keep pumping into her that's making her think she could do such a thing.

"Unfortunately, I have a text message that tells a different story."

She stays silent. What could she say?

"Your punishment is this. The knowledge that none of your 'so called' friends responded. No calls. No activity on campus. No one is coming for you."

She lets out a slow breath. "Probably not."

"So what do you think will become of you?" he taunts.

"Unknown. But I do know there are people out there who love me," she says, feeling a tightening in her chest. "And those same people hate Todd with a fiery passion. So I'd say—never say never."

He backhands her—hard. "Then why aren't they answering your text?"

"Because they aren't FUCKING STUPID!" The volume of her voice rising with each word.

He backhands her again and her groggy brain blissfully slips into unconsciousness.

86 | Shea

Shea sits dog tired on one of Cap's many couches. She tried to help with dinner, but Mrs. Cap would have none of it. So now she watches Christian animatedly recount the events of Diesel's training that day. He's so proud of the pup.

"Look. Diesel, zits!" Christian orders. The dog sits. Christian hands him a small treat.

"Diesel, heir." The dog comes to his side and sits.

"Diesel, platz." The dog lies down.

"Bravo, Diesel!" Duce says, petting the dog's head. "We all had a long day of training SBD. Diesel needs some time to relax too. You'll wear him out and he won't want to listen when he needs to."

"Oh, okay!" Christian says, sitting on the ground with Diesel.

Shea watches what happens next in what feels like slow motion. Without thinking, Duce reaches out to muss Christian's hair. A normal show of affection that turns into a full-blown incident.

As soon as Duce makes contact, his legs lock, spine straightens and eyes close.

Christian hollers, "No!" and tries to move away, but Duce's hand is locked down on his head. It only takes John a few seconds to pull him away, but it was long enough.

Christian looks at Shea, tears filling his eyes. She holds out her arms and he runs into them. John backs Duce into a seat. He looks like he's seen a ghost.

She holds and rocks Christian as he cries, and says over and over, "Me and

Diesel aren't going. No. No. No."

When Duce regains his bearings, he looks at John, who sits beside Shea, his hand rubbing up and down Christian's back.

"What. The. Fuck. Was. That?" Duce asks.

"You weren't supposed to touch him, man," John replies.

"Any one of us could have brushed against him at any point and could still. You need to tell us what we're dealing with," Duce says, looking at Christian like he's a live grenade.

"You're dealing with a child, Duce!" John snaps.

"John, whatever just happened is not natural. What the fuck was that?"

Shea speaks up. "Christian is special. We didn't want to say anything because others have tried to exploit his gift in the past. He is a gift, Duce."

"I'm not trying to say anything bad. I love the little dude, and I've only known him a couple days. But we need to know. I'm not gonna exploit him, if that's what you're worried about."

John looks over at Christian and silently asks with his eyebrows if they should tell the unit.

Christian wipes his face and turns in Shea's lap to face the room full of soldiers.

He's so brave

"I love you too, Duce," Christian says simply.

"Aw, what the fuck," John mutters.

The entire unit looks at John, confused. Shea giggles.

"I swear I'm chopped liver," he says.

Christian looks at him, and says, "John, I don't need to tell you. You know."

"Alright, enough of that. What's the call?" John asks him.

"Tell them… Or show them," he replies.

"Okay. What do you want us to do?"

He looks out at the men, who look back at him confused and fearful.

"Everyone hold hands," Christian instructs. Shea can see the hopeful look he gives the unit.

They glance at each other and then to Christian, seeming unsure.

Duce speaks up. "Do it, you assholes! I need to understand what just happened!"

They all look skeptically at Duce, who gives them all an encouraging look. They begin to hold hands one by one. Shea on one side of Christian, John on the other. Matt grabs John's hand and Duce grabs Shea's. They form a large circle and wait for Christian's instructions.

"I never done this. Let's see," he says closing his eyes.

One at a time, through their joined hands they're pulled into the same vision. The same vision he showed Gregg all those months ago.

Christian at the orphanage, alone. His visit from Todd. His mother's small shed of a house, Christian reaching out for her as she cringes away. Todd 'rescuing' him, only to put him in a cage. Alone again. Then his life with Gregg, Shea, and John. Smiling. Laughing.

Before he lets them go, he speaks to them through the bond.

"If you touch me when I'm not ready for it, my 'power,'" he says, using air quotes, "automatically engages and I see your whole life in seconds. Everything you never wanted anyone to know. Your shame. Your happiness. Your love. If I know it might happen, like during training or around a bunch of people, I keep a shield up. I just exhausted that ability today. You're right, Duce. We all deserve to relax."

"I'm so sorry, SBD. I had no idea," Duce says.

"I know. I forgive you, but maybe talk to a priest."

The unit chuckles, but Duce just nods at Christian.

"While we're here, meet Rhaego!" Christian says, excitedly.

They're all flooded with a glimpse of Shea's little bundle of joy.

When the vision fades, Shea corrects Christian. "Its name is not Rhaego!"

87 | GREGGORY

Greggory has been working on the virus riddled system for a couple of days now. Each knot he unravels leads to ten more. It's not that he can't do it. He's found his rhythm. It's just time consuming.

He stretches and turns his chair toward Dr. P, who is hunched over her desk, intensely focused. He nudges her chair with his foot. Her arms fly up as she tries to steady herself. He chuckles.

"What the hell, Greggory?" she asks, then laughs. "I thought I was gonna fall!"

"I wouldn't let that happen." He grins. "Are we hanging tonight?"

"Of course. We have to work on our blankets and that other craft we talked about. Plus, we have a few episodes left of *Severance*."

"Sounds like my kind of night."

"Is that sarcasm?" she asks.

"Hell no! I'm really excited." He chuckles.

"Okay, then come help me for a second. I'm stuck on how to get these tendrils microscopic."

"Yeah, we could use a mold. Or pour it in a sheet and cut it," he says, thinking it through.

"If we make it a bit larger, we could use a 34g needle and press it out," she says.

"Duh. What am I thinking? I'm sure this company has a 3D printer with microscopic printing capabilities. If not, we could order one. That would solve all our problems."

"That's smart. Let's do that… tomorrow, because it's five," Dr. P says.

Greggory checks his watch. "Um, it's 4:57. You have three minutes left." His face amused.

"Yeah, but it'll take longer than that to get to the guard box, so let's go!"

When they arrive at Dr. P's apartment, they decide to tackle the laptop first. Dr. P can't really help, so she works on her blanket and glances over every couple of minutes.

He doesn't think it'll be hard, he's good with computers and can sneak around without leaving a trace. He finds Clara pretty quickly because she's under the watch of medical.

"Hey, I got her!" he says.

Dr. P sits up straighter, watching the screen from beside him. "Really? It's only been like fifteen minutes."

"Yeah, well, I'm that good. Look here's her name in the medical log. I just have to figure out where they're keeping her, so I can find the right camera feed."

"Look in 25. That's where they've kept other prisoners."

"Okay… um…" he mutters, biting his bottom lip as he searches.

"There!" Dr. P says, pointing at one of the security feeds on his screen. It shows a bank of three glass enclosures. Only one is occupied. A woman lies motionless in a bed, her head turned away from the camera. A man in scrubs sits in a chair beside her.

"Oh God. Is she…" Dr. P whispers.

"No. Look at the monitor, there," he points to the screen, "behind her bed. It shows her heartbeat."

"Can you get the guy out of there so we can make sure it's her? Maybe give her a message?"

"I'll try," he says.

He works fast. A few seconds later he triggers an automated alert. An alarm blares in the cell and a red light flashes. The alert comes from a speaker overhead, "Attention. There has been a breach. All security personnel to the guard box."

They watch the man jump up and rush out of the cell.

"Hurry. I'm going to record it on my phone," Dr. P says on the edge of her seat. She opens her camera app and presses record.

Greggory taps into the intercom system, and says, "Clara?"

They watch for movement—nothing.

He says it again, firmer this time. "Clara?"

Her head snaps up.

He quickly says, "Clara, you're not alone. Don't give up."

She turns fully toward the camera and places a hand over her heart.

Dr. P gasps. "Oh, God."

They see her clearly. Her eyes and mouth are sewn shut.

Dr. P immediately sends the video, before she can even process what they just saw.

John runs drills with his team, focusing on searching for and rescuing a potentially hostile target. Gregg's been great with Dr. P, so hopefully they'll be able to convince him to come with them. But if not—they're training with tranquilizer rounds and smoke.

They tried using Tank as the hostile, but the man is exactly that, a tank. They spent forty-five minutes trying to subdue him before John had the idea of using tranq rounds.

As they finish a drill, John hears his phone ding. "Hey, let's take a minute."

He jogs over and checks it. It's a video file from Dr. P with an attached text message.

Text from Dr. P at 1415

» Show no one until you watch first

<Video File attached>

He presses play. His hand flies to his mouth. "Holy fuck!"

By the end of the video, when he sees Clara with her eyes and mouth sewn shut, he loses it. And the 'it' is his lunch, all over his boots.

He hears Matt approaching. "Fuck," John mutters.

"What is it, John?" Matt calls, getting closer.

Shea, who somehow sees fucking everything, calls out, "Are you okay?"

"I'm fine. Geez I got three mothers now?" he deflects.

"Don't bullshit me. What happened?" Matt presses, nodding toward the phone in John's hand.

"Nothing you wanna see. Lovey-dovey shit from P."

"Gimmie the phone," Matt orders.

"Fuck off, Fuggo!"

Shea, who snuck up silent as fuck, says from behind him, "Gimmie the phone. Now."

"Fuck," he says, under his breath, then hands her the phone.

Matt stands beside her. John knows the second they hit play. Both of them go pale. Tears well in their eyes. Then they see it.

Matt drops to his knees and hangs his head. "Fuck," he whispers, voice breaking.

Shea stares at the screen, tears streaming down her face. "Oh God."

"Guys, we're working on it. We have a plan. Keep your cool," John coaches.

Matt stands. His face a mask of hatred. John instinctively steps back.

"Fuck your plan! We need to go now! What if that was P? You'd wait? You a fucking coward now?" Matt screams in his face.

"We'll take it to a vote," John says, calmly.

He whistles and makes a 'round-up' motion with his arm. Matt spits in his direction, then walks over to one of the plastic chairs and sits, head in his hands.

The unit gathers around. Shea passes John his phone. She gently steers Christian away and they sit with Matt.

John clears his throat. "The question is, do we move up the timeline? Majority rules."

He presses play.

When Dr. P sees what they've done to Clara, she loses the ability to breathe properly. She knows they're evil. She saw what they did to Shea and Gregg. She shouldn't be surprised, but she is, and now she's hyperventilating.

"Okay, try to take a deep breath. Focus on your senses. Quick, tell me five things you can see," Greggory coaches.

She rolls her eyes, but then does it anyway. "Your laptop, the couch, my laptop, my blanket, and my crochet hook," she says jerkily.

"Great. Now four things you can touch," Gregg encourages.

"You, my blanket, the couch, and your laptop."

"Okay, what can you smell, three things," he continues to guide her.

She closes her eyes and takes a slow deep breath through her nose. "My perfume. You—woodsy, clean, manly. And dinner."

"I smell manly?" Gregg asks with a smile in his voice.

"Shut up. What's next? I think it's helping."

"Two things you can hear."

She closes her eyes and pays attention to her ears. "The clock ticking. And soft music, maybe from next door?"

"Last one. What do you taste?"

"My tongue?" She smiles faintly. "Hmmm, garlic."

"How do you feel?" he asks.

"Better! Where did you learn that?"

"I used to have panic attacks and anxiety. It really helped me."

"Well, thank you. I feel much better."

"I don't want to add to your anxiety, but can I ask you something?" he says, his old sheepish nature leaking through.

"Anything."

"Let me start by telling you something. I have a small device installed in my watch, you'd never know. It can pick up bug and camera frequencies. When I got home last night, it went nuts."

"Oh shit. Like in your room?" she asks, turning her body more toward him.

"Well, the whole house. But yeah, my room too."

"Shit."

"And after seeing this," he says, nodding at his laptop, "I just… I can't stay there. I have some money. I can get my own place, but I thought maybe I could stay with you. After all that I also don't like the idea of you being alone."

"Of course! This place may be tiny, but it was supposed to be temporary. Maybe we can find something bigger together?" she asks.

His shoulders sag with relief. "Yes! Ugh, I'm so relieved. Wanna look up some options?"

"Sure!"

90 | Shea

Shea suffers from all day sickness. It's a blast.

Since they've been at Cap's, she's only managed to keep down pickles and ice cream—never together! Even then it's fifty-fifty. She's starting to worry that the baby isn't getting what it needs. Those giant vitamins barely make it to the back of her throat, before they come right back up.

And the emotions—she can hardly contain them. She misses Gregg so much. He should be here to hold her hair while she pukes.

Tensions are high among the men in the unit, since the Clara vote. Matt hasn't talked to anyone. They all wanted to go immediately, but they just aren't ready. They offered a date sooner, moving up the timeline, but that's all they would do.

Matt tried to leave, but the guys formed a barricade. He's been on the buddy system ever since.

Shea sits in one of the hard plastic chairs they have in the training area and presses an ice pack to her neck. It's not helping, but at least she feels like she's doing something about the nausea.

Mrs. Cap walks toward her carrying a tray. "Come on, Preggers. Walk with me," she says.

Shea pops up and walks with the woman. She peeks over Mrs. Cap's shoulder and sees the tray contains tea, little sandwiches and cakes.

They look delicious

Mrs. Cap sets the tray on a nearby table and gestures for Shea to sit.

"I've got some ginger tea here. It should soothe your stomach. Sip it slowly, then we can try some of the treats, okay?"

"They look delicious. I'm willing to try."

She takes a careful sip. She can feel the woman's eyes on her. She meets her gaze and sees nothing but warmth.

"Do you mind if I speak freely?" Mrs. Cap asks.

"No. Of course. I welcome it," Shea says.

Her eyes lock onto Shea's. "You are a fierce woman, Shea. I've watched the way you've handled these numbskulls and how you love them, as well. How you protect and love little SBD. How you protect your unborn baby while training. But you don't treat yourself with that same love. I think maybe it's that no one has ever told you, so I'm taking it upon myself. You can chalk it up to the ramblings of the elderly or take it for what it truly is. Love." She reaches for Shea's hand and holds it tight.

"You are loved. You've got a band of misfits behind you who adore you. You have all of them wrapped around your finger, and they usually only listen to Cap—and rarely outside of an op. You've gone through something that broke you, and Gregg getting taken is just the cherry on top." She hands Shea a napkin.

There's so much snot

"So in case you never heard it growing up, or just never believed it, you are extraordinary. You are special. You are loved. And you are fierce!"

She is no longer containing the emotions. The kindness of this woman overwhelms her. She can only sit there. Staring. Crying.

Mrs. Cap offers her a kind smile, and says, "Now sip your tea before it gets cold."

"Yes, ma'am."

Dr. P and Greggory sit in silence, staring at his open laptop. After seeing Clara, they started looking for an apartment. Fifteen minutes into scrolling, he just stopped. She didn't know what to say, so here they sit.

"Maybe I should text my guy and see what we should do?" she suggests.

"Do I know him?" he asks, still staring straight ahead.

"Who?"

"Your guy. He seems to know a lot about Crown. Do I know him?"

"Greggory, I…" She shifts to face him. She doesn't know how to handle this.

"I know something happened. Or are you telling me what I've read in the code is bullshit?"

"I don't know what the code says, so I have no idea."

"I've been copy and pasting it all into a Word document. Will you read it?" he asks, his voice tight with pain.

"Of course," she agrees.

He opens the document and slides the laptop onto her lap.

"I'm gonna freshen up while you read," he says, heading toward the bathroom.

"Okay," she says, starting to read.

A few lines in, she mutters, "Shit," under her breath. She takes a picture of the screen and sends it to John.

Text to John at 2104

<Photo file>

« Please tell me what to do!

She keeps reading.

If you're reading this, something has happened and I know how Crown is, so I want to give you the basics. My name is Greggory Marsh, Gregg for short. I used to think work would be the most important thing in my life, then something changed. I met her. She has changed my life for the better and is the best thing that has ever happened to me. Shea Marsh, my wife. We adopted a child named Christian, who is wanted by Crown. We all are.

If you are reading this, it means I gave myself up, to ensure the safety of Shea, Christian and my best friend, John. Trust me when I tell you they are worth it. I'd suffer every day for the rest of my life if it meant they'd be safe. You need to know, I told them not to come for you, but they probably will. Protect them. Look into things. Todd is a really bad person. He has tortured your wife and child! You can't…

The document ends. She looks up and sees him standing behind the couch, watching her.

"Greggory," she says carefully, "I can't be the one to talk to you about this, but I contacted someone who should."

"I feel like I'm going crazy. Like. What's even real anymore?"

"You're here. Regardless of the circumstances, you're the same guy," she says.

"You knew me?"

"I…" Her phone rings and she sends up a silent prayer of gratitude.

It's John.

"Hello," she answers.

"You with him now?" John asks.

"Yes."

"Put me on speaker," he orders.

"Okay." She presses the speaker phone icon. "You're on."

"Alright. Gregg?" John says.

"Greggory. Yeah. I'm here," he corrects.

"Alright, well, I knew you as Gregg, or Greggy, or Greggy-poo, depending on the day. We met at Crown and became a family because of Shea," John reports.

"Stop. I just can't believe I married someone who treated me the way she did!" Gregg argues.

"She only ever loved you, man. You were her world and though it took her a little while to figure it out, you were always best friends."

"That's not what I remember."

"I know… But I'm telling you the truth. If you don't trust me, trust yourself!"

"How do I know that stuff in the code wasn't planted to… to confuse me?"

"I'll give you time. I'm here, man. We love you. And when you're up for it, I'm sure Shea would chew off her own arm just to talk to you."

"I'll have to think about it," Greggory says honestly.

"No problem. I do have to ask, did you shave your beard?"

"I've always been clean shaven," Greggory says, confused.

"Damn. Well, if you want to jog your memory, maybe grow it out and get some contacts," John suggests.

"Whatever you say," he says. A small smile lights up his face.

"Alright, P. Everything okay?"

"Yeah. We're gonna get a place together. We're good," she says.

"Okay, boo. Talk soon, okay?"

"Night." She ends the call and looks at Greggory. "You okay?" she asks.

"I feel like my head is gonna explode. Like there's a dam that's not letting anything through. I heard him, and I read the same thing you did. But it hits the wall and just bounces off," he says frustrated.

"That's okay. We'll figure it out." She smiles at him.

"I have a favor to ask," he says, sheepish.

"Sure."

"Will you come to Todd's with me to get my stuff?"

"Don't you think that'll cause more of a problem?"

"I think he'll keep it together if you're there. Play the lovey-dovey couple, till I can get all my stuff?"

"Okay, sweetie," she says, batting her eyelashes.

92 Shea

Shea watches John walk away to make a phone call. His face is strained, and he keeps looking around. At one point he makes eye contact with her, then looks away. He looks almost afraid.

"That's it," she mutters, marching toward him.

She hears, "Talk soon, okay?" Then he hangs up.

"Who was that, John?"

"P," he says quickly. "She and Gregg are getting a place together. The Clara stuff really freaked them out."

"You're lying to me about something," she presses.

"Shea, chill. You're like a hound dog. It was P! I came over here to talk to her privately, that's all."

"You're hiding something from me."

"Oh. I did ask. P says Gregg shaved."

"You asshole!" She turns and walks away. Her eyes burning with unshed tears.

I'm so sick of crying!

She storms into the house and heads straight for the computer that Cap said she can use. They have phones now, but those aren't used for the internet, except for the encrypted app they use.

She logs into her YouTube Music account and creates a new playlist called *Rescuing My Man*. She rips the music and transfers it to the cheap MP3 player that

Duce ordered for her online, because her iPod no longer holds a charge.

She walks back out to the training area and plugs the MP3 player into the receiver with an auxiliary cord. Several large speakers crackle to life.

She selects a song and blasts it. *We Ready* by Archie Eversole plays at full volume.

The men stop what they're doing and look over at her as she dances alone beneath the speakers. A few of them chuckle, then go right back to running their drills, using the beat to time their movements.

Shea drops into a chair and watches the finely tuned machine work.

The next song plays, *Lux Æterna* by Metallica. She sighs, takes a deeper breath and lets silent tears slide down her face.

Playlists… that's what's been missing

93 | Todd

Todd works in the kitchen beside Tina, making dinner. He sips from a glass of amber liquor. It's not his first tonight.

Tina asks him something, but he barely hears her. He's focused on his investment. This time around Greggory was supposed to be his friend. Instead he's spending all his time with his Latin lover.

Her voice is louder this time, and it makes its way through his focus.

"Todd? Hello?"

He whips his head toward her, pissed off that he has to pay attention to her. When she sees his face, she folds in on herself. She might as well be shaking like a Chihuahua.

"Yes? Dear?" he asks, each word dripping with malice.

"I was just wondering if you could pass the salt?" she asks, sheepishly.

He passes it to her without a word and turns back to his thoughts.

As they sit down to eat, the front door opens. Greggory and Dr. P walk in, hand in hand. Todd seethes. He is filled and fueled by hate, but he masks it.

"Hey, you two! How's it going?" he asks.

"Great! Actually, we decided to move in together. So I came to grab my stuff," Greggory says, hand still linked with Dr. P.

"Oh, wow! I'm so happy for you two!" Tina says excitedly.

Todd whips his head in her direction. She shrinks in her seat.

"That's moving kind of fast. I thought you we're taking things slow?" he asks, voice even, devoid of emotion.

"We are. We're getting two bedrooms. We just spend all our time together anyway. So it makes sense."

Todd's jaw tightens. "Well don't let me hold you up," he says with a forced smile.

He watches them climb the stairs, then hurries to his office to pull up the camera feed.

On screen, Greggory and Dr. P move like a single being, a well-choreographed dance. They don't speak. They just move with purpose to accomplish the task.

Todd tilts his head to the side, watching them, intrigued.

94 | GREGGORY

When all of Greggory's belongings are loaded into both of their cars, they make one last trip inside. Todd and Tina wait in the entryway.

"I just wanted to thank you both for all that you've done for me, and for letting me stay in your beautiful home. I appreciate both of you so much," Greggory says.

Tina glances at Todd, when he nods, she speaks, "If you need anything, just call. I have a bunch of old furniture in a storage unit you can have. I'm sure some of it would suit your tastes."

"Wow, that's really generous. Thank you," Dr. P says.

"No problem." Tina smiles at both of them.

Todd clears his throat and offers his hand to Greggory. "Well, whenever you want to come work out, just let me know."

"Yeah. Thanks man."

Greggory and Dr. P turn to leave.

From behind them, Todd calls, "See you at work tomorrow!"

They don't turn around. They just keep walking.

Back at Dr. P's apartment, they settle in and continue working on their blankets. The tension they felt earlier begins melting away.

"Can new babies even see color?" Greggory asks after a while.

"New?" Dr. P laughs. "Newborns, you mean?"

"Same difference." He shrugs.

"No, they don't. But I was thinking about my sister when I chose these colors. I'd like to finish them and send them as soon as possible. She might be moving, and I want to mail them to her current address."

"Well, we're making good progress. If we work on finishing them before we move, that's okay."

"Nah. I don't want you stuck without your own space for that long. I'd like to see if Tina will take us to her storage unit at lunch tomorrow. See what she has."

"Yeah. Okay."

95 | Tina

Tina sits in the dark on the hard tile floor of a bathroom. The door is locked, but she still cowers, afraid.

She didn't mean to make him that upset. It was a stupid joke. She doesn't really even remember it clearly now. Something about Gregg always choosing a girl over him.

She watched the shift happen in his eyes. Then his whole demeanor changed, all within the fraction of a second. Then came the pain.

He backhanded her with his ring still on. The pain was excruciating, and she felt warmth spill down her face.

She began begging. She hates herself for it, but she begged him to stop, from the spot on the floor where she had landed.

He didn't.

He grabbed her by her ponytail and yanked her upright. Her scalp screaming. She continued begging, but his knee found her gut. She couldn't even fall to the floor to avoid the next one because he held her there, by her hair. Like her own fucked up puppeteer.

The ability to beg or even breathe left her. His last knee knocking the wind out of her. Panic surged within her. Air would not fill her lungs.

He decided at this moment to lift her up higher, making her struggle to keep her toes on the ground, unable to get purchase.

The pain and lack of oxygen made the edges of her vision go black. She thought she was going to pass out, but it's like he could sense that and dropped her.

Then he hauled her back up by her shirt and introduced the side of her head to the edge of the table. Just before the world went black, he spit in her face.

When she came to, she was in the same spot on the floor. Todd was nowhere to be seen.

She ran.

She went to a bedroom she knew wasn't monitored and locked herself in its bathroom.

She can't tell what's blood or tears anymore. Exhausted, she lowers her head to the cool of the tile. She falls asleep.

Matt trains, eats, showers, then goes to bed. He keeps his mouth shut and his head down.

He's pissed.

If it were Gregg or Dr. P in Clara's position, they'd already be moving. No doubt in his mind. It isn't fair. But he can't leave. He knows he can't do this alone.

"Hey Fuggo!" his obnoxious brother calls from behind him.

"I'm not in the mood," Matt spits out like venom, without turning.

John shoves him from behind, gripping his right shoulder.

"Listen, fuck face," Matt snaps, spinning around ready to swing.

He stops short. The entire unit stands behind John. He lowers his fists.

"Matt," John says, stepping closer, voice steady. "You need to forgive us. Training has gone to shit because you won't communicate. That ends now. Be mad, but aim it at Todd, not us," John's voice pleading.

"What if it was Dr. P?" Matt asks.

"Then I would trust my unit and my girl. I had to sit on my hands for months while Shea was being tortured. We do what we have to for the outcome we need."

"You're a coward!" Matt hisses.

John doesn't flinch. "No. I just don't let emotions cloud my judgement!"

"Fuck you!" Matt screams, pouring everything into it twisting the love he has for John into hate.

John flinches and steps back, hurt written all over his face.

Matt smiles cruelly. "Good. Now are we done?"

"No, we're not fucking done. Fall in line with your unit, soldier," Cap says, walking forward from the back of the unit.

"Sir, this doesn't concern you," Matt says.

"Wrong. Fall in line. Now!" Cap's voice taking on the air of someone who expects to be listened to. It is a command.

Matt stands his ground.

"Are you not part of this unit, soldier?"

"I don't need this," Matt says, turning to walk away.

"Soldier, if you walk away from your commanding officer and your unit, you can keep walking."

"Good," he throws over his shoulder.

Caps tone softens. "Son, if you leave now, it takes us even longer to be ready to rescue her."

He stops. He turns back, tears burning in his eyes.

Cap steps over and pulls him into a hug. "Son, forgive the men. They're trying to do what's right. We'll get her," he speaks softly into Matts ear.

When Matt pulls away, he pats Cap on the back. "Alright, it's over."

"You sure?" John says, hesitantly.

"Yeah, fuck face. I'll be patient."

97 Dr. P

"Can you come see how this is sitting in the gel brain?" Dr. P asks Greggory.

"Sure," he says, stepping to her desk. "Yeah, this is great. See how deep it's seating itself? It's perfect."

"Thanks!" She smiles, relieved she did it right.

"Hey, you want to text Tina? It's almost lunch. Maybe we can meet her at the storage unit?" he says.

"Yeah, sure."

Text to Tina at 1153

« Hey, can we have a peek in your storage unit over lunch? Are you available?

Text from Tina at 1154

» Sure. I'll send the address. It's unit 2507

<Map attached>

"It's about ten minutes from here. You want to go now?" she asks.

"Sure."

Dr. P drives while Greggory rattles off random knowledge from the passenger seat. She smiles. He really is great company.

Pulling into the parking lot she spots Tinas Mercedes Maybach parked near the front.

"Good. She's already here," Dr. P says.

"Great. Let's do this."

They follow the signs and finally find the row with unit 2507. About a hundred feet ahead they spot a petite blond woman.

"Hey, Tina!" Greggory calls, but Tina keeps her back to them.

"Maybe she's on the phone?" Dr. P guesses.

When they reach unit 2507, Tina walks inside. Dr. P and Greggory follow. It's huge.

"It's like a furniture store in here," Dr. P says.

"Yeah. Many years of changing my mind and redecorating. Look around. Whatever you want is yours," Tina says, her back to them.

"Hey, Tina?" Dr. P calls.

"Yeah?" she says, glancing over her shoulder.

Dr. P notices the oversized sunglasses and the way Tina's hair is styled more in her face than usual.

"Are you okay?" she asks, genuinely concerned.

"Yeah. Just a bit of a headache."

"Dr. P, come look!" Greggory calls from among the maze of furniture.

"Coming!" She takes off for his location. She glances back at Tina. She's sitting on a couch, staring at her phone. Even from here, her face looks swollen, black, and blue.

"Look at this beauty!" he says, when she reaches him.

In front of him sits a beautiful, raw edged table. It's large, almost square. The middle of the table is a beautifully carved map with resin over top.

"What is it?" she asks.

"I think it's *Game of Thrones*. I love that show!" he says, excited.

"Well, it's beautiful either way. I'm in!"

"Really?" he asks, childlike.

"Really. Now find us a big comfy couch so we can get back to gel brains and viruses."

"What about the one it's arranged with? It's one of those modular boneless couches you can move into different configurations…" his voice trails off.

"Sure, we'll get a U Haul this weekend. Let's tell Tina."

"Hey, Tina!" she calls.

Tina hurries over. Up close, Dr. P gets a clearer view of Tina's face.

"Hey, Greggory, can you go see if there is any kitchen stuff?" Dr. P asks.

"Sure."

When he walks away, Dr. P turns to Tina. "Sit," she orders

"I'm fine, really. When do you want to pick this stuff up?"

"Sit."

"Seriously? I need to get back. I don't have time."

"Sit." Dr. P crosses her arms, unwilling to move.

"Fine!" Tina drops onto the couch, crossing her legs, fidgeting her dangling foot.

Dr. P steps closer. Tina shrinks back.

"I just want to look," Dr. P says, reaching out to remove Tina's sunglasses. She slides them off and gasps.

"Looks worse than it is. I'm okay, really."

"Your cheek looks like it needs stitches," Dr. P assesses.

"I can't. No medical record. I can't" Tina pleads.

"Well, I happen to have a bag of supplies in my car. Can I?"

"It has to be as minimal as possible. I can't afford another... outburst," Tina says, eyes downcast.

"You can trust me. I promise."

"Then can you do me one more favor?"

"Of course."

Tears fill her eyes and she sits back on the couch. "You can trust me too. I know who you are and who you know. My intentions were not honorable before. But they are now. Could you get her a message?"

Dr. P is taken aback and studies the woman in front of her for a minute, before saying, "Depends on what it is."

"Tell her I'm so sorry," she says, tears overflowing onto her cheeks. "She didn't deserve what was done to her, and I regret my involvement. Can you just tell her that... and if she's coming for him, I'll do what I can to help?"

Dr. P nods slowly. "Uh, yeah. I'll tell her. Let me go get my bag. I'll be right back."

While the rest of the unit confronts Matt, Christian and Duce train with Diesel. Today, they're working on silent commands, using only hand signals.

Christian watches as Duce raises his rifle toward cardboard cutouts. He shoots the ones dressed like bad guys and has the barrel pointed down when they're the image of Gregg, Dr. P, or Clara. They don't really want to shoot anyone, so the second time they run through it, he points the gun at the bad guy and Diesel growls. If the cutout moves forward, Diesel moves forward too—on high alert.

They moved on to Innie dressed in a big, padded suit, with one arm bigger than the other. They're training Diesel to attack the larger arm. The first few times, Diesel just jumps on Innie, knocking him down and licking his face. Not very ferocious. He's getting it now, though.

Duce cuts up a steak and gives Diesel a chunk each time he takes Innie down and stands over him with his teeth close to Innie's neck.

At around 8 p.m., Shea comes out, and says, "Alright, you guys. Remember, we all deserve time to relax."

Duce nods and calls Diesel to him. "You're a good boy! Good boy, Diesel!"

"Alright, c'mon SBD. Time to relax," Duce calls to him.

Christian grabs his notebook and pen and jogs over to meet them.

"What 'cha been writing?" Duce asks, curious.

"Diesel stats." Then after a pause, "And goodbye. Just in case," he says nonchalant.

"That's not going to happen. None of us will let that happen. Especially Diesel!"

"I know. But Shea says, 'shit happens.' It's okay."

99 Dr. P

Dr. P gently dabs an alcohol swab across Tina's cheek. Tina sucks air in through her teeth but remains still. She quietly watches as Dr. P draws some lidocaine into a syringe.

"Look, thank you for doing this. I'd hate to have a nasty scar."

"No problem. I'll put a few in, minimal, so no one will notice them. You'll be able to snip them and remove them in five days—or I can do it. Just find me. I only have the sutures in black, so you might need a small band-aid or something to cover them. I'm not sure what won't get you in trouble. I'll make the tails as short as possible," Dr. P explains.

Tina lets out a shaky laugh. "I honestly don't know what will set him off anymore. He used to have a clear mission, and it kept him more… docile. Now—there are so many unknowns. It makes him testy. I think if I just slap a butterfly stitch thing over it, it will be fine. He just doesn't want a record of the… episodes."

"Okay, I won't lie, this is going to burn. But I'll do one injection now, then wait like ten minutes before adding more in. It should be easier on you."

"Do it." Tina braces herself.

Dr. P does as promised. Only sticking her once, this time. While they wait for it to take effect, Tina opens up, and she is a wealth of information.

"You know Greggory picked his own furniture, right?" Tina asks suddenly.

"No shit?" Dr. P uses a pickup to gently pinch Tina's wound. "Feel anything?"

"Nope."

"Alright. I'll put some more in, just in case." She injects more lidocaine and begins suturing the wound.

"Thanks again, Doc."

"Sure," she says, focused on her task.

"Todd has been worried there is a little bit of Gregg left in ol' Greggory. Him choosing that furniture makes me think the same."

"But he had that furniture way before he came to Crown, didn't he?"

"Yeah. But Todd didn't want that furniture in our house. Said it was ugly. So he specifically erased pretty much everything except the swords."

"Wow," Dr. P says, cutting the last suture. "All done!"

"Dr. P, you two need to stick together. Todd's been distracted, but just like he went after Shea, he'll come after you. Keep Greggory close."

"Got it."

100 | Shea

"Shea! Get up! Important meeting in the living room!" John says, while shaking her entire body.

"What time is it?" she mumbles.

"0600. Time to get after it!"

She shoots upright and glares at him. "It's time to get my foot up your ass! Get the fuck out!"

"Shea, this is the big meeting. No more willy-nilly training. You have ten minutes, then I get the air horn."

FFFUUUUUUCCCCKKKKK MMMMMEEEEEE

She throws off the covers and stands from the bed. She quickly showers washing off all the night sweat. She throws a hissy fit, then gets dressed.

I've worn a sports bra every fucking day, I'm over this shit!

When she makes her way into the living room, the men hoot, holler, and applaud. She holds her middle finger up at all of them and heads straight to Christian, dropping down beside him.

"Mornin' Shea," Christian says, giving her a side hug.

"Mornin.'" She hugs him back and rests her head on his shoulder, pretending to sleep.

"I know it's early, but we have a lot of ground to cover. Someone get Shea her one coffee of the day with Truvia, or she'll never absorb all of this," Cap says.

Mrs. Cap walks over with a mug and passes it to Shea with a smile.

"Thank you," Shea says and takes a sip. She then realizes the entire room is staring at her. "Shit. Well, proceed."

"Everyone, sit in your teams. Gregg's rescue team, make your way over to Shea," Cap orders.

The men all grumble but get situated in team clusters.

"Now, as far as we know, Clara is currently the only target in true custody. Gregg and Dr. P will be easier targets. Though we know from insider information that Todd hovers in whichever building his pet project resides in. Meaning, he'll most likely be in building 4 when we breach. We also know building 25 has heavy security. John gave us some specs, but he's only seen a small fraction of 25 and none of 4," Cap says, standing as a pillar of strength.

Cap turns to Terry, and says, "Lucky for us, Terry here is an expert in drafting. And we have an expert on all of Todd's compound."

Murmurs fill the room, and the men of the unit look around.

What the hell is he talking about?

Cap holds out an arm and Christian walks to the front of the room.

"Christian here was accidentally touched by many of the staff at Crown and purposefully touched by Todd, as we all saw in the vision. He will give Terry schematics via a vision, room by room, floor by floor, building by building—until we know every inch of his compound. They will start by drafting 25 and 4 so we can commence accurate field training exercises."

Shea sits up straighter.

"For everyone else, stay in contact with the targets when possible. Keep training with Diesel, he needs to get used to commands from everyone in the unit. And take Shea to Lou at Armor Depot, let's start getting her fitted. Make 'em a little loose—we don't know how much more that belly will grow!"

"Yes, sir," several men answer, and then everyone is in motion.

Matt walks over as she finishes her coffee. "Hey, Shea. John and I are gonna take you to get fitted. Christian too."

"We're being fitted, for what?" she asks.

"Kevlar. Full body," John says, walking up and slapping Matt on the back.

"Wait. What?" Shea asks.

"You insist on going on the mission. So does Christian. We can't take a pregnant woman and a kid on a mission, unprotected. We just can't."

"So full body? Kevlar?"

"Yup!" John says, brightly, just like Christian would.

101 | GREGGORY

"These are nice pans. I can't wait to cook in them," Greggory says, pulling them from their boxes in their new apartment.

The U Haul delivered everything the day after they went to Tina's unit, but they waited until the weekend to really move in.

"Food. Gah I'm starving! Should we have some groceries delivered?" Dr. P asks.

"Sure. My wallet is on the counter if you want to use my card."

"What? My money's no good?" she teases.

He grins. "No, I'm just saying I want to get this first run, that's all."

"Okay. Well, pause what you're doing and make a list."

He walks over and sits next to her on the couch. Opening his notes app he begins typing. He pauses for a moment and watches her slowly, methodically and meticulously unpack his swords. She pulls them from their packaging and gently places them one by one on the couch with as much of the sharp edge hanging off that will balance.

"Thank you," he says quietly.

"For what?" she calls over her shoulder, slicing into another box.

"Just treating my stuff with care. I appreciate it."

"Oh, sure. I don't want to cut my own arm off, so."

He chuckles. "Oh, that's why. Got it."

"I'm just messin'. Hurry up with that list. I'm starving!"

"Okay, okay."

After the grocery order is delivered, Greggory whips up a quick quiche with bacon on the side. They eat in the living room while Dr. P passes him swords to mount on the wall.

"Oh. Maybe leave that wall there blank, and I'll get my Lego artwork to hang there," Dr. P says.

"Great idea!"

After a while she asks, "Hey, it's been a while since we talked about the code and stuff. How's that going?"

"Oh, I cracked it yesterday. Sorry, it's been busy. I forgot to tell you."

"Did you tell Todd?"

"Hell no. He approached me after we got back from Tina's storage unit and asked some really weird questions. Most of them about you actually."

"What? Why didn't you say anything?" she asks.

"Because I don't let you out of my sight, and I don't wanna worry you."

"Greggory, what was he asking?"

"If you had a boyfriend. If I knew you before. If I knew who your sister was. Weird stuff," he says, shrugging.

"Shit, this is bad," she mutters.

"You think he knows something?"

"Of course he does! He probably saw that I flew into Anchorage when the tracker went live! Fuck!"

"Tracker? What are we gonna do?"

"I need to call John," she says pulling out her phone.

"Wait." Greggory moves fast. "I have a burner that has never been in the Crown buildings—use it."

"Why? I have encryption."

"I know. But he has crazy tech—you never know."

She nods. "Oh, speaking of tech, you killed the virus?"

"Well, I left it and reinforced it. Whoever wrote it wanted me to believe Todd is a monster and that I had a whole full life that he stole. He'll never get access."

"Okay. Okay," she says, taking the burner from him and dialing John's number.

102 | JOHN

John follows behind his brother. Duce and Diesel at his six. The lights are out. They run through a mockup of building 25, trying to beat their time of five minutes to reach the glass cells. In the silence, he hears his phone ringing in his pants pocket.

"Sorry, guys. I gotta check," he says.

The lights go up and he pulls the phone out. It's an unknown number.

"This is John," he answers.

"Hey, it's me," he hears Dr. P's voice through the phone.

"Oh, what's with the number?"

"A burner of Greggory's. Just in case."

"Smart. What's up?"

He hears her talking to someone else, faintly, "Are you sure? Okay." Then louder, "Get the unit together. Shea and Christian too."

John nods to his brother, who was already eavesdropping. Matt runs off to gather everyone. Shea stalks toward John with a scowl. Matt woke her from a nap.

"What are we doing, John?" Shea grumbles.

"Just grab a seat," he answers.

"No. I'm tired and my feet hurt. What do you want?"

"Put me on speaker," Dr. P says.

"Okay, good to go," he says, pressing the speaker phone icon.

"Is everyone there?" Dr. P asks, Shea's face lights up.

"Yeah. Cap is slow walking us, but he can hear you."

"Okay. We have a problem," Dr. P says.

"Shit. What?" John says, glancing at Matt, whose face is a mask of panic.

"I think Todd knows I'm connected to you."

"Fuck. For how long?"

"A few days. Tina is trying to help us. Shea, are you there?" Dr. P asks.

"Yeah," she says, scooting closer to the phone.

"Tina asked me to tell you she's so very sorry, especially for her part in what happened. He beat the shit out of her. I had to stitch her up."

Shea's hand covers her mouth, and tears appear in her eyes. "Thank you," she whispers.

"Oh, and I sent something out in the mail for my sister. Can you see that she gets it? Open the box though, there's something for you guys in there too," Dr. P says.

"Okayyyy…" Johns says, slightly confused.

"One more thing…" Dr. P says, then there's a pause.

"Hey," comes through the phone.

Shea drops to her knees before anyone can catch her, her head hanging.

"Shit. Hold on," John says, passing the phone to Matt.

He crouches down. "C'mon Shea." He lifts her gently. "Somebody get her a chair!" he orders.

John deposits her into the chair and lifts her head. She is ghostly pale, like all the blood has drained from her face.

He walks over and mutes the call. "Matt, record this on your phone."

"Okay," Matt agrees.

John unmutes the call. "Okay, sorry about that."

"Is she okay?" Dr. P's voice again.

"Yes. Put him back on."

"Hello?" Greggory says.

Mrs. Cap is handing Shea tissues.

"Hey, man! It's great to hear your voice," John says.

"I just wanted to let you know, I reinforced the virus. I can spread it to other systems like security, whenever you need," Greggory informs them.

"Fuck yeah, man!" John says.

"I thought it would help. I don't know your timeline, but you need to make it soon. Or we'll all be in 25 before you get here."

"Copy that. We'll let you know," John says, his eyes never leaving Shea.

John hears Dr. P murmuring softly in the background but can't make out any of the words.

"Also," Greggory adds, voice softer, "I wanted to say hello to Shea. I don't remember anything. But I'm open to trying."

Shea tries to compose herself. She takes a deep breath, and says, "Hi. Whatever you're comfortable with. I'm here."

A pause. Then, "Okay."

103 | Dr. P

When they end the call, Greggory sits back on the couch. His expression, unreadable.

"Well, that went well," Dr. P says.

"I've never heard her sound like that before."

"Shea?"

"Yeah. It's always been rude or condescending," Greggory says, dragging a hand through his curls.

"Shea is a lot of things. Sweet, sassy as hell, demanding, giving, smart. But I've never seen her rude or condescending, especially toward you. Even when she had no memory of you, she loved you."

"But I don't remember that! I remember her not giving me the time of day, laughing at me, rolling her eyes, treating me like I was nothing!" He stands, agitated.

"I know that's what they… what they want you to believe. But that girl loves you with her entire being. Which is why they're coming here in the first place. I know what you think, but you're smart Greggory. Look at the facts."

"Wait. Their mission?" he asks, brow furrowing.

"Yes, it's to rescue you. Well, it was. Now it's all three of us. She's putting herself in danger—for you."

"I didn't ask her to!" he snaps.

"No. But Shea would sell both of her kidneys if it meant you were safe."

He studies her, contemplative for a moment. "Pictures. Do you have any?"

"No, but I can get some. Are you willing to come to terms with reality?" she asks, snark evident in her voice.

"I'm trying," he confesses.

She takes out her phone and opens a group text to John and Shea.

Text to John, Shea at 1305

« Send me all the pics you have with you guys and Gregg. ASAP

Text from Shea at 1307

<Image file received>

<Image file received>

<Image file received>

» It'll take too long to text. I'll email them now

» He wants to see them?

Text to John, Shea at 1309

« Yes! I'm working on him

Text from Shea at 1309

» Oh God. I'm crying

Dr. P walks to her room to grab her laptop. When she sits back on the couch next to him, she opens it and logs into her email.

When the first picture loads, she watches Greggory's face. It's a picture of Christian and Diesel, when Diesel was a puppy. They're out front of the cabin. Christian's smile is big and his arms encircle the pup.

"He's a cute kid," Greggory says softly.

"Yeah. He's an incredible kid."

She clicks to the next.

The whole gang at the hotel in Alaska. Shea is nuzzled into Gregg's side, looking up at him lovingly instead of at the camera. It also captured Diesel mid lick up Christian's face.

Greggory leans closer to the screen, like he's trying to decide if it's photoshopped or not. He keeps getting closer and closer. Then her laptop is on the ground and Greggory convulses beside it.

104 | Tina

Tina snipped her sutures and pulled them out this morning. Thanks to Dr. P, the cut had healed nicely. She still has swelling and bruising, but it's getting better.

She sits at her desk, occupying herself with busy work, when her desk phone rings.

"This is Tina."

"Tina, hi. This is Deb, Mr. Brockman's assistant."

"Oh, hey, Deb." she says. She remembers Hal Brockman from the hospital board. He got a little handsy at their Christmas party last year. Total creep.

"Mr. Brockman would like to speak with Mr. Donoghue, if he has a moment to spare."

"Let me check. Hold on a second, please."

She stands from her desk and walks into Todd's office after knocking once.

He looks up with a scowl. "What?"

"Hal Brockman's assistant is on the line. Hal would like a word."

"Fine. Put him through."

She returns to her desk. "I'm transferring you now."

"Thanks, Tina."

She puts the call on line two for Todd but doesn't hang up. She listens in, muting her line.

"This is Todd," she hears.

"Todd! It's Hal. How are you?" Mr. Brockman says.

"Great. Busy," Todd replies flatly. "What can I do for you?"

"Well," Hal says slowly. "I just saw one of your names pop up in the ER. Just arrived."

Todd's voice sharpens. "Who? For what?"

"Ah. Not too busy now, are you?" Hal teases.

"Hal…" Todd says, a threat dripping from the word.

"Let's see here… a Mr. Greggory Marsh. Had a grand mal seizure. They're running tests. The ER doc suspects a small brain bleed."

Tina's blood runs cold.

"Shit. Is anyone with him?" Todd asks.

"Yes. A woman."

"Is he stable enough to travel?"

"Via ambulance—maybe," Hal answers, sounding unsure.

"Get him here. Tell the woman nothing," Todd orders.

"I assume a donation to my ER will be forthcoming then?" Hal says.

"One hundred thousand by end of day."

"He'll be on his way then," Hal replies brightly.

Tina hangs up and whispers, "Shit."

105 | Clara

Clara is only awake, maybe, an hour a day now. They don't ask her anything. Not that she could answer. She feels like she's in a deprivation tank. Silence fills the cell. She's unsure why they even wake her anymore. Maybe it isn't every day. How would she know?

Today is different though.

Today there's a voice.

"Clara. Can you hear me?"

She doesn't recognize the voice. She nods her head once.

"I don't have much time. I'm a friend. Plans are in motion. Keep the hope. You'll be getting a new admission in the cell next door. Help him keep the hope too, okay?"

She nods again. But what is she supposed to do? She can't speak. She feels tears prickle her eyes and slip through the sutures, tracking down her face.

"I have to turn your sedation back on. I'm sorry," he says and shortly after her brain shuts down.

Sometime later, she comes out of her sedation again. This time it's not silent but no one is talking to her.

She hears, "Vitals are stable. No reaction to painful stimuli. Brain scan negative for a bleed."

"Do we think this is related to the EBW?" A voice she recognizes but has no idea who it belongs to—since her eyes have been sewn shut.

"Do we know if he had an underlying seizure disorder?"

"No. No past medical history."

"Then probably."

106 | Shea

Shea stands with her legs shoulder width apart, arms straight out at her sides. This is her second Kevlar fitting. Her belly has really popped since her first fitting.

This mission better be soon

"Shea, get the grumpus off your face," John says. "Look how happy SBD is to get his Kevlar."

She glances over. Christian stands in a fighting stance, kicking at his reflection in the mirror. She chuckles.

John's phone rings. "Hello?"

She can't hear who it is or what they're saying, but it sounds frantic. She watches John's face fall and then he's snapping his fingers at Matt.

Matt immediately starts yanking the Kevlar off Christian.

"You too. Out of the suit. Hurry," Matt orders.

"What happened?" she asks, ripping at Velcro straps.

"I don't know but he did two snaps. That means something is going down and we need to leave now."

"Shit," she says, peeling off the Kevlar. Her knees start shaking and she has to stop for a second to steady herself.

"Okay. Just go to the apartment. Lock the doors and stay put. You have a gun?" John says into the phone. He answers the caller, "No, pepper spray is not enough. I suppose those swords could kill, yes. Sleep with one by your bed. I'll call you when I know more."

John ends the call and Shea watches him take a deep breath. He looks at her, and says, "Shea, don't freak."

Matt comes up behind her and pulls her out of the Armor Depot, guiding her into the vehicle. As soon as John jumps behind the wheel they tear off.

"Tell me. Now!" she demands.

"Deep breaths, Shea," John says.

The car remains silent for several minutes.

"Helllllooooo?" she snaps, supremely agitated.

"Just wait five seconds will you?" John fires back.

Right before they pull into Cap's, Matt calls the main house phone. "Entire unit, on the field. Now."

"Guys, I'm really freaking out. Please."

"It's okay, Shea. I just don't want to have to say all of this more than once. It's okay. Deep breaths," John coaches, glancing in the rearview mirror at her.

"You say that shit one more time John and I swear it'll be the last thing you ever say!"

"There she is," John says, jubilantly.

As soon as they pull up to the field and file out, John counts heads.

"Okay, everybody, listen up." John begins.

The unit shuffles closer around them. Christian places a hand on her growing belly.

"After we got off the phone with Dr. P and Gregg earlier, she said she felt like she was really getting through to him. He asked to see pictures. We sent some over. He was looking at a picture where Shea was looking lovingly at him and apparently started seizing." He looks at Shea.

Oh no, I don't feel so good

Suddenly, Gas and Ghost are on either side of her, each with a forearm pressed into her armpit, holding her up.

"Thanks, guys," she says softly.

John continues. "She called an ambulance and met them at the hospital. After an hour or so, she said they told her to wait in the waiting room because he had scans. She waited for hours. When she finally asked what was going on, they told her they didn't have a patient by that name. That's all they would tell her."

He again looks at Shea. "Then she got a text from Tina. Todd had Gregg transferred to Crown. He's in 25. With Clara."

Cap sits in his living room with his beautiful wife beside him. He's taken his hat off and has placed it on the end of his knee. His wife runs her fingers through his hair, while he holds his head in his hands.

"This has all gone to hell in a hand basket!" he growls.

"Focus, hon. This happens all the time on an op. You got new intel, what're you going to do about it?"

"It feels personal. Watching these kids watch their loved ones suffer. I don't know what to do," he says, defeated.

"Yes, you do. Love, that's why those men are here. They would follow you to the ends of the earth. They trust you. Listen to them out there yelling and arguing. They need you. Be the man they need."

He exhales. "Shit." He sits up straighter. "Go get the little one."

"Okkaaayyyy," she says, stretching the word as she heads off.

In the time it takes her to bring the kid in, Cap has composed himself. His hat is back on. A glass of tea in his hand.

"Hi, Cap!" Christian calls from the side entrance.

"Hey, SBD. We got a lot to do still and we gotta wrangle these men in."

"Yup!"

"You get all of 4 and 25 mapped with Terry?"

"Yup!"

"Good. We're going to have to leave here soon. Have you made up your mind about what we talked about before?"

"I love Shea and Gregg and all them. I'll go."

"Are you sure? There won't be anyone to stay with if you decide you don't want to go later. Mrs. Cap will be staying here."

"I know. I can do it."

"Alright, son. If you're sure. One more thing…"

"Yes, sir?"

"Do you know what Shea's having?"

"Having?" Christian tilts his head.

"The baby. If it's a boy or a girl?"

"Oh, yes! Haven't told though," Christian admits, bashful.

"Keep it to yourself for now. I think it might help with morale to announce it."

The bate buzzer rings. Diane depresses the intercom button. "Yes?"

"Package."

She presses the button to open the gate.

Several minutes later, armed with a package Cap heads for the huddle of disarray. Getting right to the edge of it he announces himself, "Fall in, men!"

The unit disperses into lines, leaving Shea by herself. When she turns toward Cap it breaks his heart. Her face is a mask of pain, streaked with tears and snot. She seems to be barely standing on her own.

"John, get Shea a damn chair!" he orders.

John slides one under her and helps her sit. She looks at Cap with gratitude and wipes her face.

He addresses the lined-up men. "First order of business, your feelings on this mission don't matter. We finalize everything tomorrow now that we have 25 and 4 mapped. We will leave soon. End of story. Get prepped mentally, emotionally, spiritually, whatever you need to do to get on board."

Shea sniffles as more tears stream down her face.

Cap feels bad, but Clara has been captive for a while now. Matt was right. It's not fair if they drop everything now for Gregg.

"In other news, I have a package here for Shea." He carries it over and whispers to her, "Find the good Shea. It'll all be over soon."

"Okay," she says.

She studies the heavily taped box. When she looks up, Cap chuckles. Six hands extend toward her at once, each holding a knife.

Cap watches as she opens the box and pulls out a card.

108 | GREGGORY

Greggory hears beeps and quiet voices all around him, but he keeps his eyes closed. He has no idea where he is, but he assumes it's a hospital.

"The tests are all coming back normal. We assume he'll wake within the next couple of days. Because we've found no other source, we believe it's related to the EBW solution. We're hoping it was a one off, but we'll keep monitoring him closely just in case," a female voice reports.

"Alright. Keep me posted. I want a call the second he's awake."

Him. Todd's here. Sounding like he's in charge. Is this not a hospital?

The chatter stops and Greggory chances slightly opening one eye. He recognizes his surroundings immediately. He closes his eyes. He's frozen in fear. He knows they keep these cells monitored by cameras and he really doesn't want to deal with Todd yet.

His one little peek showed him that the cell he's in is the one closest to the lab, which is on his left. He slowly rolls onto his right side and again slightly opens one eye.

The middle cell, the one right next to his, is dark. Though the cells are made of some sort of glass, it appears to be slightly frosted. He can't quite see through it. He can see that there is a large shape in the center of the cell. He believes it to be a bed.

He closes his eyes. He attempts to understand what's happening by running through the events of the past day. He was looking at pictures with Dr. P—one where Shea looked up at him with the kind of adoration he used to long for. His brain couldn't come to terms with it. It's like a voice inside his head screamed, "NO! It isn't real! It can't be true! These are lies! Photoshop! It can't be!"

The more he had contemplated it, the more confused he felt and then… then the floor rushed up to meet his face.

Even now, when he tries to follow that thread of memory, his mind fuzzes out. Similar to the way one's vision might before losing consciousness. He tows the line, trying to follow the thread toward a different potential truth.

He seizes. Full large flapping motions. He is blissfully unaware.

When he regains consciousness, he's still on his side. He cracks an eye, awoken by a soft knocking sound. In the next cell he sees a human shaped shadow pressed against the glass. A fist tapping the glass over and over.

He chances a cough, to let her know he's awake and hears her. The tapping speeds up. Greggory realizes it's morse code. A single finger tapped against the glass makes a dot. A palm against the glass makes the dash.

.... .- ...- . / .... --- .--. . / - .... . -.-- .-. . / -.-. --- -- .. -. --.

Have hope they're coming

109 | Shea

Shea pulls the card with her name on it from the box. Whatever sits beneath it is wrapped in tissue paper.

Probably the gift for her sister

Shea opens the card and reads it silently.

Beautiful Shea,

I know you're missing Gregg during your pregnancy, and I'm sure when he remembers, he'll hate it that he missed it. I started us on a craft—crochet. He's pretty great at it, of course. I picked a color that I hope will bring you comfort, and he picked a marshmallow peep yellow, because he thought it would be a neutral color. I told him my sister is expecting, and I stand by that statement.

So, sister, the contents of this box are yours.

Love you always,

Dr. P

Shea wipes her eyes and passes the card to John so he can see how wonderful his lady is. She opens the first tissue papered bundle. She pulls out a blanket and lifts it up. The color is very similar to Gregg's eyes. She presses it to her chest and cries some more. None of the men move toward her. No one tries to comfort her.

She's glad. She needs a moment alone with it.

She shakes out the small blanket and drapes it over her lap.

Okay, keep it together

She reaches back into the box and pulls out the second bundle. A second card attached to it. Her hands tremble as she tears it open.

Congratulations on your bundle of joy!

Xoxo Greggory

She holds it to her heart. It's not her Gregg. But it is his handwriting. She again hands it off to John and tears the tissue paper wrapping around his blanket. The soft yellow bundle makes her feel like her heart is going to fall out of her butt. She slowly unfurls it, taking in every stitch. She slowly brings it to her face and inhales deeply.

It smells just like him!

That does it. She abruptly stands and runs into the house, clutching her little yellow blanket.

Dr. P's apartment is dark except for the thin lines of light slipping through her curtains. She doesn't dare turn on any lights. She's barricaded every door and window and lays on the couch. Gregg's He-Man sword next to her. She feels like she's unraveling. Like her mind is not her own.

She thinks she sees men in suits outside her building every so often. That makes the feeling of losing her mind and jitteriness worse.

Her phone buzzes. She nearly screams. She clamps a hand over her mouth and checks her phone.

Text from Shea at 1800

» Thank you for being the best sister I could have ever asked for

» You're amazing

She smiles and answers.

Text to Shea at 1802

« You're amazing!

She wants to text John for more details. See how Shea is really doing. She finds herself calling him instead. As the phone rings, she puts a blanket over her head to help muffle the sound.

"'Lo," John answers.

"Hey. It's me." She whispers.

"Oh, hey, boo. You just caused quite the ruckus over here."

"How is she? Really?"

"She loves them. She's currently curled up in the fetal position with the yellow blanket smashed against her face. I think maybe it smells like him?"

"Yeah, it does. He made it then I slipped it under his covers. He slept with it for a few nights. Figured she would appreciate that," she admits.

"Wow. You're amazing. That's so thoughtful."

"I try. So how long am I barricading myself in?" she asks.

"We haven't even talked about it. I'm not sure if it would be better to have you stay there or go to work and act like nothing happened. Or maybe just show concern for Gregg's well-being."

"You honestly think I won't end up in 25?"

"I don't know. Todd is smart. Evil but smart. I bet you working there and him being able to keep tabs on you will give him just enough control to keep him at bay," John hypothesizes.

"And if it doesn't?"

"Then at least you'll all be in the same place."

"John!"

"We're moving out soon either way. It won't be long."

"Still…" she trails off.

"I know it's scary, boo. There's nothing I can do until the mission is a go. I told Matt we couldn't rush in when he saw Clara in the state she's in. I can't break that rule now. Believe me, I want to come swoop in and save you right now. I just can't. You have to hold out a little while longer."

"I understand," she says, trying to be brave.

"Hey, you still have access to Gregg's laptop?"

"Um, I'm sure it's here, but it's password protected. I have no idea what the password could be."

"His passwords used to all be the same—some hacker he is. When you get a chance, try JohnSnow88. Don't log into anything. We just need to know that we can access those cameras."

"Sure."

111 | JOHN

When John hangs up with Dr. P, Cap asks him to bring Shea back out.

John sighs and marches straight into the house. When he reaches the couch, he lifts his foot and nudges Shea's butt with it.

"Go away." The muffled sound comes from under the yellow blanket.

"Cap apparently has one more trick up his sleeve. He's requesting your presence," he says, sitting on the edge of the couch. He tries to lower the blanket from her face.

"Leave me alone. I just want to breathe him in. Pretend he's with me and not locked up in 25," she sobs.

"You can't shut out the world. Everyone is worried about you. Wipe your eyes and get that round belly out there. I know it's hard, but you're like our mascot. We need you."

She huffs out a breath, a mix of emotional exhaustion and surrender. "Ugh. Fine." She stands, still clutching the yellow blanket close.

When they make it back out of the house, the unit stands silent. John watches as they offer her sad smiles. None of which reach their eyes.

Cap and Christian stand beside the chair that Shea recently vacated. As soon as she sits, Christian beams at her and slips a sash he made himself over her head. She sits back and looks down to read it, as everyone else does.

It says, "It's a…"

Shea looks at Christian, confused. "What is this, buddy?"

"Baby Shower!" he says excitedly.

As he says it, several of the men deploy poppers and confetti flies everywhere. John watches her wipe her eyes and look at Cap with the most sincere face of gratitude he's ever seen.

"Me first!" Duce rushes to her side and hands her a box. "It has nothing to do with the baby. It's for you."

She opens the box and inside are fifteen MP3 players just like hers.

"It's so you can make us all playlists," Duce explains, adjusting the bill of his hat.

"I love it!" she says, standing to hug him.

Terry steps forward next. "I made you a little something. I hope you like it."

She takes the thin envelope from him and opens it, pulling out the contents. She holds it up and John can see in her eyes that she loves it. She turns it toward him. It's a picture of Gregg, his face is awash with love and adoration. John has seen Gregg look at Shea that way before.

She puts her hand over her mouth as tears flow.

"I love it, Terry! How?" she asks, hugging him tightly.

"I had a little help," he says, nodding toward Christian.

She pulls Christian in and dampens his shoulder with her tears.

"I have another one," Christian says, pulling away from her slightly. Without waiting for a response, he says, "Now!"

Without any hesitation everyone present links hands. Shea continues to hold on to Christian. John and Matt each grab one of her shoulders. John is pulled into a vision at the riverbed of the cabin. He stands next to Matt and Shea. Christian stands in front of them.

"I wanted to offer you something before just doing it. I didn't think it would be very fair to you if I did, Shea."

"Okay. What are you offering?" she asks.

"Do you want to know if Rhaego is a girl or a boy?" he offers.

"Wait, you can tell?" John questions.

"I can show you. Then you'll know."

Shea's face lights up. "Then yes! Of course!"

"Is it okay if I bring everyone in?" Christian asks. "Cap thought it might help the group rally together before the mission."

She nods. Her voice shakes. "Yes. Of course. I'd love to share the news. I just wish Gregg were here."

112 · Shea

The riverbed recedes and then there's nothing. White nothing. One by one, the other members of the unit are brought into the nothingness. Once they're all present, Christian offers Shea one last sweet smile. Then her vision is filled with her baby.

It moves and twitches. Christian shows it from all angles. Its sweet face, with its eyes closed. One small hand rolled into a fist rests beside its cheek, tiny fingernails on display. A sparse flocking of fine hair covers the fetus, blond in color, except for the hair on its head, which is dark brown.

No surprise there

Then Christian shifts the image to more of a far away view, allowing her to see the whole baby at once. Without needing it pointed out Shea gasps and covers her mouth. Her hair pin trigger emotions, explode. She barely hears it when the men around her cheer and clap.

Sensing her emotional state, Christian amplifies the baby's heartbeat for her to hear. Something to focus on, to calm herself.

The vision fades and she clutches Christian even tighter. "Thank you, buddy. I needed that."

He buries his face into her hair. "Gonna be brothers," he whispers.

Greggory hears a commotion in the next cell, without thinking, sits up and turns toward the frosted glass. Two figures lift Clara from her position on the floor against the glass. She doesn't struggle, at least not from what he can see. Of course, she doesn't make a sound. He keeps watching, hoping his presence alone might deter them from any abuse behaviors.

As he watches the scene, the large glass door to his cell opens. Turning his head toward the sound he watches Todd strut in, followed by a team of medical personnel. He attempts to school his emotions.

"Greggory, so glad to see you sitting up. You had several seizures during the night, but they have slowed down over the last few hours. Are you aware they're happening?" Todd asks, standing at Greggory's side.

"No," Greggory answers. "I remember feeling funny before the first one, but I've been really out of it since then. Why am I locked up here instead of in a hospital? Aren't seizures kind of a big deal?"

"They can be. But our team and technology are miles ahead of a local hospital. I wanted you to have the best care possible," Todd replies smoothly.

"Oh." Greggory gestures at the semi-transparent walls. "Then why the cell?"

Todd laughs through his nose. "Greggory, I apologize if you thought we put you in a cell. These rooms are very private and function as a clean room of sorts. This is the best place to recoup and recover."

"That's... very generous of you, Todd," Greggory says. His voice betrays his doubt. "So where do we go from here?"

"We'll monitor you and try some different medications to stop the seizures. As soon as you're back to normal, out you pop."

"Okay. Am I allowed to do some work while I'm being monitored?"

"Unfortunately, screens can trigger a seizure. So we brought you some of your favorite books and a blank notebook. You can journal or make lists—whatever you want."

"Thanks," he says, unenthused.

"I'm sorry, man. I gotta jet. Leads to follow and such. I'll check in tomorrow, see how you're feeling."

"Alright," Greggory says, picking up one of the books Todd brought. It just happens to be the book he's been reading.

As soon as Todd is gone, Greggory begins thinking about the picture that started all this. He's not sure what's happening. But he feels some sort of break from reality, just before he seizes.

And he likes it.

114  Mrs. Cap

Mrs. Cap watches the men celebrate and come up with names for their little friend. Shea sits in the chair, still clutching onto Christian.

Walking over Mrs. Cap taps Christian on the shoulder, giving him a small nod. She has learned how to send him specific thoughts so he doesn't get overwhelmed when she touches him.

She gathers the blankets and other gifts, then extends her hand to Shea. Shea takes it, and they walk into the house together.

When they reach Mrs. Cap's office, she guides Shea into one of the large armchairs.

"Sit. We need to talk," Mrs. Cap instructs.

"Am I in trouble?" Shea asks, her anxiety evident in her voice.

"No, sweet girl. We just need to chat, us women. Cap is having a similar talk with the boys," she says, sitting in the armchair across from Shea.

Mrs. Cap notices how Shea's hand moves protectively across her belly and smiles. "Any thoughts on a name for the sweet angel?"

She hesitates, now fidgeting with her crucifix. "Gregg and I never really discussed the future. Not that we didn't want a baby. Things have just been kind of life and death for a while."

"You think he wants children?"

"Oh yes," Shea says without hesitation. "Gregg will make a fantastic father."

"So. A name?"

"I will definitely not be naming him Rhaego," she says, chuckling.

Mrs. Cap laughs softly. "I don't blame you."

"But I think I'd like to name him after my dad," she says finally. "It's a great name, and he deserves to be remembered that way."

"I'm on the edge of my seat here," Mrs. Cap says.

"Abel," Shea whispers, her smile trembling. "Like in the Bible. A righteous man who pleased the Lord."

"That's a lovely name. You think Gregg will agree?"

"Absolutely. Well, my Gregg would have. I don't know about Greggory."

"We'll cross that bridge when we get to it. For now, I wanted to tell you that a flight will leave here at 0400. Ten hours from now."

She reaches down and grabs a package, handing it to Shea. "This is yours and SBD's Kevlar. I have checked and re-checked with him. He wants to go. But you don't have to. You can stay here with me and let the boys do the heavy lifting. Keep Abel safe," she offers.

Shea shakes her head. "I can't. I know it would be best, but I can't stay. He was there for me. I won't abandon him now."

Mrs. Cap nods slowly. "Okay, I had to offer."

She continues, her tone firm. "If you're going, then listen close. Wear the Kevlar at all times. Even on the plane. We've been picking up some chatter out of Crown. They're speculating what our plans might be. You'll fly into Orlando, putting you very close to Crown. Cap has a hotel booked in Satellite Beach, so you'll be close but not too close. A couple of days later, you'll be reunited with your love, Clara, and Dr. P."

She places a gentle hand over Shea's. "Take this seriously. Keep the Kevlar on. You're a primary target for Todd."

"Yes, ma'am."

"One more thing, Shea." Mrs. Cap's tone softens. "Little Abel is a blessing. Things may look bleak now, but it'll work out. I just know it."

"That kid is gonna be a lady killer," Duce says, folding his clothes and dropping them into his duffel bag.

"You see all that hair?!" Innie adds.

"If he makes it through this," Gas mutters.

Duce's head snaps up. "What the fuck, dude? Shea will be fine. We'll protect her and she's got all that Kevlar."

"Yeah, but you know she's Todd's public enemy number one. From what we know about him, he'll do whatever it takes to get her alone and do something fucked up. Like make Gregg kill her," Teddy predicts.

"Enough!" Cap's voice booms as he strides into the barracks. "I have hats, MP3 players loaded with Shea's battle playlist, and op tags for each of you."

"Sweet. What's the finalized op name?" Duce asks.

Cap stands tall. "The mission is as follows, rescue three friendlies—one potentially hostile. Detain primary target AKA Todd Donoghue. The military base close to Crown will be backing us, but will not breach until rescue targets are secured and primary target is detained."

Cap lifts a Velcro patch embroidered with gold thread. "Operation codename is Abel."

The men erupt into cheers and Duce takes his goodies from Christian, who's darting between bunks like an eager supply runner.

"We board at 0355. Wheels up at 0400. Get some rest boys!" Cap turns and leaves the barracks.

Duce inspects the goods that Christian gave him. The op patch is embroidered with the name Abel with a crown above it—fitting. Mrs. Cap sure does work fast.

"Hey, SBD," Duce calls Christian over after he's delivered all the goodies that Cap gave him.

"Yup," he calls back, skipping toward him.

When the kid is right in front of him, he asks, "You ready for this?"

"Yup!"

"You okay being in the back and letting me call Diesel's commands."

"Yup!"

"You trust me? Even after everything you saw?" Duce asks earnestly.

Christian's eyes soften. "Yup! You change. All good."

Duce feels that one right in his chest. "Alright. You have your bag packed?"

"Yup!"

"Make sure you wear your Kevlar outta here and until we're far away from Crown. Got it?"

"Sure. Why?"

"You're one of Todd's high value targets. That means he might be willing to hurt you, if it means taking you into custody. You know all of us would never let that happen. But you've seen how an op can go sideways," he says, tapping the side of his head.

Christian nods solemnly. "Okay. I wear it."

"Good kid. Now go check and make sure Shea has all the help she needs."

"Okay!" he says, then skips out of the barracks.

Duce chuckles to himself and zips up his duffle.

"I don't know about you assholes," he announces to the room, grinning. "But I'm having a hankering for the beach!"

116 | Dr. P

Quietly getting ready for bed, Dr. P runs though the senses exercise that Greggory taught her. She's been on the edge of panic all day, thinking about going to work tomorrow like nothing happened.

By the third round of 'what can I taste,' her phone rings. She knows by the ringtone that it's John.

"Oh, thank God," she murmurs, accepting the call. "Hello?"

"Hey, boo! How're you holding up?" he asks.

"Not good. I want to lie and sound tough, but I'm freaking out."

"We finally have a plan. We leave tonight for Orlando. We'll get a hotel and then in a day or two, we'll go in."

Relief floods through her, relaxing the tension she was carrying in her shoulders. "Oh, thank goodness. What does that mean for me?"

"We can't come get you because there are definitely goons on your location. You can't come to us for the same reason. The plan right now is for you to go in tomorrow. Act like you're worried about Gregg, but normal otherwise. You'll take a late lunch off campus. I'll tell you the location when it's closer. You'll be followed. That's fine. You'll slip out the back with us, and we'll take it from there."

"So I'll get to stay with you guys?"

"Yes. You'll have to go back to crown when we go in. We can't chance leaving you alone. I'll protect you though."

"As long as I'm not there alone." Her voice falters. "What if they don't let me leave? Or throw me in 25 the second I get there?"

"Then at least you know we're on the way," he says gently. "You gotta be brave. I'll do everything I can to keep you safe."

She takes a slow breath. "I can do this."

"That's my girl. Pack a bag. Bring some beach clothes. I'll bring fatigues for you. I gotta get some rest. Gotta be ready for Operation Abel."

"Abel?" she repeats.

"Yeah. It was Shea's dad's name. She's naming the baby after him."

Her jaw drops. "It's a boy?!"

John laughs. "Wow. I suck at giving good news."

"Yeah, you do!" she says, laughing softly for the first time in a couple of days.

Shea's alarm begins singing the song of its people at 0345. She immediately launches her phone across the room. She then hears Diesel growling at it, while it continues to wail.

"Ugh! FINE!" she yells, switching on the light.

When her eyes adjust, she doubles over laughing, clutching her side. Diesel lies next to her phone with his teeth bared, while the alarm continues. And Christian sits on top of his duffel bag wearing nothing but his Kevlar suit.

She walks (okay, waddles) over and retrieves her phone, silencing it.

"Christian, buddy… I love the enthusiasm, but that suit goes under your clothes."

"Really?"

"Yes. Didn't you notice your bum is in the wind?" she asks, chuckling.

He jumps up and looks in the mirror. His eyes going wide. He immediately places one hand over the front and the other over the back, saying, "It was dark!"

She shakes her head, still laughing. "I'll go get ready in the bathroom. Underpants first, then the Kevlar, then clothes over that."

"Got it!"

She grabs her duffle bag. She already packed everything last night so she wouldn't have to do it at four o'clock in the morning.

After a quick shower, she puts on her granny-est of panties and most comfortable bra. Then slips into a thin pair of leggings and a long-sleeved top so the

Kevlar doesn't chafe.

The suit's Velcro crackles as she rips it apart and re-straps it in place on her body. The straps over her stomach only adhere with a small amount of Velcro. Meaning she's already almost outgrown it.

She examines herself in the mirror. The Kevlar compresses her curves, making her belly stand out. Large and in charge.

She places her right hand over it and closes her eyes.

She prays, "Dear Heavenly Father, please keep us safe. Allow us to rescue our loved ones and move on with our lives. Please help him remember me. Amen."

The doctors and nurses are gathered around Greggory, pushing meds and trying to fix the 'problem'. He's had over twenty seizures in the last twenty-four hours. Each one, self-induced.

At around seizure number fifteen, he really honed it in. It takes only seconds to cause it. He lies there letting them do what they're going to do, hoping the medication doesn't work.

Test after test shows no brain damage, but the lead doctor keeps talking about inducing a coma. He's been quietly listening, not putting up a fight—but a coma doesn't work for him. Not when he feels like he's finally getting somewhere.

"Doc, I feel great. No need to put me in a coma. Let the meds do their job."

The doctor frowns. "I hear you, Mr. Marsh. But just because there's no brain damage yet doesn't mean it isn't coming. I need to think long-term."

"Well, what's another twenty-four hours? Every scientific study has some risk," Greggory says with a slight smile. "I don't even notice the seizures. They don't bother me."

"They will if you wake-up without any memories, or as a vegetable…or not at all."

"Can't you just give the meds a little bit of time? Please," he pleads.

The doctor only hesitates for a second. "Fine. Let's clear out," he says to the team, then addresses Greggory, "I'll give you three more seizures, then I'm doing what I think is best. Which is a medically induced coma."

"Thanks, doc," he says, closing his eyes.

It's almost like a tickle or like he knows a tickle is about to happen, or maybe it's having to sneeze. He waits until his room is empty and tries again. He pictures the photo in his mind. All of their smiling faces. He stays on it, analyzing their faces of genuine happiness. He feels fine, but this is the way it's gone each time before, nothing new.

It isn't until he focuses on Shea's upturned face, gazing at his own. He appears completely oblivious in the photo—that someone could be looking at him like that. Or is it such a normal occurrence that this version of himself thinks nothing of it.

The pre-tickle feeling comes. But something different happens this time. The image moves and changes in his mind, like he can see what played out before the picture was taken.

Greggory pulls the kid in front of himself, pressing his fingers into the child's neck, tickling him

Dr. P enters the frame, and says, "In five!"

The kid scrunches up his shoulders and squeals.

Shea playfully slaps his arm. He turns to her, and says, "Watch it, or your next." Then quickly looks at the camera and smiles.

The photo captures that very next moment. Where the look Shea gives him is just what it looks like. Unguarded love and adoration.

The seizure never comes.

He thinks he just had a memory.

119 | Todd

Todd sits in his sauna, scrolling through Greggory's medical record. He's still unsure what's causing the seizures. Their first EBW subject never had this issue.

He dials Tina's cell. When she answers, he says, "Come down to the sauna." He ends the call and sets his phone screen down on the bench.

She knocks on the door before entering. He chuckles.

"You rang?" she asks.

"Come in. You're letting the heat out."

She steps inside, slips off her heels, and leaves them by the door. She plops down on the bench across from him.

"It's nice, isn't it?" he says.

"It's hot. What can I do for you?"

"Tell me where you found our lovely Dr. P."

Tina stiffens. "The board picked her resume and set up an interview with you. You were busy with Greggory, so I met with her. That's it."

"Did you do your due diligence?" he probes.

"Yes. She checked out. She came highly recommended and had the kind of experience that fit what we were looking for perfectly," she says, defensively.

"And her personal background?" he prods.

"I did a background check and had Mitch do some personal digging. Nothing came of it. She's clean."

"I had a nice talk with Mitch yesterday. He told me the same. Except when

I started asking about where she's from in Alaska, he seemed to have no recollection of that."

Tina's posture becomes more guarded. "Of her being from Alaska?"

"Yes, Tina," he says, malice dripping from each word.

"I gave him her whole file. Besides she's great. What's the problem?"

"The problem is our treacherous little friends were in Alaska. After just a small amount of digging, I learned she was at the airport when the trash can tracker went live. You think that was a coincidence?"

"Honestly, yes. We've seen no behavior that leads me to believe that she's with them."

He studies her. "She was quick to cozy up to Greggory. And she hasn't left her apartment since he was transferred to 25. You don't find that odd? Tina?"

She swallows. "No. I texted her. I knew she was freaking out. She's solid, Todd."

"You think she's showing up to work in the morning?"

"Yes."

"If she does, do you think I'm going to just throw her in a glass cell?"

"You shouldn't. She's made amazing progress."

"We'll see. You're dismissed."

He picks his phone back up, but his eyes never focus on the screen. He stays there a while longer, contemplating the right move. Tina is useless. So he'll have to play it by ear.

Christian carries his large duffel bag in front of him, both hands gripping it tight. John offered to carry it, but it's time for Christian to man up. The bag slaps against his legs as he walks across the big parking lot. There are lots of big trucks, Cap calls them Hum-bees. But they aren't taking those. They're all walking past them, to a plane in the distance. Of course it's the farthest thing away.

Diesel walks right next to him, nose in the air, sniffing around. Christian can tell when he gets a good smell because Diesel's nose follows it, but he never runs off. He's a good boy.

"Are you sure you don't want me to take that, bud? We gotta get to the plane before it takes off without us," John says.

Christian looks around. John is the only one left in the parking lot with him.

"Okay. But don't tell."

"You got it. You made it most of the way."

"It's heavy!" he exclaims.

"I know!" John exclaims right back at him.

They make it to the plane. John hands the duffle back to him just before they go up the stairs. Christian carries it onto the plane and drops it in the aisle, hurrying to claim the seat next to Shea.

"There you are! I was saving that seat for you," Shea says.

"Thanks."

He hears John call his name, grumbling about the bag he left in the aisle and how he could have broken his neck.

"Sorry, John."

Christian looks around, making sure everyone is here. Everybody looks grouchy and tired. They'll probably all sleep on the way. He turns to Shea and notices she has the green blanket over her legs and the yellow one tucked under her chin, covering her chest.

He reaches over and places a hand on her stomach, but the image of Abel is fuzzy. Like he has a bad connection. He can see well enough to know the baby is fine, but it's unsettling.

"Everything okay with Abel?" Shea asks.

"Yeah, but… fuzzy," he says, his face pinched in confusion.

"Hmm. Maybe because of the Kevlar?" she asks.

"Maybe," he says, not convinced.

"Here," she says, reaching out her bare hand. "Try just touching my bare skin."

He does and what he experiences is love flooding through him. Shea is telling him without words that Abel coming doesn't mean she'll love him less.

He opens his eyes and looks at her with surprise.

"I've been practicing with Mrs. Cap. She showed me how to tell you stuff with my thoughts. She told the unit too, in case something happens and we can't communicate. You can be our walkie-talkie."

"Cool!"

121 | CAP

After the rowdiness of everyone getting settled on the plane, Cap leans back and thinks. His eyes are closed, but he's not going to waste this time sleeping. The symphony of snores made him chuckle at first, but after about thirty minutes of John sounding like he was trying to start an old tractor engine, Cap slipped in his ear buds playing Shea's mix.

He's run through the operation in his mind at least a dozen times. He made a mistake and he's kicking himself for just now realizing it. He gave in to the demands of emotional children, instead of being their leader. Well time to shake shit up.

When there is about an hour left in the flight, Cap removes his earbuds and stands. He walks down the aisle, slapping boots, shoulders, and the occasional head as he passes. He doesn't say anything, just disrupts their slumber.

Once the men are groaning and upright, he kneels in front of Shea and Christian. Taking a much gentler approach with them, he places a hand on her arm and gently shakes it, saying, "Shea, wake up."

In true Shea fashion, she opens her eyes and sneers at him until recognition crosses her face.

"Is everything okay?" she asks.

"Yeah. We just need a quick meeting before we land. Wake the kid up, would ya?"

He stands. Taking deep breaths, he calms himself. He knows this is going to go over like a fart in church.

"Listen up," he projects his voice above the grumbles. "We land in about an hour. Before we're boots on the ground, I need to correct a mistake."

The plane quiets. All eyes are on him. They're paying attention.

"Teams and objectives are being reformed based on intel and emotional states. I know what you're all capable of. These orders are within your capabilities."

The men murmur to themselves. Shea looks alarmed.

"Let's start—Team A will go straight for the cells in 25. Extracting both Clara and Gregg. You'll then make your way to the meeting point in 4, like we planned. Team A will include Terry, Teddy, Gas, John, Tank, Hoover, DD, and myself."

"What the hell, Cap?" Matt shoots to his feet.

"Sit!" Cap snaps. Then addressing him directly, "Deal with it. This is the way it needs to go. You should never have been on Clara's rescue team, and you know it! It's just even more obvious now that Gregg's in the cell next to her. You think I'm gonna send you, John, Shea, and Christian in there together? It would be a shit show!"

He takes off his hat and runs a hand through his hair. "The only reason John is on Team A is because Dr. P will be with him and Gregg knows her. Their presence might convince him to come with us," he says a little softer.

He looks around the plane. "Team B, will sweep building 4, clearing it so it will be safe for us to all convene there once the rescue targets are in our custody. According to our latest bit of intel, this is where Todd has been spending his days. Remember the goal is detainment, not lethal force. Tranq rounds only. Side arms are to only be used if there's no other option. Team B will include Matt, Duce, Shea, Christian, Diesel, Ghost, and Innie."

The cabin goes quiet—eerily so.

"If you have a valid objection I'll hear you out," Cap offers, even though they don't have the time or resources for another course of action. "Otherwise, come to terms with it and get on board."

Shea wipes at her eyes but remains quiet. Matt's jaw tightens, but he gives Cap a single nod. This appears to send a message to the rest of the unit. They all nod accepting their missions.

122 | Clara

Clara slowly becomes aware. Her consciousness sharpening, thoughts coming into focus. She stays exactly as she wakes, motionless, braced for whatever torture they have planned for her today.

Voices drift from the next cell, but they're too muffled for her to understand.

Warm air brushes her ear and struggles not to react. She hears the quiet churn of a stomach and the rhythm of breath from the mouth hovering over her. She remains still, she can't let them win.

A whisper, so soft she would think she imagined it if she had not felt the breath.

"Clara, they're coming in a couple of days," he says.

Then the sedative creeps back in. Not enough to pull her under, just enough to make her float and the world tilt.

123 | GREGGORY

"Well, I guess you were right," the doctor says, scanning the chart like he still can't quite believe it.

"So no coma for me?" Greggory asks.

"Not if you keep this up. It seems the medications are working."

"Awesome. So when can I get out of here? Or at least have my phone? A tablet? Something?"

"I suppose if you stay seizure free for a few more hours, we could introduce a screen, test it out. Your phone came with your belongings from the hospital. I'll make sure it's charged."

"Thanks, doc!"

The medical team files out, leaving him in the quiet. He closes his eyes and pictures the faces from the photo. Trying so hard just to remember. He hears faint tapping noises from the next cell. Not on the glass like before, they're farther away this time.

... --- --- -.

"Soon"

124 | Dr. P

Dr. P sits in her car outside of building 4, trying to find the courage to go in. She rechecks that Greggory's laptop is still under her duffel bag on the passenger side floorboard. She checks her hair and make-up in the visor mirror. She closes her eyes, drags in a breath—it's not helping.

"Come on, you can do this. If you get locked up, he'll be here in a couple of days." She closes the mirror, muttering to herself, "I can do this."

She opens her texts and stares at the message from John. Her thumb hovers over his name like it could change something.

Text from John at 0655

» We're taking off now. I'll see you around 1330. I'll call you at 1300

Text to John at 0656

« Okay!

She grabs her purse and locks the car behind her. She holds her head high, trying to exude a confidence she doesn't feel. Inside building 4, Tina stands in the lobby, wringing her hands and tapping the toe of her six-inch heel on the tile. Her brows are furrowed, half her bottom lip caught between her teeth.

When Tina spots her, she immediately walks over. "There you are. Come with me to get a bagel," she says. She hooks her arm through Dr. P's and steers them into the first-floor kitchen.

Tina walks over to the spread of bagels and begins examining one closely. Dr. P steps up beside her and looks over to her.

"Is everything okay?" Dr. P asks, her voice shaking slightly.

"Great! They brought the asiago ones from Panera that I like," Tina says, spreading cream cheese across the bagel.

"Okay." Dr. P picks up a bagel and mirrors Tina's movements.

Tina puts her bagel on a plate, and says, "Let's go enjoy the sunshine while we eat these." She urges Dr. P with her eyes.

"Okay."

They sit at a picnic table in a small gathering area outside of building 8. Tina sits, putting her plate on the table. She holds her head in her hands.

Dr. P reaches over and places a hand on her forearm. "Hey, what's going on?"

Tina looks up. "Todd questioned me this weekend. Asking a lot of questions about you. He knows something is off. I tried to brush him off, but he probably couldn't care less about what I said. I don't know if you're safe here."

"I appreciate you letting me know. There is a plan in place. I'm supposed to leave here at lunch. You think I'll make it that long, or will I end up in 25 as soon as I walk in?"

"Well, I booked him up with meetings all this morning. Since you guys have done such a great job with the neural implant, he wants to start meeting with interested parties. He should be unavailable for taking prisoners until about three."

"Okay, the only reason I came in is to show him I'm not guilty and to ask about Gregg. If he's not even available, should I stay?"

"Yes. Leaving for lunch is normal enough, but right after you got here? You have a detail, there's no way they aren't right on top of you. I can see three of them right now. Far enough away that you might miss them. Close enough that they could act at any moment."

"You think they'll follow if I leave here for lunch?" Dr. P asks.

"Definitely. I'm sure there is a plan in place for that. Keep it casual though, if they suspect anything you're never going to be able to enact that plan."

"Thank you for your help, it won't be forgotten," Dr. P says, taking a bite of her bagel.

"It's the least I could do." She breaks off a small piece of bagel and wipes the cream cheese off on the edge of the plate before popping it into her mouth.

"Can you tell me anything about Clara and Gregg?" Dr. P asks.

"I've been keeping an eye on the medical records. If I ask Todd directly, he'll lock me out of the system. Clara is the same. Sedated, only up like every other day now. Gregg had a total of like twenty-seven seizures. They pumped him full of several different anti-seizure meds, and he hasn't had one since. They're going to give him his phone later today. I don't know if he'll risk texting you, but keep an eye out," Tina reports.

"He has crazy encryption that will make it look like he's texting his mom or something if anyone checks. He's so good with computers."

Tina studies her for a moment. "I have a question. Did he figure out the code?" Tina asks, seeming to be curious not malicious.

"Yeah, he did. He said there was like a hidden message to himself. He didn't believe it, but it made him hesitate before handing the system over to Todd. He said he actually reinforced the virus and that he could manipulate it if necessary."

"Wow. Todd is wrong at every turn. I bet he hates that." Tina leans closer. "I have to warn you. Even if it seems like Gregg seems like he is warming up to the idea of Shea, it will be different in person. There is a deep hatred planted in his brain. Not just a dislike or non-belief that his life was different. It's the kind of hate that laughs while you're disemboweled. Just be careful right away," Tina advises.

Dr. P swallows. "Damn, okay. He did seem to be trying."

"Right, but she's not in front of him. It might be different when she is."

"Thank you for all your help," she says.

She looks sincerely at Tina, and because she's leaving and because she really has nothing to lose, she asks, "Why don't you leave? If Todd is going down, that will implicate you too. Why stay?"

Tina goes still. "I know looking at us now, it probably makes no sense," she says quietly. "I knew Todd before all of this. When we were struggling. He used to braid my hair for me. The man that held me when I kept miscarrying and couldn't get out of bed. He ran me baths and rubbed my feet. He brought me back from the dead emotionally. I still see the man I fell in love with."

Her voice steadies. "I went along with horrible things because I loved him. I believed there was a good reason. I was blinded by that love. Now that the blinders have literally been knocked off my face, I see with a sort of clarity. Whatever comes my way, I deserve it. I'll stay to take it."

Dr. P can feel tears stinging her eyes, but she works hard to hold them back. Tina is keeping her composure, she would too.

125 | GHOST

Ghost sets up his sniper rifle at the top of the plane's stairs. Several blacked-out SUVs wait for them below. The sun is at its zenith, local time is 1230. He clips a sunshade onto his scope and scans the area, looking for any signs of a threat. If it were just the unit, he would have called it good an oscillation ago. With the presence of two high-value targets in their care, a pregnant woman and a small child, he continues scanning.

He glances over his shoulder, at the rest of the unit, all dressed in black cargo pants and black Under Armor shirts. "I need a man on the ground with me to cover while I survey the other side of the plane."

He doesn't wait for someone to volunteer. He picks up his rifle, folds in the bipod legs, and descends the stairs with the weapon raised. He chances a quick look over his shoulder and sees Duce right behind him, scanning the area with the butt of his rifle at his shoulder. Diesel stays tight at Duce's six.

Ghost drops to the pavement beneath the plane, rifle balanced on its bipod. Duce and Diesel pace back and forth under the plane, checking every angle as they go. After several slow sweeps with his high-powered scope, Ghost calls the all-clear.

He keeps his rifle pressed into his shoulder, watching still, as the unit descends the stairs. Shea and Christian are kept in the middle of the formation. Shea's head is down, her hand resting on top of Christian's head. She's always protective of him. Ghost respects that. Even now, she moves like a shield.

Cap gives seating assignments across the four SUVs. He separates Shea and Christian and places them in the middle of the vehicle they are assigned to. Ghost takes the cargo area of the third SUV, just in case.

As they head toward the hotel, there is no music. They stay in contact via the comms in their ears. They're all on the lookout for anything suspicious, on high alert.

126 | Shea

Shea worries about Christian and all her new friends the entire drive to the hotel. Her knee won't stop bouncing, fingers tugging at the straps on her suit. Cap reaches over and rests a reassuring hand on her knee. She looks over at him. His soft smile helps a little.

I can't believe I'm back in hell…

When they pull up to the beachfront hotel, Cap explains it's actually a timeshare he's had for a long time. The property consists of two buildings, each five stories. The SUVs pull in front of the office, parallel to the distance between the two buildings.

Shea is told to remain in the vehicle until the unit clears the property and the route to their room. Cap remains with her, for her protection. She hears over the comms that John is staying with Christian.

She watches through the tinted window as the unit moves with practiced grace toward the building their room is in. She's amazed at how well Diesel has taken to his training, he walks practically attached to Duce's right leg. Diesel pausing when he pauses and moving when he moves. The unit splits and half the men go to clear the entire property. The other half takes the exterior elevator and stairs to the fifth floor.

Fifteen minutes later, they return. The unit surrounds Shea and Christian as they move to the elevator. Shea rides up with Christian, Cap, Matt, Duce, and Diesel. The others run up the stairs to meet them at the room. On the fifth floor, their door is directly ahead, with other rooms to the left and right. They stand there waiting for Cap, who had gone to the front office to check in.

"Alright, watch out," he says, as he steps off the elevator.

The unit forms a half circle around Shea, Cap, and Christian, letting them enter first.

"I'll stay on watch for a little while, make sure everything is copesetic," Teddy says, standing guard at the door.

Once everyone except Teddy is in the condo, Cap says, "This unit has two bedrooms and a pullout. Considering several of you will be on watch overnight, this shouldn't be a problem. Shea, John, Dr. P, Christian, and Diesel will take the master. The second room has two beds. There is a pullout, another couch, and a few reclining chairs besides that. You can figure it out. I'll take watch tonight, but tomorrow I expect one of those beds."

Shea listens, but she must admit she's distracted.

Christian walks enthusiastically around the condo, checking everything out. He opens the fridge in the full kitchen, then disappears down the hall to the bedrooms. A second later, he reappears through a set of double doors at the far end of the unit. He peeks through one of the long floor-length curtains and gasps. His pure excitement shining out of him.

As soon as Cap finishes talking, Shea heads over to Christian. He grabs a wand hanging from the curtain, and pushes it open several feet. Sunlight hits her full in the face, reflecting off the ocean. The beauty of it renders her speechless. As she stands there stunned, Christian is trying to get the sliding door open.

Cap starts over to them as soon as the curtain is open and closes it swiftly.

"Hey!" Christian protests.

"SBD, you're in danger here. We need to be careful," Cap explains.

"He's never seen a beach…" Shea says, hurt for him.

"I understand, but we're on a mission, not a vacation."

"Fuck that," Shea says, almost surprising herself.

The room goes silent and turns toward her.

"We have plenty of protection. You guys cleared the property, and this is a private beach from what I can tell. He's a kid. He's had a life of captivity. You're not gonna drop us on a beach and tell us we can't touch!" she complains, voice slightly raised.

"Shea, it isn't safe!"

"Todd has no idea we're here yet. We would know if he did. We have more than one person on the inside! His goons aren't just combing the beaches of Florida. Once Dr. P gets here, I'll understand added security. But we can't not live. This man has taken enough from us."

She looks over at Christian, and says, "Go put on some shorts. I have some sunscreen. We're going to the beach!"

127 | JOHN

John watches Shea stand her ground. The second she mentions Dr. P, he checks his watch. "Shit!"

He runs to the second bedroom and dials her number. She answers on the second ring.

"Hello?"

"I'm so sorry I'm late. Are you okay?" he asks.

"Yeah, I'm fine. Are you okay?"

"Yeah. Sorry. Shea's pushing back against Cap. I got pulled into their orbit."

"So what's the plan? Tina kept Todd busy all morning, but that window is quickly closing. I need to go to lunch."

"Okay. There's a Publix on A1A in Satellite. It should take you like forty-five minutes to get there. It's going to make your goons suspicious, so play it cool when you walk in. Slow walk it to produce, look around a bit. I'll see you there."

"Okay, I'll leave here now. Will you stay on the phone, just so you can hear that I make it out? I'll hang up once I'm in my car."

"Of course. Put me in your pocket."

"Thank you!"

He stays on the line, walking back out to the living room. Shea is now crying and the men have clearly picked sides.

He continues to listen to the phone, but knows he needs to intervene here, or it's gonna get ugly.

"Matt, Terry, Hoover, and Innie, grab Teddy and get in civvies. You're coming with me to get P," he orders.

"Copy," Matt says, pulling hoover with him toward the back bedroom as the other men follow.

He can hear Dr. P, muffled and steady. So far, so good.

"Duce, Diesel, Gas, and Tank, take Shea and Christian to the damn beach!"

"Eye-eye CAP-tain!" Duce jokes.

"Okay, I'm leaving now. See you soon," he hears Dr. P say softly through the phone.

"Cap and DD, guard the room. Ghost you're on overwatch with a spotting scope from the balcony. Keep them safe."

"Who died and made you boss?" Cap asks, half-grin obvious in his voice.

"Cap, she's right. You can't just lock them up. There are plenty of us to ensure their safety. You're being un-yielding. I don't know if you haven't learned this about Shea yet, but she doesn't do well with that. Especially when it's regarding Christian. If there's even a sniff of danger they'll come back up, right Shea?"

"Yes. Of course," she says, sniffling.

"Fine. But it's your ass if something happens!" Cap says.

A few minutes later Matt, Terry, Hoover, Teddy, and Innie parade into the living room in the ugliest Hawaiian shirts John has ever seen.

"What is this?" he asks.

"Trying to blend in with the locals, bro," Matt says.

"Go through my bag, each of you pick a shirt. Take these off and burn them!"

They come back out wearing brands like Hurley, Nike, and Columbia fishing.

"That's better. Now let's move!"

Dr. P drives the speed limit. It's taking everything in her not to press the pedal to the floor. She keeps an eye on her rearview mirror. One vehicle seems to make all the same lane changes she does. There appears to only be two men in the car, both wearing suits. But they aren't close enough for her to be sure.

She finds the Publix John told her about and parks. This time she doesn't need to psych herself up to leave the car. She has to talk herself down from sprinting for the automatic doors. She puts one heeled foot in front of the other, pretending to be on a leisurely walk in the Florida heat, bags slung over her shoulder.

When she enters the building the blast of air-conditioning instantly cools her skin. She starts out for the produce section, chancing a glance over her shoulder. There are two men in suits trailing her about ten feet back. They aren't even pretending to do anything other than follow her. She moseys by the bakery and the deli, pausing here and there to make it look like she's trying to make a selection for lunch.

When she gets to produce she stops in front of each item. Staring at the lettuce, then potatoes, bananas, and so on. The men linger around the deli, keeping a little more distance now. As she looks at the precut fruit, she hears a man's voice behind her.

"Go through the double doors to the back of the store. Don't rush. Just go."

This is it. Her legs are shaking now. She's so close.

She pushes one of the large grey swinging doors open and walks through. She hears arguing behind her as soon as she's on the other side of the door. She looks around but doesn't see anyone back here. Was there a problem?

She hears a whistle and looks toward the sound. A loading bay door in the very back is open. Several feet below it, stands John with another man. She jogs over to him, sits on the edge and drops down the distance to the ground outside.

John catches her and pulls her into his arms, wrapping her in his warmth. He pulls her away from himself slightly, looks into her eyes then kisses her.

She forgets the world she is running from and sinks deeper into him. The kiss telling her something he has never said out loud.

He breaks the kiss at the persistence of his friend, and they pile into a nearby SUV. They drive without speeding down the highway.

"What about your friend?" she asks. "The one who told me to head to the back?"

"He has his own SUV. He's going to take them on a wild goose chase. That was Matt, my brother," John explains.

"Oh, I didn't see him. Just heard him. How far are we from the hotel? I can't wait to get my hands on Shea!"

John smiles. "We're going in the wrong direction, just in case. We'll probably drive around for an hour or so, before we head back."

129 | GREGGORY

Greggory tries to replay the picture in his mind, over and over, but nothing else comes. He burns through the few hours he has to wait until the doctor returns to his cell.

"Alright, you have remained seizure free, so we will allow you one hour of screen time. If you are able to tolerate that, a couple of hours later we'll test it again."

"So I can have my phone?" Greggory asks.

"Yes. But there is no reception down here, and the Wi-Fi is encrypted. Usually personal devices aren't allowed."

"No problem. I have a game on there that I like to play," Greggory says.

"Alright. Let us know if you develop a headache or any neurological symptoms," the doctor orders, handing the phone to him.

Greggory sets it in his lap and waits for the doctor to leave. The second the cell door closes, he's hacking the network. Within just a couple minutes he's in and has the encrypted text messaging app open. He texts Dr. P.

Text to Dr. P at 1440

« I need more pictures, ASAP. As many as you can send of me with Shea. I only have one hour. Please hurry!

He sets his phone down. Something about a watched pot never boiling. He closes his eyes. Minutes crawl by. Anxiety builds. What if she doesn't answer him in time?

At the thirty-minute mark, he grabs his phone again and picks a different contact, one Dr. P added in case of an emergency.

Text to ICE at 1515

« This is Greggory. I need as many pictures as you can send that include both Shea
and me. Please hurry. I don't have much time.

130 | Shea

Shea reads the text from her lounge chair on the beach. Christian plays at the water's edge, giggling as he runs from the waves.

Duce approaches, he probably saw the shift in her posture from relaxed to rigid.

"You okay, Shea?" he asks.

"Yeah. I just got a text that said it's from Gregg. Is that possible?"

"I can check with our inside man. He can find out."

"It says to hurry. That he doesn't have much time. Can you find out like right now?" Urgency in every word.

"Yeah. I'll have Cap call. Gimme just a minute."

She waits rereading the words. It sounds like he didn't know who he was texting. If it's even him at all.

I hope it is him…

She forces herself to focus on Christian instead, pointing out shells for him to collect. He rinses each one in the surf before bringing it to her and displaying it like treasure.

Duce returns. "Cap says he does have his phone, but not for much longer."

"Thank you, Duce."

She opens the message thread and attaches the entire folder of photos that include him.

Text to Gregg at 1522

<142 photos attached>

Text from Gregg at 1522

» Thank you!

131 | GREGGORY

As soon as the text comes through, Greggory opens the file. He scrolls quickly through the photos, wanting to see them all. But his time's running out. He picks five pictures, each one a different scene, and memorizes as many details as he can.

He saves the original file to a password protected folder on his phone, which doesn't show up without a perfectly placed thumbprint. With only minutes left, he disconnects from the network and opens a simple search-and-find game he has downloaded to his phone.

The doctor arrives right on time, walking into the room with an air of authority.

"Well, that went well. Any symptoms?" he asks, taking the phone from Greggory's outstretched hand.

"No. I feel great. No headache or anything."

"Great. We'll give that a couple of hours and work on titrating down the medications in the meantime. You could be out of here in a few days at this rate."

"I'm sure I will," Greggory says, thinking of Clara's message.

"We'll leave you to it. Get some rest. I'll be back in a few hours, or sooner if there's any seizure activity."

"Thanks, doc."

When the glass door to his cell is closed, he lays back on his pillow and closes his eyes. He brings one of the images to his mind. That pre-seizure sensation flutters at the edge of his awareness. But the seizure never comes. Instead, the picture comes to life.

It's him, Shea, and a tiny puppy. Shea has her hand outstretched toward the camera. His own face watches her, appearing elated. The puppy has its forepaws on Greggory's chest, and its neck is stretched toward his face, tongue out in preparation for a lick. He focuses on it, waiting.

The moment expands. A tall man stands in front of them, smiling, holding the dog. He watches himself carrying Shea, their faces aglow with love. They sit on the couch. She kisses his face, which is covered in a short beard. The puppy jumps into his lap. She throws her head back laughing. She extends her arm and flicks down her hand. A diamond ring sparkles in the light.

He watches that version of himself watch her, like he can't believe how happy she is about it.

He wants to imagine all five pictures right away, but he decides to sit with this one a little while longer.

John focuses on the task at hand, watching for any signs of a tail. Thirty minutes in, no sign of Todd's goons. He starts to relax, just a little. Terry continues to drive cautiously, edging slightly above the speed limit to keep up with traffic. Hoover and Teddy sit in the back row of the SUV. Dr. P sits alone in the middle. John turns in his seat and sees the tension written all over her.

"Hey. It's okay. We haven't seen anyone," he says to Dr. P.

"I feel like all my nerves are exposed, or something. I'm trying to use a trick that Gregg taught me, but I can't stop watching the window. I keep thinking every car that gets close to us is full of men in suits."

"You don't need to be on lookout. You're in a vehicle full of men that know what to watch for and when to act. You're safe." He reaches back and squeezes her knee.

"I know. I just can't believe it could have been that easy," she says.

"You said yourself he's tied up in meetings until around this time, right? We're making sure we're back at the condo as soon as possible. We'll be okay."

"Alright," she agrees, though her eyes stray to the window again.

John turns back toward the front and goes back to his watch. A few minutes later, his phone dings with a text.

Text from Matt at 1605

» No tail, kind of weird. Making return path now

Text to Matt at 1605

« No tail here either. Us too. How far out are you?

Text from Matt at 1605

» Like 10 min, wish it was sooner… Innie is farting this SUV up and I can't roll down the window! Help!

Text to Matt at 1606

« LOL that's why I sent him with you in the first place! We're 15 out. Stay by the outdoor elevator til we pull in

Text from Matt at 1606

» 10-4

Thirteen or so minutes later, their SUV pulls up in front of their building. The men get out and surround Dr. P, guiding her to the elevator. Once she is safely inside the condo, John breathes a sigh of relief.

Though, he does feel like that went a little too smoothly.

133 | Todd

"What do you mean you lost her?" Todd asks into his phone, calmly.

"Sir, there were several men and multiple vehicles. They were on the road before we even got back to the car. They distracted us," his man answers, voice trembling with fear.

"Mistakes happen. Get back to campus. I appreciate the update," Todd says, ending the call.

He presses the intercom button on his desk phone, summoning Tina without a word.

When she enters his office, he can tell she has been crying. Her eyes are puffy and red. She keeps sniffling.

"Yes, sir," she says, devoid of emotion.

"Tina. Take a seat."

She perches on the edge of the chair, wringing her hands in her lap.

"I assume you held up your end of the bargain?" he asks, a smile in his voice.

"Yes."

"Fantastic. I think I'll keep your collateral a little while longer, just in case you get any ideas about helping the prisoners," he says, his words dripping with malice.

"Please, Todd. Hurt me. Punish me. Leave them out of it. Please," she begs, emotion thick in her voice.

He smirks. "Now, Tina, what would be the fun in that? They're safe and will stay that way, until you fuck up."

"I'll do whatever you ask. Please. Just let me take Ren and Stimpy home. You don't need them anymore. I put the tracker on Dr. P this morning, just like you asked. Please!"

"Do as I say, or I'll return those rats to you piece by piece. Go clean yourself up and get back to work."

He turns his attention to his desktop computer. He pulls up the tracker beacon, already planning his next move before she even reaches the door.

134 | Shea

Shea treks up the beach toward the condo, Christian's hand in hers. When Duce came and alerted them Dr. P had arrived, Shea started packing up immediately. She glances down at Christian's face, lit up with excitement.

"You excited to see Dr. P, bud?" she asks.

"Yeah. More excited that it's close now. Plus, goofy-happy John."

"Closer to rescuing everyone?"

"Yeah!"

"And goofy-happy John because he's in llllooOoooovveeee?" she sing-songs.

Christian chuckles, and matter-of-factly says, "They both are."

Shea smiles to herself and presses the button to call the elevator. When the elevator rises to their floor, Shea is practically tackled as soon as it opens. Dr. P holds her tightly, her body shaking.

"Hey. Are you okay?" Shea whispers in her ear.

Dr. P pulls back a foot and places her hands on either side of Shea's pregnant belly. Her expression is unreadable, but tears shine in her eyes.

"Hey. What's going on? Talk to me," Shea encourages.

"It sounds horrible, but I'm just so grateful you needed a doctor all those months ago. Things are crazy, but I'm just so grateful," she says, tears spilling onto her cheeks. "And I'm so excited to meet little Abel! Did you like the blankets?"

Instead of answering Shea leads her into the master suite and gestures to both blankets spread out on the bed.

"I love them. That was such a thoughtful gift. Thank you."

"It was fun working on them with Gregg. He's fun to be around still. He's in there. Tina warned me he might be hostile in person at first, but I'm sure we'll figure it out," Dr. P reports.

"He texted me today. It seemed like he didn't know it was me. He was asking for more pictures. You know anything about that?"

"Yeah, I saved your number as ICE—in case of emergency. He must have thought it was one?"

"I guess he only had his phone for a short time and needed the pictures before they took it," Shea speculates.

"That's good. He's trying. I saw a missed text on my phone, but the content was deleted. I should have known it was him. I was busy getting rescued."

"So you met everyone, already?" Shea asks, sitting on the edge of the bed.

"Yeah. They're all hilarious. Although I think Innie needs to see a gastroenterologist for a serious case of flatulence."

Shea chuckles. "So he needs a stomach doctor for farting in other words?"

"Ha, yeah."

"Let's go figure out what's for dinner. Abel's hungry," Shea says, standing from her spot on the edge of the bed.

When they walk into the living room, they descend into chaos. They hear the voice of Ghost, who is on overwatch on the roof, through the comms.

"Two inbound SUVs. Blacked out. No visible license plates. Men inside appear to be wearing suits. Half a click out. Advise."

135 | Tina

Tina sits in her office, waiting for Todd to leave. He's been shut in his office for hours. She needs him gone—long enough to find Ren and Stimpy. She risks pulling up the video feeds, searching for any signs of them. But nothing.

Frustrated, she grabs her laptop and leaves building 4.

She takes a golf cart across campus and enters building 25. She uses her credentials to ride the high security elevator to the fifth floor, and stalks across the floor to the pod of glass cells.

At the entrance, she hesitates. What if Todd sees the footage before Greggory can wipe it? The thought makes her stomach twist. He'll take it out on her babies. But knowing there's no other option, she opens the glass cell.

She finds Greggory awake. He looks surprised to see her. She stays outside of the room, in a camera blind spot. "I need your help," she says, unshed tears clogging her throat.

"Okay," he agrees, no questions asked.

"I'm going to put my laptop on this tray and roll it into the room. I need you to access the cameras and see if you can find my ferrets. Please." Her voice pleading even though he's already agreed.

"Ren and Stimpy? Is everything okay?"

"I don't know…we don't have a lot of time," she says, pushing the cart to his bedside.

She watches him—she can tell by his face that he's on the network within seconds. She stays where she is, keeping a look out. She remains quiet, letting him work.

"I'm not seeing anything, Tina. I've checked everywhere, even the stairwells. I'd assume they'd be in a carrier or a cage, but I just don't see anything. I'm sorry," he says.

"Shit, okay. Okay, I'll figure it out. Thank you, Greggory."

He holds out the laptop, saying, "I erased the footage from the time you got here. In self-interest I looped the footage in the glass cells. There will be no way for them to know. It won't come back on you."

She walks forward into his cell and grabs the laptop. She looks at him with newfound admiration. "You're a really great guy, Greggory. I hope all this works out for you. I'm sorry for my part in it." Tears run down her face.

"Why is this door open?" She hears from the doorway.

Tina panics. She stammers out an answer, "I…well…Todd…"

Greggory saves her with his quick thinking. "She was sent to see how I'd do with a larger screen. They thought you had gone home since you were late to do the test. She let me type a letter for my mom. She was going to send it out for me, I missed her birthday."

Tina's shocked at first, then she schools her features and nods along with what Greggory says.

"Well then, that's great! Brain function remained normal, I assume?" the doctor asks.

"Yes, sir. I'm feeling great, really. Can I get out of here soon?"

"Soon. We're still titrating down the medications. We need to get them as low as we can or get you off them. If you stay seizure free—then yes, you're out of here. I'll speed up the titration since you're doing so well."

"Awesome. Thanks, doc."

Tina is amazed. Even she believes his excitement. She holds her laptop against her chest, and says, "Well, it's getting close to quitting time. I'll go print this letter and get it sent." She nods at Greggory, then to the doctor, and slips out of the room.

She walks straight out of the building and takes the golf cart to her car. Once inside she breaks. She sits there for over half an hour, crying. She tells herself she deserves this.

Ghost awaits orders, eyes locked on the approaching vehicles. Just in case, he grips the bolt handle, lifts it up and pulls it back. The chamber is empty. They didn't want any of their guns hot around Christian. He pushes the bolt forward and hears the solid thunk as a round is chambered. He shoves the bolt handle home.

"Are they still approaching?" Cap's voice comes over the comms.

"10-4. Four hundred yards and closing."

"How's traffic?" Cap asks.

"Pretty heavy. No clear shot."

"Shit. John's gonna bring you up one of the tranq rifles. All valuable targets will be in east bedroom."

"Copy."

Ghost lays down his rifle and carefully moves to the roof access. When the hatch opens, he sees a tranq rifle being passed up through it.

"John, I know you need to get back down there, but there has to be a tracker on her. This makes no sense. You did everything right. Sweep her," Ghost says, pulling the rifle through.

"Fuck. Yeah. Okay. Shit. She's gonna blame herself..." his voice trails off as he lowers himself down the ladder.

"Fuck!" is the last thing Ghost hears from him.

A second later, John's voice comes through comms. "Somebody sweep P, and potentially the entire suite."

Ghost slides back down to his position on the roof. He sets the tranq rifle down and picks his tried and true back up, settling behind the scope. It's still just the two vehicles approaching. But they're much closer now. And there is still no real plan in place. He keeps them centered in his sights and waits.

137 | JOHN

John rushes down the ladder and back to the suite. Hoover and Innie open the door as he reaches it.

"Hey, we're on perimeter. Gas and Tank are heading out too. The plan is to tranq and relocate the suits. We're gonna have to get out of here soon. P's freaking out about a tracker, locked herself in the bathroom. They need your help," Tank reports.

"Got it. Thanks. Be safe out there."

John heads to the back bedroom and walks straight to the bathroom. He knocks. "Boo, you need to come out. They're almost done sweeping the condo and they need to sweep you. This isn't your fault. We should have swept you at Publix."

She opens the door, tears in her eyes. "This feels like my fault," she says, her voice cracking.

"I know, but it's not," he says, pulling her against his chest. "We have to check you out. Go to Cap."

He watches as she stands in front of Cap, head hanging in shame. There was no way for her, or any of them, to know. But that doesn't matter and he knows it. She will blame herself until this is all over.

Cap waves the detector over her and nothing happens.

"Shit, it's not in the room?" John asks.

"No, I checked," Cap says.

"Everyone line up. It might have transferred," John orders.

The remainder of the unit, along with Christian and Shea, line up in front of

Cap. One by one he waves the detector over each of them.

When it's Shea's turn, the detector chirps near her upper arm.

Dr. P gasps, clamping a hand over her mouth. "I'm so sorry. It must have been when I hugged you."

John rushes over. He and Cap lean in close to Shea's arm, trying to see what the detector picked up on. Finally, they spot it. It's smaller than a grain of rice. Cap plucks it free, brings it close to his face, then tosses it on the ground and crushes it under his boot.

John looks at him like he's lost his mind. "We could have burned it?"

"It wasn't just a tracker. It was also a mic. Have we talked about operations since Dr. P got here?" Cap asks.

"I don't think so," John says, eyes wide.

"Inbound. Pulling into the parking lot. Advise!" Ghost says over comms.

138 | Tina

After regaining her composure, Tina opens the laptop she brought into the car. She checks Todd's mission status to estimate how long he'll be occupied. According to the log, they're just now pulling into Dr. P's location. She should have plenty of time.

She's not going to run. She knows what she deserves. But her babies are innocent, and they don't deserve whatever he's plans to do to them. She makes a couple of calls, one to her lawyer and one to Dr. P.

When Dr. P answers, it's at a whisper, "Hello?"

"I'm so sorry, P. I had to. I had no choice. I'm sure everything is popping off over there, but I needed to tell you. And I know I shouldn't ask, because of everything, but I need you to watch after my ferrets, when… when…"

"I understand. I will."

The line goes dead. That's one thing handled.

After meeting with her lawyer for thirty minutes, she heads to their massive empty house. She unlocks the door and walks straight to Todd's office. It's locked, of course, but she's not letting that stop her today.

She goes out to the garage and finds a small four-pound sledgehammer. When she lifts it, it feels way heavier than four pounds. She carries it with both hands.

Arriving back at the office door, she allows the disappointment, abuse, and hate to flow freely, for the first time.

She breathes in ragged pants, as she lifts the hammer over her head and brings it down on the door handle with everything she has. She hits the handle and the space where the door meets the door jam, the wood splintering. In a blind fury, she keeps smashing until there's a jagged hole where the latch used to sit in the door frame. Wiping sweat from her brow, she uses a heeled foot to kick the door all the way open.

Inside, she goes through his unlocked drawers first. Nothing useful. She takes the sledgehammer to the locked drawers, breaking them open and searching through the contents. She takes several files and drops them near the door.

Finally, she turns and faces his wall of screens. Disgust coils in her stomach at the lack of privacy he forced on her.

She takes a step towards them. Her knees go out from under her. The sledgehammer slips from her hand onto the hardwood floor with a loud thud.

139 | GHOST

Ghost hears over comms, "Tranq rounds only. Take them down. Ghost—Hoover, Innie, Gas, and Tank are under your overwatch."

Ghost switches back to the tranq rifle now that the SUVs have pulled into the lot. The scope isn't the same, but he can see what he needs to just fine.

He hasn't seen Hoover, Innie, Gas, or Tank, yet. He assumes they are still under the cover of the building, waiting for the suits to move.

He watches through the scope. Although all the windows are blacked out, he can see through the windshields. In one SUV, the driver glances at the passenger, who is on the phone, probably awaiting orders. In the second SUV, the men sit perfectly still, eerily so.

Ghost shifts between the two vehicles, waiting for movement.

Ten minutes pass. "No movement. Is someone watching the back?"

"10-4. No goons," Cap replies.

"This is weird…" Ghost mutters.

After a few more minutes, all of the doors to both SUVs open at once.

"We've got movement," Ghost says.

The men are a well-coordinated unit, stepping out and standing behind their respective doors as cover. There is no sound, just eight identical movements as they all reach for their sidearms. Ghost tracks the first group as they close their doors one by one and head under the cover of the building. Just before they slip out of his eyeline, they crumble to the ground.

The second group raises their weapons toward the building but they don't fire. One of them breaks off and heads around the back of the building.

"One incoming to the rear," he says, over comms.

"Got him," Teddy replies.

The remaining three hold their ground. Seeing no other choice, Ghost orders, "Hoover, Tank, flank them and take them out quietly."

He watches Hoover slip around the exterior elevator, using it as cover. He takes the two men on his side out. Tank doesn't have the benefit of cover on his side. He sprints low to the front of the SUV, drops to a knee and fires. Shooting the final man in the leg with a tranq.

"All targets are down," Ghost confirms.

140 | GREGGORY

Greggory sits with his eyes closed, replaying the photos he saw earlier. He's surprised when he hears the door to his cell open. He assumed the doctor went home after their interaction.

When he opens his eyes, a tall man in fatigues stands in the doorway. Greggory's never seen him before. He watches curiously as the man walks toward him.

"I'm sure you don't recognize me. That's by design. I'm friends with some friends of your friends—who have run into a bit of trouble. I'm here because things are about to get a little… interesting," the man says.

Greggory pushes himself upright. "Is everyone okay? What's going to happen?"

"Everyone is fine. There's no sneaking up on that group of guys. Here's this," the man says, handing Greggory a tech device of some sort. It's the size of a standard smartphone but four times thicker. "It's on the network. One of their PDAs—mobile surveillance and control. I was told you would know what to do with it when the time comes."

"Yeah. Thanks," Greggory says, tapping through the different options on the screen to see what it can do.

"I don't know when it'll happen, but you'll know. Stay put until then and be safe."

"Okay. Are you helping Clara too?"

"No. You will. Just wait, okay? If an alarm goes off before it's supposed to, it could ruin everything. Dr. P vouched for you, said you could be trusted with this."

"I can, I will—thank you."

"Alright. I have to get back to my post. It'll be noticed if I'm gone too long. Trust your friends," he says, backing out of the cell and closing the door.

Since Greggory already looped the cameras, he continues investigating the device. It gives him access to every camera in the compound, all locks, alarms, and communications.

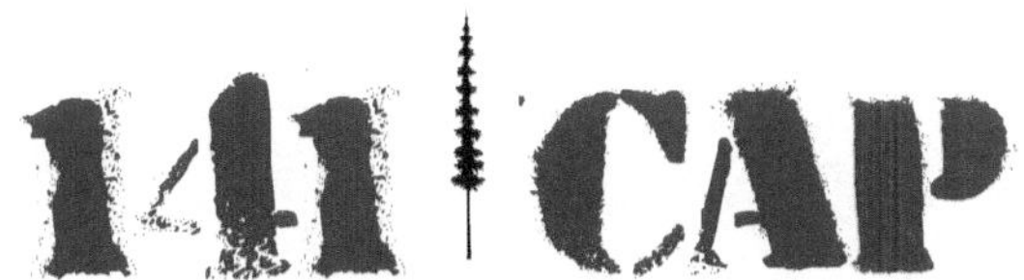

141 | CAP

"Alright, everybody, our hand has been forced," Cap says to the room full of his men, along with Shea, Christian, and Dr. P. Ghost listens over comms.

"Hoover and Tank finish what you started. Drive the unconscious men in their SUVs to the beach, ten minutes out. Gas, follow them in one of ours and bring them back here. After that, we clear the property. It's too hot to stay. All in favor of ending this tonight?"

Every hand shoots up, except Shea's. He looks at her, confused.

"Believe me, I want Gregg out of there like yesterday. I just worry because we've all been up since before four this morning. Are we going to be at our best? I mean, by time we actually get there… will we?" she asks.

"I understand your concerns. But we've all been deployed to unsafe regions, only sleeping for minutes at a time over several weeks. Anyone who feels like they need a snooze, grab it on the ride. There's also a vending machine full of energy drinks in the parking garage. Dealer's choice," Cap says, the men let out a few hoots.

His men thrive on this, they would be fine. He is worried about Shea, but the adrenaline will carry her once they get moving.

"I just don't want anyone getting hurt," she says, wiping her eyes.

"I know it's easy to get sucked into this band of nitwits, but worry is our enemy. We all have our missions, and that's where our focus needs to be. Worry gets in the way of focus. Is everyone clear on their assignment?" he asks.

"Yes, sir," comes from around the room.

Shea meets his eyes and shrugs. He knows she can't help it. Once they get moving, she'll get some pep in her step.

142 | Tina

From her spot on the floor, Tina can see all the screens clearly.

She weeps.

She can't believe she fell for it. He lied to her. He was so convincing to get her to do exactly what he wanted. Tina knows this is part of the problem. He's become so evil, that she never even questioned him. She believed him capable of what he said.

She stands and with a bit less gusto, destroys the screens with her sledgehammer. When she finishes, she drops the hammer and runs through the house, desperate to see with her own eyes.

She reaches the room and flings the door open. Her knees buckle again.

Ren and Stimpy run through clear tubes mounted along the wall. They are currently modeling one of Tina's favorite behaviors. They enter the tube from opposite ends, meeting somewhere in the middle. Once there, they nip and slap each other and engage in what she likes to call hippo play. They open their mouths as wide as they can, not biting, just taunting the other with their powerful teeth. It looks just like tiny hippos fighting.

She composes herself and walks into the room. She glides her nails along the ribbed surface of the tube, eliciting a noise that the ferrets love to follow. They follow the noise right out of the tube and tumble into a large ball pit. They dance and dook, making the happy noise of their species.

She scoops them up—no easy feat while they're mid-play, all wriggles and joy. She kisses their small faces and breaks down again.

This was going to be so hard.

She loves her ferrets just like a mother loves her children. They're her babies. She never thought anything would come between them, but she has to do what is right.

She deposits them back in the ball pit and walks over to the closet. Grabbing a large bag, resembling a diaper bag, she begins packing. She puts all the pillowcases they like sleeping in, blankets, food, treats, and toys in the bag.

Reaching deeper into the closet, she pulls out a cage, still in its box. She's gained their attention now. They both stand with their front paws on her lower legs. Stimpy digging at her for attention.

"I know, babies. I'm sorry," she whispers, as tears stream down her face.

"You'll be with Mama until the last minute, boys," she promises, sitting on the floor and soaking in every second of them. Before she can no longer…

She puts the cage together, wiping tears as she works. By the end, she is emotionally exhausted, and her ferrets sleep nearby. She stocks the cage with food, water, and their pillowcases before heading over to where they sleep.

She takes her time, scooping up Ren first. He stretches and yawns in her arms. She gently strokes his face, softly speaking words of undying love. After she puts him in the cage she reaches for his brother. Stimpy wakes up while she holds him, stretching his face toward hers and repeatedly licking her tear-streaked cheeks.

"Mama loves you so much. Thank you for the kisses," she coos at him, broken.

143 | Shea

Shea stands surrounded by tall, muscular men. Her Kevlar is strapped on, with loose fitting fatigues over it. Her hair is twisted into a messy bun. One hand holds Christian's hand and the other holds Dr. P's. They wait in a corner of the parking garage for Hoover, Tank, and Gas to return. They have been instructed to keep their mouths shut.

I think I might shit myself…

Her legs are shaking. Nervous energy courses through her. Her senses are on high alert. She is acutely aware of the salty smell of the ocean air and the stickiness of the humidity. She worries about what Gregg will say when he sees her. Will he ever remember her? She can't go on without him… raise his child, without him.

Christian's hand feels like it's coated in a thin layer of jelly, which is an actual possibility. She opens her hand taking a peek. It's clean.

He chuckles quietly. With constant connection to him, her thoughts aren't safe. She shoots him a mischievous grin. He doesn't seem worried at all. He's cool, calm, and collected.

Must be nice…

She watches as men peel off one at a time toward the vending machine. All of them purchase at least one can of energy drink, if not two. As one steps out of formation the others shift and sidestep to close the gap.

Shit, I should have brought a coffee

When the SUV containing Hoover, Gas, and Tank pulls into the parking garage beside the other three, Cap steps forward and faces them.

"Alright, same seating assignments as before. Dr. P in the third SUV. They're all unlocked. Before we load up, comms check?"

"Check, check, check," echoes all around the garage.

"Time?" Cap asks.

They all raise their wrists, comparing watches.

Cap says, "Time is 19:23:45…46…47."

"10-4," resounds around.

"Does everyone have a tranq rifle and sidearm?"

Each man lifts up his weapons for Cap to see. Shea raises her Security-9 pistol. Dr. P holds up a tranq rifle. Christian gives Diesel the command to 'speak'. His bark ringing out and echoing in the parking garage.

"We need guns hot, now."

Most had already ensured they had one in the chamber, but a few rack one in now. Shea and Dr. P do the same.

"Who has the laptop?" Cap asks.

"Got it, Cap," John says, holding it up.

"Concerns?" Cap asks.

The group goes silent.

"Alright then. Load up. Estimated time of breach of 25 and 4, 2130."

144 | Tina

Tina carries the bag and cage into the multi-car garage. She scans the row of vehicles, searching for an SUV large enough to fit the cage. She decides the 2025 Jeep Grand Wagoneer looks spacious enough. She takes all of her cargo over to it, loading the ferrets into the back. They climb around and push their noses through the bars of the cage. She closes the hatch and tries to keep herself together.

Using the running board, she climbs in and presses the push to start button. The keys sit in the cup holder. She opens the garage door, backs into the circle drive, and turns around. As she drives down the long driveway, the ferrets attack the bars of the cage, wanting out. She takes slow breaths and runs through her plan over and over again.

She's not afraid for herself. She genuinely believes that she deserves what is coming. But her chest twists at the thought of anything happening to her babies. She worries about the life they'll have without her. Will they be taken care of properly and be loved.

She feels selfish that she's destroyed by the fact that she won't get another sweet kiss, or feel the unconditional love of these sweet, loving creatures. What if they decide to just bring them to a shelter?

She knows she's done all of them wrong, very wrong—but she hopes Ren and Stimpy won't be punished for her mistakes. The people she has wronged are all very caring. All she can do is hope and trust.

She pulls up to building 25 and parks right out front. She pops open the hatch, closes the driver's side door, and walks around. The ferrets continue to attack the cage as she pulls it out. She makes sure her keycard is in her right hand for the sensors, pulls the bag strap across her body, and picks up the cage.

She opens the main door to 25 easily enough but has to put the cage down to access the elevator. Once she reaches Todd's uninhabited office, she places the now calm ferrets beside the desk and covers the cage with a sheet.

She sits behind the desk, feeling like an imposter and logs onto the computer. Her last act as a free woman will be to document everything Todd has done over the years. She will make sure he also gets what he deserves.

145 ✝ Todd

Todd stares at the mission log, irate. His men are MIA, as is his secretary. He switches the screen, logging into his home camera server. He doesn't see Tina anywhere, but the destruction she left stares back at him. His anger rises.

"Stupid bitch," he mutters, clicking through cameras.

He notices the ferret room door is slightly open. She never leaves it like that…smart girl.

He flips to the cameras within the compound and finds her quickly. She is sitting at his desk in 25… stupid girl.

With one phone call, he orders Mr. Time to pay her a visit. He sits back, enlarging the camera view and watches. There's no sound, he didn't want his privacy to be invaded in that way. But the picture is enough.

Mr. Time walks into his office in 25 with a large duffel bag slung over his shoulder. Tina stands behind his desk, hands splayed out on the desk, head down. As Mr. Time approaches her, his lips move. Tina remains still.

Todd's anger begins to ebb, turning into wrathful vengeance in his veins.

"You'll get what you deserve bitch," he mutters, reclining in his chair, closely watching the screen.

146 | GHOST

Ghost sits in the cargo area of the third SUV with his rifle at his side. He watches through a spotting scope, giving each window thirty seconds before shifting to the next. The rest of the SUV sits heavy and silent, like a held breath.

He knows they're all fraying when Gas opens an energy drink and the others start giggling.

"Slap happy, much?" Dr. P says, which is met with more laughter. "Seriously, we could be walking into our deaths, and you guys are laughing?"

That's apparently the funniest thing any of them have ever heard. Ghost chuckles as he continues watch.

"It's nervous energy. We've all been to war. Instinct will take over, but for now… Yeah, slap happy is a good way to describe it," Gas explains to Dr. P.

"Oh, so no laughing when we're in the compound?" she asks.

"No way, that's work time—always serious when it's work time."

"We never know what's gonna happen. It can be scary, so why be so serious all the way there? There's nothing we can do until we're there. Besides that, if we don't get it out now, who knows what would happen during the op," Innie adds.

Ghost continues his watch as the vehicle goes silent again. He hasn't seen any threats but remains vigilant.

"We're about five miles from the access road according to the GPS. Get your game faces on," Teddy says, as he drives.

When they get about a mile and a half out, Teddy pulls the SUV over to the side of the road, in line with the others. Without needing a command, Ghost opens the hatch and hops out with his rifle. He climbs onto the roof of the SUV, lies flat on his stomach, and sets up his rifle.

Over comms, Cap says, "Ghost is on watch. Once he gives the okay, we will unload one SUV at a time. Starting with one."

As Ghost studies the compound, he can see the guard box and the single guard within. There are only ten vehicles within the compound. With three rotating guard shifts patrolling the buildings they needed access to.

"Clear from us to the guard box," he reports.

"Alright men, you know what to do. It's time. Keep the high value targets in the middle of formation," Cap orders.

As soon as Cap gives the order, all the SUV doors swing open wide.

147 | Tina

The moment the door opens, Tina knows it's bad news. She looks up to see Mr. Time standing at the door, duffel bag over his shoulder. She hasn't had much interaction with him, making her unsure about what's going to happen. She did have a feeling someone would come but honestly thought it would be Todd himself.

She stands, placing her hands on the desk. Her head hung, she asks, "Are you here to kill me?"

He walks a few steps closer, closing the door. "No. I've been ordered to remove any of Crown's property from your person."

She looks up at him, confused. "What, like my badge?" She pulls it from her top and tosses it at him. "Here."

"That, and…" he trails off, letting the rest hang.

While she thinks about it, he walks over and places the duffel bag on the edge of the large desk. Opening it, he removes a paper drape and spreads it out. He places alcohol swabs, a scalpel, mosquito hemostat and sutures on top of it.

Watching him, the reality of her situation dawns on her. "No…"

"Yes. I'm sorry. This room has no audio. Do you have your affairs in order?"

"What do you care?" she spits.

"I work for Crown for a paycheck. I work for someone else out of loyalty."

"What, like God?" she asks, confused.

"No. Like my old military buddies who are going to level this place in a few hours. You have been the source of a lot of pain for them, but you've also done a lot to make up for it. So I'll ask again. Are your affairs in order?"

"Yes. I just… I was finishing some stuff up, but it's fine. I guess none of it matters now anyway."

"Are you going to cooperate? I brought some feel-good drugs if you do," he says.

"Yes, I just…" she pauses, unable to say it before tears are rolling down her cheeks.

He notices her eyes fixed on the cage nearby, and nods.

She walks over and pulls the sheet off the cage. They both look up at her from their hammock. She opens the cage and lifts Ren, who is lying with his head on Stimpy's back. She holds him close, trying to memorize every detail of his face, even though she knows the memory will soon be gone. She does the same with Stimpy, who is more affectionate than Ren. He licks her face as she tries to memorize his, as well.

She places them back in the hammock. She can feel his eyes on her, but she needs a proper goodbye.

"You'll be okay. I wouldn't leave you with just anyone. I love you both so much. I'm sorry it has to be like this. I wish I could stay with you forever. Bye, babies," she says through the bars, then pulls the sheet back over them.

Turning to Mr. Time, she wipes her face and nods.

"I am sorry about this, but he's watching. I have to complete the task. You're sure everything is in place that needs to be?" he asks again.

"Yes. Can I lay on the couch for this?"

"Yeah. That's fine."

She walks over and lies down, her head resting on the armrest. She closes her eyes.

"I'm going to give you some IV meds. They'll work fast. You'll feel a little pinch."

"Okay."

She feels the pinch. Within a few seconds, she feels almost nothing—not in her body, or in her heart. She hears him speaking but can't make out the words. She feels stinging on her scalp, but within a few seconds that's gone too.

Her eyes remain closed. She feels like she's floating.

His voice breaks through the fog this time. "I'm sorry, Tina. I'm going to pull the implant now. I know Shea got back her memories, but your implant has had more time to burrow into your brain. I'm not sure if it will be the same for you. Are you ready?" he asks.

"Make sure nothing happens to them. Please. Dr. P agreed to take them. Just make sure he doesn't get to them. Please?"

"I'll move them somewhere safe. They should be here soon. Ready?"

"Yes."

She feels a pulling sensation, then loses all manner of thought.

148 | MR. TIME

Mr. Time pulls the implant from the small hole in Tina's skull and drops it into the trash. He reinstalls the plug and sutures the wound shut. He makes sure she's still breathing, then picks up the diaper bag and the cage and leaves the room.

He doesn't have to carry it far. There's only one place he thinks will be safe until the unit arrives.

He swipes his keycard to access the cell. The door opens to a confused looking Greggory.

"I don't have much time. These are Tina's ferrets. I'm putting you in charge of keeping them safe. Everything they need is in this diaper-bag-looking thing. I'm also leaving this duffel bag, so you don't have to carry the cage when they come for you. We'll come by later to grab it. They should be contacting you any minute. They should be here soon. I need to get back, so they don't suspect me until the last moment. Can you do this?"

"Uh, yeah. I love animals. I've got this," Greggory answers.

"Good. Keep that device on and ready. It should be any minute."

"Okay."

Greggory gets off of his bed and crouches near the cage.

Mr. Time leaves and opens Clara's cell. He knows she isn't completely sedated because he's the one that turned it down. He walks to her bedside and again adjusts the rate of her infusion. Her head tilts slightly toward him.

"Very soon now. I'm putting a pair of small scissors in the drawer back here so Greggory can snip your sutures. He'll need to turn off the machines you're hooked to, clamp the lines, and detach them. There are caps for each line in the drawer too.

Can you remember that?"

Her head nods faintly.

"Good. You're barely getting any sedation now. By the time he comes in to help you, you should barely even feel high."

He heads out to the guard box to get an update on how many men Todd has put on the night shift. As he steps inside, he can see Jeff—the current guard—is nodding off. Excellent.

"Hey, Jeff. How many we got on tonight?" he asks.

"Uh, Todd just ordered increased patrols to the perimeter and around 4 and 25. We currently have twenty-two guards on duty, another eight are MIA, and he wants me to call ten more in before ten tonight. He's offering double time to any guard that makes it in. I'm sure I'll have no trouble staffing."

"So by ten tonight, we'll be at thirty-two on duty with another eight unaccounted for?" Mr. Time clarifies.

"Yeah. He said to be on high alert. He sounded pissed. I'd steer clear."

"I know you would, Jeff. I'm a different type of creature," he says, walking out of the guard box. He texts John again on his way to report to Todd.

When he gets to Todd's office, he isn't surprised. Todd grills him for over thirty minutes about what he said to Tina and where he took her ferrets. He simply tells Todd that he told her to cooperate or else, and that he took the ferrets to the large trash compactor in 25.

Todd was exceptionally happy when Mr. Time left his presence.

149 · Shea

Shea walks with her knees bent as much as she can. The men move in a low crouch, closer to the ground, rifles pressed to their shoulders. But Shea is pregnant and sore, and that ain't happenin' for her. They move together, each a few feet apart, comms silent.

The sun has set, and the air is slightly cooler than it was during the day, though it's still humid as hell. Over ten acres of local flora surround the compound on all sides. Among the fields are several patches of palm trees, Brazilian pepper trees, saw palmetto, oak trees, and pine trees—offering dashes of cover.

Ahead of her, Cap holds up a fist. She watches as the men immediately find a bit of foliage to squat behind, so she does the same. She guides Christian behind cover, making sure he stays low. Shea leans against a tall pine tree and feels Abel thrash her bladder.

Oh shit.

She spots Dr. P at the next tree and waves her hand up and down to get her attention. Dr. P slides over and bends down close to Shea's face, so her voice won't carry.

"I have to pee!" Shea admits.

Dr. P stifles a laugh and looks around. Most of the men already have one eye on them. When Dr. P waves to John, he hustles right over.

"Shea has to pee," she whispers into John's ear from her tiptoes.

He doesn't laugh, which surprises Shea. He really does have his game face on. Instead, he presses the button for comms, and says, "All men turn away from my current position until further notice."

As one, the unit turns away, now facing out in all directions, keeping watch. Shea listens as John quietly tells her what she needs to do. She feels incredibly embarrassed, heat creeps up her face.

Thank God it's dark…

As she was instructed, she pulls down her pants then pulls her underwear to the side. She squats with her back against the tree and pees through the gap in her Kevlar suit. John, Dr. P, and Christian stand with their backs to her, blocking anyone's view. John holds a pack of tissues behind his back, wordlessly, like it's just another part of the mission.

"Okay," she whispers once she has herself back together. "Sorry, guys. Abel is doing somersaults or something."

"Don't apologize," Dr. P says. "Maybe he senses his daddy is near."

John presses the comms again. "As you were." They all return to their formation and keep pushing forward.

Every ten minutes or so, Ghost gets down on the ground and scans. Probably to make sure no alarm has been rung yet. Shea is certain that it happens every time they pass a certain distance, but she has no idea what it is. They are moving slowly. They have only covered about half the ground so far.

150 | GREGGORY

While Greggory waits for the word or signal to move, he changes into the sweats Mr. Time left for him. He packs the other set, which he assumes is for Clara, into the duffel bag also left by Mr. Time. Then he sits on the floor of his cell, playing with Tina's ferrets. They're playful and sweet creatures. He hopes they'll be okay, with whatever is going to happen. As he wiggles his fingers across the belly of one, the other pounces on his hand and his brother. He laughs.

As he amuses himself, the handheld device which sits on the bed suddenly crackles with static. He jumps from his spot on the floor and reaches for it immediately. Across the screen flashes: *COMMUNICATION REQUESTED*. Followed by two buttons beneath it: *ACCEPT* and *REJECT*.

He carefully presses *ACCEPT*. He watches the screen change into a night sky and trees. He hears someone say, "Tilt it down, you dolt!" The screen changes again, to include a face—the top of which he recognizes from the photos.

"John?" he asks.

"Hell yeah, man! We're getting close. Checking comms before we need you," John answers.

"Okay. Everything going okay?"

"Yeah. No alarm so far. We're close. We'll probably call back in ten minutes or so.".

"Great."

Dr. P suddenly shoves John's face aside and waves at Greggory, a huge smile on her face.

Greggory waves back, smiling when he sees she is safe. Then the call ends.

He scrambles to put the diaper bag and duffel on the bed. He hesitates before placing the ferrets in the duffel. He doesn't want them without food, or water, or a poop pad. But he only has what he has.

He sits on the edge of the bed, hands shaking. What if he fucks it up?

Lost in thought time passes, and he curses when the device he holds starts it's staticky call, "Fuck!"

He again hits *ACCEPT*. This time there's no video, just audio.

"Hello?" he says.

"Hey. I need you to listen very carefully."

"Sure, of course."

"When we end this call, I need you to trigger all perimeter alarms on the northeast side of the property, plus the building alarm on 15. We will be entering the property on the southwest side, closest to 25 and 4. Disable all alarms and keycard access points on those two buildings," John instructs. "Good so far?"

"Got it," Greggory says.

"When the alarm goes up, grab your stuff and go to Clara's cell. Liberate her from her binds, then head to Todd's office in that building. Tina is in there, unconscious. Check and make sure she's okay and hunker down there. We'll be in soon. There's a pistol in that diaper bag, I'm told… but we're trying to keep things non-lethal. Only use it if you absolutely have to," John finishes.

"Got it. Anything else?"

"Stay vigilant. If you're in a bad way, send a communication."

The line goes dead.

Greggory immediately snaps into action. He disables the alarms and locks in 25 and 4. He then triggers the perimeter alarm on the northeast side and the building alarm on 15.

He unlocks their cells. He slips the device into his pocket and gently transfers the sleeping ferrets into the duffel bag.

With both bags over his shoulder, he pushes open the cell door and carefully scans the hallway. He slinks to the cell next door, opens it, and quietly slips inside.

151 | Clara

Someone just entered Clara's cell so quietly she barely heard them. As she listens, she hears distant alarms and the sound of something scraping against canvas piques her curiosity.

"Oh, come on. It's okay, guys. It'll only be for a little while," she hears, a voice she hasn't heard in a long time.

She sits straight up in bed, feeling safe with the man in her presence.

"Hey, Clara. Hang tight. I'll get you sorted out," he says.

She points toward the spot where she heard the other man give her the instructions. Still wondering why he told her, someone with their mouth sewn shut. She'll never understand.

She hears Gregg move over to the area, opening cupboards and drawers. She flaps her hand at him and mimes opening a drawer. She has no idea if he gets it. She's never been all that great at charades, but she's trying.

"I see it. I got it," he says.

He comes to her bedside and she feels the weight of something he places on the bed, and it's moving. She jerks away, unsure what is happening.

"It's okay, Clara. Lie back. I need to remove the sutures. You're feeling Tina's ferrets. They're contained and unhappy about it. Nothing's gonna get you."

She lays her head back onto the pillow and grips the sheet beneath her tight in her fists. She feels the cold of the scissors resting on her cheek as he snips the sutures on her left eye, relieving painful tension with each snip. When she can open the eye fully, a tear slips from it. The lights are too bright. The colors too vivid.

"One more. Hang in there," he says.

She looks at him through one eye, trying to convey a look of true gratitude. Then remembering the rest of her face is still stitched, she thinks she might have come off more pirate or *Billy Butcherson.*

Gregg makes quick work of the other eye and moves to her mouth. When the final sutures come free, her jaw clicks and pops repeatedly as she opens it. The smell of her own breath nearly makes her gag. Looking at him, she squints, her eyes fight to adjust to the light.

"Ah, hold on. Mr. Time really thought of everything," Gregg says, placing a small bottle of mouthwash in one of her hands and a pair of sunglasses in the other.

She slips the glasses on her face and dumps the entire bottle of mouthwash into her mouth. She swishes hard, running her tongue across her teeth. A cup is deposited in her hand that she spits in to. Finally, she looks up at Gregg, a smile spreads across her face.

"Gregg! It's so good to see your face! I can't believe you're here to rescue me. Let's get out of here," she says, her voice hoarse from lack of use.

"Hi, Clara. It's nice to meet you. I go by Greggory now. I assume you knew me… in another life?"

"Oh. Greggory, okay. Yes, I did. I'm still glad you're here!"

"Good, um…bear with me. I have to unhook all these lines and cap them. You have a tube in every orifice it seems."

"Yeah. I'm pretty excited to piss, shit, and eat on my own when all this is over."

"I bet."

Once all the lines are capped, she carefully stands from the bed. Her knees wobble, nausea rolls through her, but there is no time for that now. As soon as she's standing, she throws her arms around him and hugs him tight. When she pulls away, she can see a dark blush rising in his ears and cheeks.

He hands her the sweats and turns away while she changes and tucks in her capped lines. Once she's put back together, they slip out of the cell and move as quickly and quietly as possible toward Todd's office.

Inside, they make sure Tina's breathing. They then hunker down under the desk, waiting. Every so often, they reach into the duffel and feed the ferrets while they listen for the chaos to reach them.

152 | Shea

Shea is huddled with Team B just outside the southwest perimeter. Ghost passes her the spotting scope so she can see building 4 and the path they plan to take to it. As she lifts it to her eye, she realizes Cap was right. Nervous energy courses through her, making her hands shake as she tries to stabilize the scope. It also doesn't help that Abel has been non-stop abusing her internal organs.

After trying for a few seconds, she gives up and passes it to Duce on her other side. She's too jittery to do anything helpful.

Team A breached the perimeter a minute ago. Team B is waiting for a light to flicker on the fifth floor of 25. That's their cue to move.

Christian sits beside her, watching Diesel flit from person to person, awaiting a command. As she watches, Matt crouches and leans close to her ear.

"Hey, Preggers. You feeling tired?" he asks, referencing her earlier comment, a mischievous grin on his face.

"Alright, I was wrong. Really funny," she says, crossing her arms over her belly.

"C'mon. You would've made fun of us too. I just wanted to see how you were holding up. We both have something to lose in that building… I'm a wreck, if I'm honest."

"I honestly haven't thought about it much. I'm trying to listen to Cap and keep my mind on our mission. But this kid is tap-dancing on my bladder, so that's been a distraction to say the least."

"Oh, that sucks. Our inside guy helped them a lot. I'm sure Gregg is killin' it. You know him. He's like a dog with a bone when he gets a task," Matt muses.

"Yeah, but is it Gregg? Or Greggory? Dr. P said he might want to hurt me when he sees me. It's not just me anymore. If it was, I'd take the risk. But I can't let anything happen to Abel."

"That motherly instinct is real. We've got your back. Even if we have to tranq his ass. We'll make sure you're safe..."

153 | JOHN

As soon as John gives Greggory his orders, he ends the communication and squats with his team, awaiting the alarm.

The second they hear it, Terry, Teddy, Gas, Tank, Hoover, DD, Dr. P, and John move in formation over the concrete wall behind Cap. John keeps his rifle to his shoulder and scans back and forth through the scope. He tries to also keep P in his sightline as much as possible. She is directly in front of him.

As they move toward building 25, his phone dings. Cap holds up a fist for them to stop.

Text from Time at 2124

» 26 men reporting on perimeter and 15. 4 men on guard in 4. 2 in 25. I'm in 4, See you soon!

John reads it quietly to the rest of the unit, and they continue their careful march to 25. At the front of the building, Cap halts them. They press against the building, each rifle angled in different directions, ensuring they cover all the surrounding buildings. Gas steps in front of Cap and opens the door wide, confirming the locks have been disabled.

They file through one at a time. Gas takes up the rear manually locking the door behind them. Terry and Teddy begin clearing the first floor as the rest head up the stairs. Gas and Hoover take the second and third floors. Tank and DD move to the fourth. John, Dr. P, and Cap head to the fifth.

Since John is well acquainted with this floor, he leads. This floor is covered in individual pods, so they start at the end closest to the stairs and make their way across the floor.

The pod with the cells is one of the first. John exhales a sigh of relief when he clears both cells. Empty. He watches some of the worry ease from Dr. P's face. The entire floor is deserted. No guards in sight. Hopefully his men on other floors are careful.

When they reach the pod with the time machine, he's shocked to see most of it disassembled. From there, they stop by the armory. The three of them stock up quickly.

John leads them to the back hallway of the last pod. They clear the office that used to belong to Shea and him, then move to the final door. Anticipation bubbles through him, steady and electric. He glances at Cap and Dr. P. Cap nods but Dr. P shrugs as if to say, what're you waiting for?

He takes position beside the door. Cap steps up and kicks it—hard. The door sends splinters into the air. John enters with his rifle tight to his shoulder. He immediately notices that Tina's on the couch. He walks over to clear behind the desk and finds Greggory and Clara crouched underneath, heads tucked to their knees.

John pushes his rifle to his side and moves the chair they had pulled in front of themselves.

"Hey, guys. It's me. You're safe."

154 | TERRY

Terry leads with Teddy close behind as they clear doors on the first floor of building 25. The glass walls make it easy to clear most of it quickly, but there are a couple of rooms they need to breach. One is the bathroom. Now they stand on either side of a door, ready to breach.

Teddy silently raises three fingers and counts them down. On one he kicks in the door. Terry immediately enters the room, rifle up, Teddy on his six. Inside, two suited guards scramble to stand. They appear to have been napping in the kitchen break room.

Before either man fully stands, Terry has pulled the trigger on one. Followed by Teddy taking down the second. Two muted pops. Suppressors doing their job.

"Clear," Terry says, while Teddy checks the hallway for anyone responding to the noise.

Terry steps over to the downed men and zip ties their hands behind their backs. They are out cold and would stay that way for a while, but he isn't taking any chances. He has no idea how long this op will take.

When he is done with his task, he joins Teddy in the hallway. Together they continue clearing the rest of the floor. When they complete their circuit, they take the stairs to the fifth floor. As soon as they reach the fourth floor, their comms crackle in their ears.

"Three friendlies in custody."

Terry presses his comms button. "Two hostiles down."

Greggory climbs out from under the desk, then reaches back to help Clara up. He puts both of the bags over his shoulder, ensuring the duffel with Tina's ferrets is tucked tight to his side. They keep digging at the bag, restless little prisoners themselves, but they'll have to hang in there for just a little while longer.

"Are you guys okay?" Dr. P asks, pushing John aside so she can hug them both, tears in her eyes.

"I'm starving, but super stoked I'll actually get to eat when this is over," Clara says.

"I bet. You're skin and bones, girl." Dr. P says.

Greggory stands there awkwardly watching John talk to the new arrivals. A man walks over to him that he doesn't recognize from any photos.

"It's great to meet you. I've heard a lot about you. Are you going to cooperate and come with us? Or?" the man asks.

"Sir, I didn't catch your name?"

"Sorry about that. You can call me Cap."

"Well, Cap, as you know, I don't really remember anything. But I know the way I've been treated here isn't right. I'd rather figure things out with you all," Greggory admits.

"Fantastic. Stick with Dr. P. I'm not gonna arm you. No offence, but we're unsure how you'll react when you see Shea," Cap says. "Can you pass me the pistol that's in that diaper bag? Grip toward me. Please."

"Oh, okay," he says, slightly disappointed he won't be able to defend himself. He runs his hands along several compartments before finding what he's looking for. He passes Cap the weapon with his hand wrapped around the barrel.

"Alright, is everybody up here, now?" Cap asks, while dropping the magazine from the gun and clearing the chamber. He drops the ammunition into one pocket and the weapon into another.

"Yes, sir," John reports.

"Signal Team B with two flicks. Tell them their mission is a go. Have them report when they breach the building, then we'll head over," Cap says.

John presses his comms. "Team B, mission is a go. Report when the building is breached."

John then turns to Gregg, grinning. "Hey, Gregg! Man, it's great to see you. I can't wait to see Shea's face when she sees you. That beard's coming in nice. No contacts though, huh? Guess prison doesn't stock those."

"Uh, thanks? I prefer Greggory. I thought you had a beard?" Greggory asks.

"Yeah, I shaved it when we went on the run. It's coming in though," John says, stroking the half an inch or so of facial hair on his jaw. He reaches into his back pocket and pulls out a black hat. He hands it to Greggory. "It's the Op hat. You should wear it."

"Okay." Greggory glances at the logo briefly before pulling it on. "Did Shea alter her appearance, too?"

"Uh… you could say that. We cut a lot of her hair off. She was pissed."

"Oh. She had really long hair, right?"

"Yeah."

Before John can say more, they hear Matt's voice over comms.

"Breach. Breach. Breach.

A gun shot cracks. Diesel barks. Then a single shout, "FUCK!"

The unit turns as one and heads for the stairs. John grabs Clara and Dr. P by the arm, pulling them along with him. Terry pulls Tina up and over his shoulder like she's nothing but a rag doll. Greggory follows.

156 | Shea

Shea hears the order for them to move to building 4. Team B advances as a stealth unit. Diesel is tucked close to Duce's right leg, silent and alert. As they line up against the building, Matt takes position beside the door, ready to open it.

Matt presses the comms button. "Breach. Breach. Breach," as says, pulling the door open.

Innie enters first, followed by Duce and Diesel, then Shea, Christian, and Ghost. Matt plans to enter last after holding the door for everyone.

The second Shea steps inside, she sees that they are well and truly fucked. She clamps an arm around Christian, pulling him tight to her side.

A gunshot cracks.

Duce drops before anyone can react.

Diesel barks and moves to stand over Duce, teeth bared and growling.

Matt shouts, "FUCK!"

The comms go dead.

WHAT THE FUCKKKKKK

This building is like all the others she's seen, complete with a large entry way. Shea looks around taking in her surroundings.

Fifteen suited guards encircle them. The door they came through is already blocked with guards. Within the circle stands Todd, gun in his hand. A man in fatigues kneels in front of Todd, nose and mouth bloodied. Todd presses the gun to the back of the man's head.

There's only one other man inside the circle. He looks incredibly jacked compared to the last time Shea saw him. It's the man who shot Gregg. Anger and confusion rise within her. She can hear and feel her heartbeat in her ears.

She tries to calm herself, but there are currently fifteen guns pointed directly at her. She shifts side to side slightly, testing it. Every muzzle tracks her. Out the corner of her eye, she sees Matt inch closer. Each step slow, deliberate.

She's so focused on him, that when she is grabbed from behind, Christian wrenched from her side, she feels like her brain is melting. Time is moving fast and her brain slow, she can't keep up.

NO! Christian…

A guard walks her toward the center of the circle. Another shoves Christian to the ground closer to the circle, then steps away. They walk past Duce. Diesel still stands over him. Duce appears to still be breathing—for now.

The guard presses his gun to her temple and forces her to stand in front of Todd and his hostage.

"Shea. We really need to quit meeting like this," he says with a devilish grin.

Matt watched the guard move on Shea. He almost pulled the trigger, until he saw every gun in the room trained on her.

As Shea stands in front of Todd, Matt listens for any hints of communication in his ear. Any instructions. Any sign.

His attention is brought back to Todd when he hears a sharp crack. Looking over he watches Todd wipe his face, disgusted. Shea cups a hand over her cheek. It clicks. She spit in his face, and he slapped her. Atta girl!

Todd's voice cuts through the near silent room. "You're lucky I haven't shot you yet. But Greggory will want to watch. I can be patient. Maybe."

He jams the barrel harder against his hostage's head. "I'll make you a deal. You get rid of this man for me. He's the one that got rid of all your husband's memories, after all. And I won't kill you. You or him."

Matt clenches his jaw. He needs a plan. Now. For Shea. For Time. And before Clara walks through that door.

Shea speaks, steady. "Todd, I'm not taking a life. And like you said, you want Gregg here when you kill me, so can we just chill for a couple minutes?"

"First of all, it's Greggory. Second, chill? Sure. Oh, while were chillin' all your men need to drop their weapons. I know it's only silly tranquilizer rounds, but I'm not really in the mood for a nap."

Matt nods and they all drop their weapons. Coincidentally, that's when Team A pushes in. Several muted gunshots sound through the room, then suddenly stop. Four guards slump before they notice the gun pressed to Shea's head. They drop their weapons as they file into the situation.

Clara runs to Matt. He doesn't think. He pulls her close. He breathes her in. Not a pleasant experience at the moment, but she's here.

"Ah! Family reunion. So touching."

He scans the room and enjoys the spotlight. "I have a bargain for all of you Leave now. Leave Shea, Greggory, and the child behind. I'll let you walk off this property alive. You can even take this traitor with you. I'll trade you the one I shot. Sorry about that."

"Absolutely the fuck not!" John says.

"Ah, John. So nice to see you. You can stay too, if you wish," Todd offers.

John stays silent, eyes shifting to Cap, waiting for orders. Cap surveys the room, taking a silent head count. When he finishes, he steps over to Diesel and gently coaxes him over to Christian, so he can examine Duce.

John watches everyone, trying to think what the best next move is, but he's drawing a blank.

"Nothing? Come on," Todd taunts. "My guards could kill you all where you stand. There is no move here. I won. You lost. Greggory, why don't you come on over here?"

John turns. Gregg had stationed himself in the back of the group, but his height makes him hard to miss. John looks back to the center of the circle and watches Shea struggle against her captive. Her face a mask of terror. Greggory walks between the men of the unit. As he passes each of them, they lay a hand on his shoulder. Silent support.

"I'm here, Todd. No need to shoot anyone," Greggory says, stepping into the center of the circle.

Todd laughs—maniacal and creepy as hell. He slaps Greggory on the back and pulls him to his side, speaking quietly in his ear. John can't hear any of it. He drops to a knee beside Cap.

Speaking in hushed tones, he asks, "How bad is it, Cap?"

Cap drags a hand down his face. "He's gone, son."

Around them, the unit inhales sharply as one.

Diesel sits at Christian's side, gently nudging the boy with his nose as Christian cries into his shirt, the fabric pulled up over his face.

Cap drops his head and places a hand over Duce's chest. "Rest easy, soldier."

John's jaw tightens. He shoves his grief down hard. There's no time for it now. Not with a psychopathic asshole on the rampage.

Behind him the men murmur Duce's name. Not loud. Just scattered, like a quiet prayer.

John looks up and sees that Shea is still fighting her captor, tears streaming down her face.

Diesel stays seated at Christian's side, but he keeps half rising, shifting his front paws, eyes locked on the circle.

Waiting for a command.

159 | GREGGORY

Greggory listens to Todd's promises of fame and fortune, a life of absolute privilege. He listens while his eyes scan the room. Todd simply has too many weapons. And by the look of them, the men that came to rescue them are truly broken by their friend's death.

"Todd, this all sounds great, but that wouldn't be privilege. It would be a gilded existence. I don't know what path is right for me, but I don't want fame and fortune at the expense of other people's lives. If you let everyone go, and live, I'll stay," Greggory negotiates.

Todd smiles. "Well, I guess what I meant was, you have two choices. Privilege or servitude. It's your decision. But either way, Shea and this traitor don't walk out of here."

"Oh. I see…" Greggory says, desperately trying to think of a way out of this, without anyone else getting shot.

"Why don't we have a reunion first? Then we'll see how you feel about staying, how about that? Paul, bring her in front of Greggory."

Greggory hasn't looked at her. He avoided it. He knows he had a different life before. But also knows what Tina told Dr. P. There is a very real chance he will find pleasure in her pain or even her death. He doesn't think he could, he could never—not even after everything he believed Shea had done.

While watching his bare feet, a shadow falls in front of him—Shea and Paul.

Greggory looks up and meets the saddest face he's ever seen. She won't meet his eyes. Probably just as afraid of what he might do, or what she'll see in him. He doesn't know what he feels. But her sadness makes him falter.

"I'm pretty sure she's in full Kevlar, sir. I can feel it through her fatigues,"

Paul reports.

"Very good find. Well done. Open the fatigues," Todd orders.

"No, please, just stop. I'll stay. I'll be your servant, or whatever you want… Please just stop, Todd!" Shea begs.

Greggory watches the men of the unit all take a tentative step forward. They are ready to die, if it means protecting her.

"Must I say it, Shea? I. Don't. Want. You. I never have. You know this. Paul, proceed."

Paul holds the gun to her head with one hand and starts unbuttoning her fatigue top with the other. She jerks, trying to break free, but Paul's fast. He slams the butt of the gun into her temple.

She crumbles to the floor.

Greggory smiles.

He doesn't know why. He isn't happy, he just can't help himself. He tries to quickly school his features, but he isn't fast enough. Todd noticed. Todd throws his arm around him and pulls him close as they stand over Shea, who is already starting to stir on the floor.

"Ah ha!" Todd says, delighted. "I knew you'd enjoy a little violence toward the woman that broke your heart. Paul, pick her up."

Paul hauls her to her feet and makes quick work of the buttons, pulling her top off of her.

The room begins to spin. He is met with an intense version of the pre-seizure feeling. He knows he's slipping. Down becomes up and up becomes down. He can't stop it. He's falling backwards. His body hits the floor and he seizes.

160 | MR. TIME

The second Greggory drops to the ground, flopping around, Mr. Time the pressure of the gun on the back of his head ease. He makes a quick, calculated glance over his shoulder. Todd's attention has shifted toward Greggory, in motion to move to Greggory's side. Knowing he won't get another chance like this, he lifts one knee after the other, getting his feet under him. He stands quickly, aiming the back of his head at Todd's well sculpted nose.

The gun flies from Todd's hand and slides across the floor, stopping against Shea's boot. It takes her a second to realize what just happened. When she does, she reaches down and grabs it, bringing it up and aiming at Todd. Greggory's flapping has slowed, but he's still going.

He feels the tension in the room shift, a spark he can't help but relish.

"Tell your men to drop their weapons," Shea orders.

Todd sneers. "Or what? You'll shoot me? Please."

"I won't become you, no. You're right. But I might be the only person in this room who feels that way," she spits.

Todd looks around the room, noting the imposing ex-military presence. "For now," he says coldly, "holster your weapons."

The suited men relax their arms to their sides. Mr. Time goes to Greggory's side. Not because he thinks Greggory won't be fine on his own, but because the eyes of every man in his unit are urging him to do so.

He kneels at Greggory's side and uses his fisted knuckles to perform a sternum rub. Greggory rouses. Mr. Time backs away, letting him breathe. Greggory rouses. He looks confused, like he just woke from a deep sleep.

Mr. Time studies him. "Do you remember?"

He can tell they both know exactly what he means.

Greggory swallows. "Yeah… along with some other things."

161 | Shea

He looks up at Shea with those seafoam green eyes, and she breaks. Her arms, holding the gun up at Todd, are shaking. Mr. Time steps in and gently takes the weapon from her so she can go to her husband's side.

"What just happened?" she asks, afraid to get too close.

He stares at her, unblinking. "Um, first, you're pregnant?!" he blurts, unbelieving.

"Yeah… It's yours, if that's what you're thinking," she says, defensive.

The unit chuckles behind her.

So much for professionalism

"There she is," he says softly. "I know it's mine, Shea… Is it a boy or a girl?" he asks, timid.

"Um, hello? This is not the time for this. Do you all have a death wish or something? This is ridiculous!" Todd snaps.

Mr. Time pulls his arm back and hits Todd in the temple with the butt of his gun, dropping him instantly.

"Was that necessary?" Shea asks.

"He's quiet now, isn't he? Proceed," Mr. Time says.

"It's a boy," Shea says, rubbing her hand over the Kevlar covering her belly.

Greggory's eyes widen. He pulls off his hat and finally reads the embroidered op name. "Abel? After your dad?"

"Yes. Now tell me what happened. We'll celebrate later. Hurry up before he wakes up."

"When I got the serum, Mr. Time leaned in close to give it to me. That memory was erased with everything else. He whispered, 'I'm only giving you a partial dose. Todd expects you to want Shea dead when you see her, but I replaced those commands with one of my own. When you see her, and truly look at her, you will remember.'"

Shea looks at Mr. Time, who is smiling broadly. She moves to him and wraps him in a tight embrace, before even hugging her husband. His actions deserving her immediate attention.

She then throws her arms around Greggory. "Wait, what's your name?" she asks, gazing lovingly at him as he presses his palm over her belly.

"Gregg… Like always?"

"You required we call you Greggory during the… well."

"What a twat!" he says, then leans in and kisses her like it had been years, not months, since he's seen her.

"You're all fucking dead!" Todd growls, getting up from the floor. He wipes his nose and spits on the floor next to Shea.

"Actually, we're not," Dr. P says, walking in the door, a wriggling duffel slung over her shoulder. Like it's no big deal.

162 | JOHN

John's head snaps toward Dr. P. He left her outside with Tina's unconscious form and the ferrets for a reason. He watches her walk among the men and lock eyes with Gregg. He nods, affirming he is himself again.

She stands there unmoving, eyeing Todd like her gaze could pin him where he stands. The next several minutes of his life, of all their lives, unfold in slow motion.

Several military men descend the stairs behind Todd. None of his guards notice because they're all so focused on Todd. The soldiers stay hidden behind the stair pony wall. John subtlety signals in the direction of the staircase, for his men to watch as well. They all slowly reach for their rifles, to assist if able.

Their CO peeks around the end of the pony wall, signaling to Cap (who is standing right next to John) that they're going to take out the eight men closest to them. Cap nods and signals to his own men to take the remaining four closest to them.

"You're just going to hold a gun on me all day?" Todd snarks.

"Nah," Mr. Time says.

The soldiers rise from behind the wall and fire. Eight guards drop. At the same time, the men of Op Abel turn, taking out the other four. John's eyes flick between Shea and Dr. P.

As the suited guards hit the floor, Todd completely loses his shit. He lunges for Shea. He pulls her from Gregg's side, who's momentarily distracted by everything happening at once. Todd drags her in front of him and locks an arm around her throat. Her face reddens fast. Every rifle in the room trains on Todd as he backs away.

"Shoot me," Todd hisses, "and I swear I will cut that parasite from her gut before I pass out."

He presses a pocketknife against the Kevlar covering her belly.

John's mind goes blank. He can't risk Shea or Abel. The soldiers on the stairs look at Cap. Cap gives one small shake of his head.

Stunned silence.

Then a small but confident voice breaks it. "Fass!" Christian orders.

Diesel, who had been antsy since they entered the building launches like a bullet aimed straight at Todd. He leaps through the air, carefully avoiding Shea. He latches on to Todd's neck from Todd's left side and drags him down and away from Shea. Diesel shakes his head, teeth buried deep in Todd's neck. Todd works to attack his assailant. The knife slices down Diesels left shoulder blade. He doesn't even flinch.

A collective gasp fills the room. Gregg runs to Shea and drops beside her, checking her over.

Todd gurgles and gasps from the ground. Diesel stands over him, muzzle a hair's breadth away from Todd's face, teeth bared. Blood pours from the wound on Diesel's shoulder.

They all stand silent, in shock. Shea collapses in a heap on the ground, sobbing.

"Heir!" Christian calls.

When Diesel makes his way to the child, his muzzle is covered in Todd's blood.

Christian strokes his face, and lovingly says, "Good boy, Diesel!"

"YEAH!" Teddy shouts.

"Good boy, D!" Innie adds.

The unit joins in, chanting for him and carefully petting him. Job well done.

Diesel stands proud, soaking up the attention.

163 | Shea

Todd gasps and gurgles beside her. His eyes, once so full of hate, now hold something closer to fear.

She waits.

It might sound twisted, but she needs to know he is dead. The gasping stops. His eyes go cold. She collapses into tears. That dog is a gift from God. He did the one thing she never could, and he did it to save her.

Gregg wraps his arms around her, like he can sense what she is feeling. She welcomes his missed embrace and melts into him.

The military men move through the room, ensuring all targets are actually down. The unit drifts toward them, needing to see for themselves that she's okay.

Dr. P drops to her knees next to them and pulls them both into a loving embrace. Tears trail down her face too. Shea can tell Dr. P considers Gregg a great friend now too.

Sitting there, the sorrow of Duce's death threatens to overwhelm her. The men all around her, that risked their lives to save her loved ones, they lost one of their own. The tears feel like they will never stop. The hurt so deep her chest feels like it's cracking open.

Gregg brushes her hair away from her face, saying, "Shea, love. It's okay, beautiful." He pulls her in tighter.

Her eyes are closed to the world, she doesn't want to see the damage. She feels responsible for all of it.

She hears John step closer. "Hey, man. Will you forgive me?" he asks Gregg, a smile in his voice.

"I'm sorry about that, man. And actually, I feel like I don't have the right words to thank you," he says, his voice tight with emotion.

"No need. I'm just glad you're okay," he says walking away.

Shea keeps her eyes shut tightly. She would disappear in this moment if she could. To be alone with the heavy weight of her grief.

"I'm gonna be a dad," Gregg says softly, and life comes rushing back in. The joy in that simple statement is palpable. Through all the bad, a new life awaited. The family she always wanted for herself.

Regaining some sense of control she moves to stand, hugging members of the unit. Christian walks over to her and the grief threatens to overtake her again. She looks at his innocent face, he's seen too much in his short life.

She drops to her knees in front of him. "I'm so sorry, Christian. You should have never had to give that command. But thank you. You saved my life."

Diesel pads over and licks her face. She assesses his wound and cries even harder, her forehead pressed to Diesel's.

"P… can you?" she asks, in-between sobs.

Dr. P nods and heads out to grab her kit.

Her attention lands back on Christian.

"Don't be sorry. I glad," he says, confidently. "Now little brother will be safe."

She falls apart all over again.

164 | Shea

Four months later

"Guys, wake up! We have to be at the facility in thirty minutes!" Shea says, frantically trying to find a pacifier while also making sure everyone is awake.

"This house is too small for all these men. The toilets are atrocious!" Dr. P says, coming up behind her, pacifier in hand.

"No kidding. They said they wanted to be here to see what would happen with Tina, but they're all obsessed with Abel. They're never gonna leave!" Shea says, smiling despite herself.

"Well, none of us have jobs either, that doesn't help," Dr. P says.

"I wasn't talking about you guys. Ugh. I love that you're here. It's just, when Gregg and I picked this place, we thought it'd just be us, as friends, temporarily. I love this house and the pool. This is where we fell in love. It's just not very big. Especially with a band of military misfits, three couples, a one-hundred-twenty-four-year-old child, and a baby," Shea complains.

"Matt and Clara really are leaving tomorrow. They booked the flight," Dr. P reminds her.

Shea looks around, still too many sleeping bodies. The baby in her arms smiles in his sleep.

"Christian!" she calls.

When he arrives in front of her, she whispers in his ear. He giggles and takes off running.

He comes back into the living room carrying a bullhorn.

He says into the mouthpiece, "WAKIE WAKIE!"

Men shoot upright from couches and air mattresses all over the living room. Shea chuckles.

"THIRTY MINUTES!" Christian continues.

"Breakfast is ready. I made four dozen eggs and four packs of bacon this morning. The amount of food we go through is ridiculous," Gregg announces, reaching for Abel.

"Thank goodness. He's been so cute this morning, but my arm is tingling," Shea says, passing over the baby.

Thirty minutes later, they all sit in a visitor room at the facility. Mr. Kline walks in carrying a legal document. He sits across the table from all of them.

"She'll be in shortly. I'd like to go over the legal details before she comes in. It'll overwhelm her," he says, opening the folder.

He reads, "The Revocable Living Trust of Tina Donoghue. Named trustees are Shea Marsh, Greggory Marsh, Dr. Amber Pontes, and Johnathan Krieger. Assets in trust include the entirety of Crown Skull Laboratories, all properties owned by Todd and Tina Donoghue, and four bank accounts totaling approximately 4.3 billion dollars."

He pauses, and rightly so. Everyone in the room gasps.

I think I just shit myself

After the shock settles, he continues. "In the event of the death of Todd

Donoghue and the legal or mental incapacitation of Tina Donoghue, the trust will be placed in the care of the trustees. Also to include a pet trust in the name of Ren and Stimpy, to be overseen by the same trustees."

He nodes, then stands and opens the door, signaling to the guard that they are ready.

Shea can't believe her eyes. Guards lead Tina into the room, sitting her beside Mr. Kline. She sits, still, almost statue like, but her eyes still rove around the room.

Then they stop, and something like light shines there. Shea follows her gaze. Without speaking, she walks to the cage and pulls back the sheet.

Ren and Stimpy look up from their spots on the hammock. Tina's head tilts, watching them sniff the air. She doesn't say anything. No smile lights up her face. But Shea can tell she's still in there somewhere, because of the single tear that traces its way down Tina's face.

The four trustees met, and with Gregg's encouragement took over Crown. Innovating in a much healthier way. Deciding to create for good, Crown became the forefront of technological advancement.

No one left after that meeting. Instead, they all moved into Todd's mansion. Odd at first—but there was plenty of space. The ferrets even got their old room back, which Christian would hang out in every chance he got. They were well loved. Diesel healed quickly and loved all the attention he got from the many inhabitants of the mansion.

The Mark Cahill Fund for Veterans' Mental Health was created to honor the memory of Duce, a loyal friend and soldier. The fund provides support to organizations that offer counseling, crisis intervention, and mental health resources to veterans and their families.

Shea ended up with a bigger family than she could have ever imagined.

And she's loving every second of it.

Epilogue

Abel
Twenty years later

"I called you in today, because it's time," Abel says to the room filled with his family.

He stands at the front of the room. He's tall, with seafoam eyes like his father. The dark brown waves he inherited from his mother crown his head.

His parents sit at the head of the table, his brother beside them. His uncles John and Matt sit with his aunts Amber (Dr. P), and Clara. Next to them sits John and Amber's daughter Katherine—his fiancé. The rest of his family sit surrounding the table, not at it, since they are not board members.

"Not yet, Abel. You rush things," his mother says, in her 'I know better' voice.

"Mom, you and Dad handed me this company several years ago. I was raised in this place. Dad took me under his wing on this project before I could even write my name. It's time."

"Are you certain?" Dr. P asks.

"Just watch the news! The world is filled with murder, famine, homelessness, climate change, war. We're approaching the point of no return! It's time!" he urges.

"We have a government contract, and they're willing to push it worldwide. Dad c'mon. You know I'm right," he continues.

"Son, I know the program is ready. But are we?"

"I am! And so is S.E.R.A!"

"Ah, finally landed on a name, huh?" Christian asks, smiling.

"Yeah. It stands for Synthetic Enhanced Reasoning AI. She'll be our saving angel," Abel says.

"Sera, like Seraphim?" Shea asks, fingers resting on the crucifix around her neck.

"Yeah, Mom. The best AI ever created. And a neural implant that does good for humanity. It will change the world!" Abel says.

Font Attribution:

HVD Peace https://www.fontspace.com/hvd-peace-font-f23071

Mathilde https://www.fontspace.com/mathilde-font-f16297

Ambery Garden https://www.fontspace.com/ambery-garden-font-f88768

Uncanny https://www.fontspace.com/uncanny-font-f28133

Hacked https://www.fontspace.com/hacked-font-f28425

Thank you for reading
Lone Pine
Please leave a review on
Amazon and Goodreads.